THE MOSLEMS ARE COMING

ENCOUNTERS WITH A DESKTOP TERRORIST

Azad Essa

Foreword by Ferial Haffajee

HarperCollins *Publishers* India

First published by Burnet Media in South Africa in 2010

First published in India by
HarperCollins *Publishers* in 2012

Building 10, Tower A, 4th Floor, DLF Cyber City, Phase II,
Gurugram Haryana – 122002, India
www.harpercollins.co.in

2 4 6 8 10 9 7 5 3

P-ISBN: 978-93-5029-439-0
E-ISBN: 978-93-5029-532-8

Typeset in 11/14 PalmSprings at
SURYA

Printed and bound at
MicroPrints India, New Delhi

For my mother Rooksana,
my father Ebrahim,
my sister Shenaaz,
and our friend Sibongile 'Angel' Bhengu

CONTENTS

Foreword

The first title of this book, 'Zuma's Bastard', in reference to South Africa's president and with an ironic play on his playboy ways, was an insight into a new brand of journalism in South Africa. Azad is of a generation of South Africans who reached political maturity in the era of liberation but who owed no particular loyalty to The Leader of any stripe.

It's fitting then that a second iteration carries as provocative a title, 'The Muslims Are Coming' – a title to incite the conservatives and annoy the liberals who like to think they are not Islamophobic.

Azad is of a generation with none of the old loyalties or fractured identities or outmoded ideologies of those of us who reached adulthood in the eighties and before. He is a journalist of the twenty-first century. His book emerged from his award-winning blog on Thought Leader, South Africa's leading blogging platform. It is a collection of writing from blogs, to journals, to diaries and old-style articles, so the voice through the book is varied and fresh. Now he finds himself working with *Al Jazeera*, again at the cutting edge of where journalism is headed.

I've watched him blossom out of South Africa and into the world. So it's fitting that he turns his quizzical (and very funny) eye on the uprisings of northern Africa to ask an important question: when will the tide of revolution slip down into sub-Saharan Africa?

And, can Twitter seriously cause a revolution?

He is a quintessential voice of the Born Frees, the generation of

South Africans whose lives have largely been lived in a democratic country, free of the worst ravages of apartheid. Of course, there are many young people born free but still in chains; Azad is part of the lucky cut. His voice is individual (but still fiercely engaged), liberated, non-racial, questioning, querying, connected but free to roam. It is a delight.

And roam he does. From South Africa, travel with him this time to Kashmir and Norway, Kenya and the Democratic Republic of Congo.

As an editor, I have to look hard for young journalists who are interested in a world beyond Mzansi, so Azad Essa is part of a generation of new internationalists crafted in the mould of the campaigning John Pilger, the broadcaster Rageh Omaar or the Zimbabwean film-maker Hopewell Chin'ono. They are journalists with a keen sense of geopolitics who track the changing world but also remind us that so much remains mired in poverty and oppression even in the era of being so wired.

Azad looks beyond the bling that can characterize writing about developing countries like India and South Africa. I remember that during the glitzy Indian Premier League in 2009, Azad called up wanting to write a feature on stadium workers who were paid such a pittance they could not afford to buy food, nor could they travel home. So they slept in the sheltered eves of the stadium.

Azad is a very funny writer. To wit, his column on being a teetotaller bar-hopper sent to in a representative set of pubs to see if anybody is watching Zuma's first state of the nation address broadcast live. Nobody was.

This time, he is still funny but deeply touched by the world he has discovered while with *Al Jazeera* – an often tragic and dangerous world. He writes:

> I sat up repeatedly until the wee hours of the morning chatting on instant messenger with a grief-stricken Libyan doctor who passed on valuable information on the acts of violence in the streets, the state of the hospitals and the

> movements of marauding mercenaries . . . I was his lifeline. He was our window into the streets of Tripoli. No wire carried his story . . . On more than one occasion he told me not to ask him to calm down. On more than one occasion I came home and cried myself to sleep.

When I studied at Wits University, Johannesburg, in the eighties, I often wondered why it was that fellow Muslim students were so deeply apathetic about the struggle against apartheid, then in its fiery final stages. The issue that provoked their revolutionary rage was Palestine. Azad deals with this occasional activism at some length in the book as he grapples in very personal and evocative ways with how to oppose Zionism but not allow this to tip into racism against Jewish people.

While the book is South African, Azad's sphere is global and this second imprint of his writings will take this mad-cap to a different audience. The Islamophobia expressed in the ban in burqas in several European countries has human rights activists incensed. And while the author cuts into the regressive politics this move exemplifies, he also lets rip like this:

> [T]he burqa may have made sense five hundred years ago when it deflected dust and pervy male stares, but it doesn't today on the nicely paved streets of twenty-first-century Paris, where every woman has more rights than God (and likely owns a vacuum cleaner). In fact, it achieves the opposite effect today: it brings unwanted attention to the wearer . . .
>
> Truth is, I often don't know how to act around a woman in such attire because no one teaches you what etiquette to follow when someone pitches a tent around her body and then stands next to you. Should you greet her? Should you ignore her? Should you lower your gaze and dare to check out her Nik-Nak-shaped toes? Even non-burqa-wearing Muslim women – in headscarves or without – can feel uncomfortable around their swathed sisters. A troop of

> ninjas looking down with (supposed) disdain at regular Muslim women in hipsters and short-sleeve tops can be quite terrifying.

The man is funny. It is always sad to see great journalists leave our shores. Azad is at the beginning of a professional life of activism, action and a whole lot of fun. I have no doubt that this will be the first book of many. I am honoured to be associated with it.

March 2012 FERIAL HAFFAJEE

Introduction

It all began in a dingy office full of mice, mites and spineless books at the University of KwaZulu-Natal in 2005. I was hired as a researcher and part-time lecturer in the labour studies department to write research reports destined for our dusty bookshelves. It wasn't quite the dream job I had imagined. I always figured I'd find myself batting alongside Hashim Amla at Eden Gardens in Calcutta one day, taking on the 'motherland'. We would flay the Indian attack with our nifty wrists and long beards, shrugging off the burdens of adulthood with the flourish of willow on leather – but instead I had become an academic.

Puke.

Having just returned from perusing the world as a vagabond student, I knew nothing and had loans to repay, so I had to mortgage my ideals for a salary. Such is life. Truth be told, I joined an incredibly smart and passionate team of academics who challenged my every rant, with a mad scientist–poet with bushy eyebrows for a boss who urged me to push the limits. He is a lyrical man, Ari Sitas, and anarchy seemed destined for greatness around him.

Academia still remained a drag. So I wrote up the research and did my teaching, and bummed about on the beach when no one was watching.

But while I mucked about quietly among the mice and moths, South Africa's political climate was shifting gears. Suddenly, a country lauded as the light of the African continent began flickering ominously. Journalists and analysts did their part force-feeding us a narrative of doom and gloom. Africa's oldest liberation movement, South Africa's ruling party, the ANC, was falling apart before our very eyes. Internal fighting, rape charges, hate speech and hairy political conspiracies do not combine into a pretty sight, I assure you.

Gradually, South Africans still cocky enough to call themselves young, myself included, began to realize that history has little time for pussies. I found myself ambushed at a crucial juncture in the great South African story without the leverage of political history to propel me forward, no allegiance to a party to blind me to the idiocy of our politicians, no uncles in high office to pave the convenient way ahead for me and not even a grandfather coolie connection to Gandhi to help me along. History, it appeared, really wasn't on my side. But I realized that if I wanted to hang about and wait for destiny to take shape, I might as well have stayed at madrasah.

Unable to take up arms, jaded by the daily political spectacle and suffering from too much self-importance to self-immolate, I did the unthinkable and rallied to make use of my halcyon years – my college education. I began to write about the events unfolding around me every day – I wrote about South Africa, the world, and some of the more peculiar misdemeanours plaguing us all. I came without the baggage that would sink me to the level of political rhetoric filling most of our newspapers. Nor did I have any pretentious reverence for elite academia. Crucially, I just wanted to say it as I saw it, and I wrote as I wanted to hear it. I didn't have to toe any line, except my own.

Of course, no newspaper would publish the seething fumes that I soon vented (this was before I was forced to learn a measure of self-restraint), and so the Accidental Academic blog on the *Mail & Guardian*'s Thought Leader platform was created. But even this premier online portal took ages to grant me a spot; the Internet may be a free-for-all but the *M&G* still had standards to consider, and I had to beg for the blog. My first post went online on 13 June 2008.

I didn't realize it at the time, but my disdain for the political hocus pocus at play in my country spilled over into a blatant disregard for the bullshit that surrounded me. While Jacob Zuma may have fathered the Accidental Academic – along with his other bastard children – my foray into writing was no longer just about South Africa and the dawning political apocalypse.

I found that the more I wrote, whether it was about xenophobia, the Dalai Lama or, oddly enough, crawling pubs for a story, the more my identity began to unravel.

I soon realized that no matter how much I protested otherwise, readers wanted a semblance of coherent politics; they needed me categorized, framed and archived or, at the very least, fried. They needed to box the speaker in order to code the message.

Despite all the globalization talk, they craved a polemic.

Considering that I had always battled to identify with my brethren and in consequence felt more at ease with the common infidel for much of my life, I was now forced to deal with a new breed of bigots who hid behind the safety of the screens only to crawl out of the online woodwork to spew vile, venomous vitriol. They were like little widgets that clung to regressive politics like parasites on red blood cells.

It seemed to me that though the world had become smaller, closer than it had ever been – since Tintin went to the Soviet Union at least – we still knew so little about one another. Worse, we still seemed obsessed with defending our own, terrified to speak truth to power and we couldn't be bothered to find out more.

While my cousins back home irritated me with their racism, religious intolerance and oily obsession with heaven, the rednecks and two-timing liberals seemed to turn a blind eye to glaring injustices and allowed a new narrative of silly hate to slip beneath their radar.

So *the Moslem was born*.

Mos-lem, adjective, noun, plural: a homogenous group of idiots, claiming a lofty edification, with a constant resort to regressive tribalism. Distinguished by a lust for blood in the name of jihad, they are also known for an unreasonable attachment to a murky morass known as 'Sharia'. As unthinking as a stack of French crêpes, they defecate with devious derision on modernity. They pursue world domination through prolific procreation and they are *coming* – en masse.

I know many Moslems. They're my next of kin, who've banished me for teasing their sisters (or nieces), questioned my allegiances, interrogated my intentions and breathed hell-fire down my neck. Trust me, I've had to check myself mid-sentence for being among the believers.

And as you are about to discover, I had grown used to lambasting my community for being primitive prudes. I've had no qualms about exposing the double standards my brethren are too often guilty of.

But to castigate the entire Muslim civilization by way of the subtle roll of the tongue (read the Moslems) and to insinuate that we are a type of archaic memento which will one day modernize, develop, break free of the shackles of the Islamic Middle Ages and reach a type of Enlightenment, is just downright childish, if not precariously irrational, anti-intellectual and, weirdly enough, Moslem in nature.

The Moslems needed to grow up, yes, but the clash of civilizations should have been a Hollywood film, not the foundation of a prolonged witch-hunt.

And so I found myself whiling away my day at the university and then donning a cape at night and brandishing my keyboard like a sword out to slay demons of holy bigotry.

I wrote about packing condoms in my travel bag instead of Qur'anic verses to avoid being profiled at airports in Europe, advised young Muslim lasses to strap on dildos to take a stand against workplace machismos, and fictitiously handed out tank tops to one-time burqa-chicks in Paris. It was really nothing out of the ordinary daily life of the urban Muslim anywhere in the world. But it proved quite a big deal for the haters.

The rousing response online surprised me. It also encouraged me to quit my job in 2009 and embark on another type of suicide mission: journalism. Writing had reignited the other dream that lay dormant all these years and it was time to take the plunge.

And whereas the online world could push and pull and open new spaces for discussion and debate – often spitting back with equal venom – the newspapers wanted me to keep it clean, and refused to publish the damning, dirty stuff . . . So I've had to trawl the online world. Until now, that is.

Now my nighttime misdemeanours are a book: replete with illegitimate perspectives, comparisons and anecdotes from a kid who wasn't even alive 'during the Soweto riots', who never 'suffered from communal unrest', and who never 'went skateboarding in downtown Tel Aviv with RDX strapped to his knee caps'.

What on earth do I know, right?

Funny, that's also what the Moslems thought.

ACROSS THE DIVIDE

'The blacks have fucked it up, haven't they?'

It's a glorious summer morning in Istanbul. The colours of the sky resemble a messy oil painting, both resplendent and melancholic at the same time. The Divan Yolu, once the imperial road that ran all the way from Constantinople to Rome, and now the central thoroughfare at the heart of the Sultanahmet district, is alive with culture, history and the promise of a cheap and tasty breakfast. I find myself standing outside a quaint café, watching a young man set freshly baked cheese pastries on a plate.

Having attended a friend's wedding in the small town of Kirsehir, near the Turkish capital of Ankara, and then spending a couple of weeks meandering through the country's central regions, I have finally made my way back to 'the City'. Istanbul, touted for centuries as the grand juncture between the East and the West, turns splendour into the spectacular. It is difficult to imagine a more extravagant ancient city, and it's especially thrilling for me to be visiting a place that straddles both Europe and Asia in a cacophony of opposing cultures, belief systems and ideologies. In many ways, Istanbul is the original city, the only capital of three consecutive empires, from the Romans to the Byzantines to the Ottomans. It is good to be here on this glorious morning, and enjoying a fresh pastry along the Divan Yolu as I plan my day ahead seems a fine thing to do.

I order a bottle of Coke at the counter before taking my place at a communal table. A well-built Turkish man who looks to be in his early fifties sits opposite. He's impossible to ignore: besides sporting a moustache, shoulder-length curly dark hair and a blue NYPD t-shirt, his defining feature is his physical size. He is a real Rambo. A He-man. Except for that seemingly incongruous t-shirt, he could well be the Turkish version of Hulk Hogan. Sure, both Rambo and He-man avoided the moustachioed look, and Hulk Hogan is blonde even in old age, but you get the picture: this guy's huge.

Turkish Rambo chews loudly, scanning the scenes outside with empty eyes. 'I am from South Africa,' I say by way of introduction.

'Oh. You're a long way from home,' he replies. He has a strong American accent that suddenly brings to life the bodacious letters across his chest. I agree that I am indeed a long way from home, since Durban is, well, some distance from Istanbul.

'I moved to the States some sixteen years back,' he tells me. 'This is not the place it once was.'

He takes a bite of his delicious-looking pastry, glances back at me and asks a question, almost in passing: 'So, how's South Africa doing since the blacks took over? They have fucked it up, haven't they?'

I almost choke on the ice-cold Coke streaming down my throat. No exchanging of names, no discussion of what we did outside pastry cafés, no shared vision on the long legs of the passing dame – no icebreaker at all – this guy just goes right for the jugular. And with a perfectly straight face.

'They're all a bunch of monkeys,' he continues as he takes another bite of his pastry.

I try not to react, but my face creases and my eyes squint unceremoniously – and, possibly, steam escapes from my ears – as I try, literally, to stomach his comments. I feel rage creeping up my oesophagus and I vow to myself never to sit next to a stranger and gulp ice-cold Coke on an empty stomach again.

'I see you don't like what I say,' he says nonchalantly, as a waiter comes over and delivers my spinach-and-feta pastry.

'Look,' I respond, trying to tread carefully, 'our new government has done some really irresponsible things and, yes, things aren't rosy. But it's not as if they inherited a country in good shape, you know.'

'But the country is not the same as it used to be,' he replies flatly. 'These niggers can't do anything right.'

I'm gobsmacked. The vulgarity of this bloke, unashamed to throw racist expletives at a perfect stranger – what did his mother teach him? As I use my bread knife to slice my pastry into little cubes, I envision it morphing into a silver-plated machete . . . This could only mean war.

Except, I'm wary. It's easy enough to remind a fellow South African that his or her overt racism is unwelcome, and to be outraged and offended if necessary. Hell, back home you can throw the first punch and be touted a hero for fighting for the cause. But I don't recall agreeing to face up to a Master of the Universe on the matter. This was not on the memo; certainly not in Istanbul, at least.

A knot of trepidation tightens in my chest. Seriously now, is this really the moment for *that* fight?

I take a bite of my pastry to mull over the situation. The cheese spreads slowly in my mouth, sending love to all parts of the solar system. For a split second my bitter disposition is forgotten – then it returns even drier. Why couldn't he have said that Gandhi was really a homosexual Moslem or that Osama bin Laden was a recovering alcoholic? That would at least have been a little entertaining. This conversation was just not funny – not in this century, at least.

I have to do something, I decide, even though my options are limited. I could express my disgust by clearing the table with one violent sweep of my arms and walking away in a huff, or I can tackle that which offends me. Option two it is. He may break my kneecaps and dunk me into the Bosphorus, sure, but I feel a deep-seated sense of righteousness bidding me to correct his misconstrued sense of history.

But how do I get him to reconsider his racist views and deter him from equating poor governance with 'the blacks', without tangibly addressing his racist remarks? This guy obviously gets a hard-on from his bigoted talk, and I refuse to consummate it by acknowledging it. So how do I overcome his racism without calling him a racist?

Beyond these technical points, I really don't want to be overtly defensive about the South African government, in whom I have limited faith but for entirely different reasons. Only a fool can defend our country's rampant corruption, failing health sector and horrifying crime with a straight face. Affirmative action, BEE and BBBEE gimmicks notwithstanding, we're fast becoming the most unequal country on earth, breeding a new type of restlessness and frustration for all to see. So while I may think our politicians are a bunch of wankers, concerned only with mining our pockets and lining theirs, simply put, it's what politicians do. It's a worldwide phenomenon.

Life or, in this case, bloodshed, is about timing. This, I conclude, just doesn't seem like the appropriate time to sound like a brownish pink-faced liberal defending the natives.

Right, so here goes.

'I don't know what you know about South Africa,' I begin politely, 'but it wasn't one country before 1994. With the arrival of democracy, two totally different, unequal worlds merged into one complicated nation. Also, the idea that South Africa was some thriving country before the new government took over is just wrong.'

'But they've taken a beautiful country and messed it up!' the enormous Turk counters.

I shake my head, determined to chew my food slowly, just how my mother taught me.

'If you really want to talk black and white,' I try again, 'South Africa had a white face, with a black behind. The country that you saw thriving in the past was the front end of a farce, while it attempted to hide all its shitty politics, inequality and prejudice, along with everything else that detergent couldn't whiten, in its backside!'

Rambo's mouth opens to advance a retort, but I interject: 'Look, what I'm trying to say is that the country was pretty fucked up already.'

His mouth freezes and his eyebrows rise as he stares at me with scepticism. The man, it seems, is not accustomed to backchat.

'Oh,' he says after a sizeable, contemplative silence has permeated the air. 'So do you think there's hope for your country?'

'I'm not sure. There was a bunch of politicians running a brutal system before, and now, after "freedom", we have a new troop . . . Whether they care about the ordinary South African is up for debate. This has nothing to do with being black or white. This is just politics.'

I really didn't want to be pedantic about colour; I'd failed.

I think to myself: will I have to be pedantic about colour my entire life? Is this the legacy we have to bear as those growing up as South Africans in the twenty-first century? Was this the price of 'freedom'? Standing up to insignificant racists the world over?

The bodybuilder eventually stops staring at me and continues eating his pastry. I order a fresh orange juice.

POSTSCRIPT

The original version of this piece became one of the most visited pages on my blog. I was accused of writing fiction and of being a scandalmonger, both brave and cowardly in the same breath. Much of it was a case of the title instantly ringing the Political Correctness bell.

I knew I would be lynched online, but I knew also that it was an important story to tell. I felt I had failed in my response at that moment, yet even in retrospect I wasn't quite sure how far I was meant to take the fight. (I'm still not.) And on top of the obvious affront, there was the fact that this guy was not white; he was Turkish. This was racism from a man whose countrymen face discrimination in western Europe every day. It was a sad but poignant encounter for me – and reflective of man's penchant to trample on whomsoever he may.

Across the divide with my Jewish cousin

I

The first time I met a real-life superhero I was eleven years old. He was known as Mighty Mouse and we played soccer together for Chiltern Park FC in the local under-12 league in Durban.

The year was 1994 – a good time for heroes. This particular one was small in stature and lightning quick, and he continued running even after the final whistle. Legend had it that Mighty Mouse even ran in his sleep; he was just never short of breath or energy. In fact, he embodied a frenetic vigour that rendered Jonty Rhodes' efforts, in comparison, the creaky lassitude of a wrecked old tank from the Great War.

Of course, Mighty Mouse had a mild-mannered alter ego and a real name to go along with it but, as with Superman, it was his heroic title that defined who he was and how everyone knew him.

My second encounter with a real-life superhero was with Mighty Mouse's little brother. While not as fit as his elder brother, he had a zest for life, amplified by an implausibly prodigious smile on his tiny face, that left me wanting to give him a big-brotherly hug whenever I saw him. He was affectionately dubbed Mickey Mouse.

But everything changed when I found out that Mighty and Mickey Mouse were Jewish, as was their father, our coach, Peter. On hearing the news, I promptly pulled out of the soccer team, disposed off all my soccer apparel that might have been tainted by their presence, and refused to ever again watch Mighty Mouse trump Oil Can Harry and save Pearl Pure Heart on the VCR . . .

Don't be daft.

In reality, Mighty Mouse and I became the engine of our football team. We formed a great partnership, controlling the midfield and literally outrunning our opposition season after season – until, of course, we grew up and discovered that *shibobo* was more exciting when practised with the ladies. Mighty Mouse started growing at last and shed the superhero cape; I involuntarily reached puberty myself, acquired a covering of permanent stubble and urgently started searching for a life. We eventually moved on from our soccer club to different schools.

Ten years later I bumped into my childhood hero. He was now a university student. Our meeting transported me back to the immortality of those pre-teen years – to the guile, resilience and fun of unimpeded youth (and unbreakable Matchbox cars made in Macau). Remembering it all, it occurred to me just how much his dad, Peter, had influenced my life.

As our coach, Peter was inspirational, even though he was a dictator of note. He had huge Arnold Vosloo eyes set into the canvas of his big, bald head, and he screamed with an accent that made me feel like I was in the English Premier League, not some backwater club in Durban. He was measured in praise, fair in criticism and hard on discipline – but even though his eyes were scary big, his voice was warm, compassionate and thoughtful.

I realized that I had missed the little superhero and his family immensely.

II

On a trip to India a while back I had picked up a copy of *Tales from One Thousand and One Nights* at a local book fair, partly to satisfy my quest to start reading more and to bolster my imagination, but mostly because I harbour secret dreams of having a harem of my own some day.

The book sat unread on my shelf for almost a year, but eventually I got around to opening it up and reading 'Aladdin and the Wonderful Lamp', one of the many stories in the anthology. My knowledge of Aladdin was, until then, largely limited to a dark and disturbing Japanese feature-length animation (which still gives me nightmares) and, of course, the Walt Disney 'I can show you the world' version, complete with flying carpets and the voluptuous Jasmine all carefully wrapped in cheesy but greasy Orientalist ideology.

When I began reading the story, I assumed I would soon be soaking up the magic from the sleeves of this classic fairy tale as I bid for an escape from my benign adult life. But just as I began losing myself in the words of the enchanted text, Aladdin decided to piss on my dreams – by getting ripped off by a Jew.

As the story tells it, when Aladdin returns from the desert with a load of chinaware provided by the perverted genie, he approaches a merchant to sell his goods. But this isn't just any old merchant; this is an 'unscrupulous Jewish merchant' who tries his darndest to swindle our beloved Aladdin. Needless to say, our hero finally meets an old Muslim sheikh who gives him 'the right price' for his merchandise and he lives happily ever after . . .

Now, it wasn't a case of Aladdin being ripped off that upset me. The merchant, the sultan or even the genie could've humped that delinquent brat Aladdin and dumped him into an open gutter for all I cared. But was the acute anti-Semitism really necessary?

Sure, this was a fable written a thousand years ago, before hate speech was outlawed on Constitution Hill, but what purpose did such anti-Semitism in a story – seen widely (and quite sadly so) as the quintessential window to the Orient – serve in a modern world already so divided along ethnic and religious lines?

Call me naïve, call me sensitive, call me a Jew-lover, but is this type of storytelling not precisely the soft ammunition used in demonizing 'the other' that is responsible for stirring communalism and exacerbating it across the globe? Is this not a clear example of a carefully constructed mythology designed to maintain a status quo of the 'behavioural tendencies' of a certain ethnic group, and keep people clutching onto structures of power, such as religion, government and the army, 'to protect them'?

The 'unscrupulous Jewish merchant' could, in other stories, as easily be the 'money-laundering Russians' at Bahnhof Zoo in Berlin or the 'fanatic Muslims' in Mohammed Ali Road in Bombay (who calls it Mumbai anyway?) or the 'drug-dealing Nigerians' in downtown Durban.

I put down the book.

III

Bumping into a 'cousin' of mine in the corridors of Howard College at the University of KwaZulu-Natal, I narrated in earnest the shock of coming across such clear anti-Semitic sentiment in the sacred *Arabian Nights* volume.

This woman is not actually my first, second or even third cousin. Still, we've affectionately called each other cousin ever since we spoke about her circumcised son (an odd discussion), kosher meat and our similar perspectives on peace and justice in the Middle East. (Yes, she's Jewish.)

I concluded my *Arabian Nights* experience by promising to steal Jasmine away from a clearly unworthy Aladdin as punishment for not standing up to hate speech and all that.

'If you think that's bad, go read Roald Dahl,' said my cousin, who thought my defence of the former slaves of Egypt was just precious. She went on to point out that a mild form of anti-Semitism still exists even in South Africa, home of the brave, free and occasionally xenophobic. I was aware that Muslim South Africans tended to throw anti-Semitic remarks every time a couple of Palestinians died for daring to stand up to an Israeli tank, but surely she knew that these were misdirected chants meant for the we-want-all-your-land Zionist type of folk?

'Of course,' she said. 'But I'm talking about anti-Semitic white South African Christians.'

To my shock, she explained that her son avoided revealing his Jewish background in school, to strangers and to the local yoga instructor.

'You won't believe the prejudice among the people here.'

Here we are, a decade into the new millennium, and a kid feels the need to conceal his Jewish identity from white Christian South Africans.

Jesus. Who would have thought?

IV

As a kid, I used to spend a great deal of time with my grandfather at his cosy house in Morewood Road in Durban. My Nana, as we called him, looked more like an ageing Moses than Charlton Heston did in *The Ten Commandments*, with his long, white beard, serene eyes and mouldy toenails. He would sit in bed or in his dilapidated chair and watch CNN all day. Broadcasting war LIVE on television was quite a revelation back in the 1990s and, if ratings are to go by, it's still good business. Of course, by then Rambo was no longer in Vietnam and broadcasting from the Middle East was the new 'in' thing. (A trend that hasn't died off.)

The early 1990s also witnessed the first Palestinian uprising, or Intifada, and this seemed to drown out all other news.

Because I was a kid, my sense of the Middle East conflict as a chronicled dilemma was not developed enough for me to be able to tell the good guys from the bad. All I understood was that Muslims and Jews were killing each other for land or something. But I'm pretty certain that, even as an eleven-year-old, I knew whose side I was on.

And despite my good friendship with Mighty Mouse and his family, I clearly recall how my just-over-a-decade-old self reacted when I overheard Dad telling Mum that Coach Peter and his family were Jews. It was just a passing comment but I remember my body responding to the news.

They were *Jewish*.

It's not like my grandfather went on anti-Semitic tirades every time a couple of Palestinian kids were shot at for throwing stones at Israeli officers. Likewise, when I was in my own home, it wasn't as if my father propagated anti-Israeli sentiment through crass outbursts of profanity against God's 'chosen people'. My father taught me to be such a non-confrontational-turn-the-other-cheek wuss that I felt ashamed whenever I heard about suicide bombers blowing up school kids in Israeli busses.

Yet, in spite of all the positive construction of the oneness of humanity created by my folks, I still squirmed when I heard that my friends were Jewish.

And nothing exemplified this internal disturbance like the evening I remember arriving at soccer practice with the car radio blaring out news of a fatal bomb blast in Jerusalem, or possibly Tel Aviv, and distinctly wondering what Mighty Mouse and his family thought. Were they pro 'the Jews' and anti 'the Muslims' because they were Jews, or were they pro 'the Muslims' and anti 'the Jews' *even though* they were Jews? Or were they just indifferent because they thought both sides were crazy?

I remember thinking how their perception of the conflict affected the way they related to me. Would my good attitude, polite demeanour and slick passing skills shift their possibly jaundiced notion of 'the Muslims'? Did it even matter? It was confusing. I desperately wanted to know the answers to these and other questions. But then, being Jewish or Muslim, could we simply act as if outside events did not affect us, or did real friendship mean we would have to eventually engage each other on the conflict?

But, most importantly, what did my mate Mighty Mouse think?

To be eleven years old is a remarkable thing: you're old enough to think, but young enough not to dwell. So I simply moved on. Besides, my father always brought doughnuts when he picked me up from soccer practice; that was probably enough to distract me.

Of course, today I know the situation in the Middle East is not about 'the Muslims' or 'the Jews', even if they are apparently the main protagonists. It took me long enough, but today I realize how influential the soft signs offered by allegories in fairy tales can be on children and the manners in which they construct their world. Kids don't need to be forcibly indoctrinated to pick up vibes, or to feel awkward about a situation thousands of kilometres away even if they hardly know a thing about the topic. In an age of psychedelic information exchange, where identity remains a highly contested product, there is simply no room for the 'unscrupulous Jewish merchant' if we have any serious aspiration to bridge our shattered worlds.

Today, Mighty Mouse and I have found each other on Facebook. He is always going to be Mighty Mouse. But I think it's time we had a chat.

POSTSCRIPT

A version of this piece was first published towards the end of 2009 in the community magazine *Al Huda*. The magazine was celebrating ten years in print, and it was perhaps apt that Editor Khadija Patel selected the Israel–Palestine issue as a theme since it was a year after the deadly invasion of Gaza – a good time, perhaps, to restart a conversation about the conflict and the prospects for peace and justice. While the issue was laced with a pro-Palestinian stance, Patel carefully commissioned articles that moved away from the usual religious dogma that often plagues commentary on the crisis, and placed reconciliation and dialogue as the motto for the bumper edition.

I was pleased because it has always been my concern that South African lobbying for Palestine is too Muslim in character. Even though the African National Congress (ANC) has historical struggle linkages with the Palestinian Liberation Organization, to use this old linkage as proof that the pro-Palestinian lobby in the country is made up of a diverse set of South Africans is a self-defeating lie. The fact that protest marches against Israeli aggression or in solidarity with Palestinians are overwhelmingly Muslim in nature means there is a huge gap between the liberal intelligentsia pushing for action against Israel and the general South African public who think it's just a Muslim issue.

The Palestinian issue is about an illegal occupation – but you wouldn't know that if you went to a march in Durban, Johannesburg or Cape Town. In South Africa (unlike in certain other countries), it is almost impossible to extricate the land issue from its religious branding, which in all frankness is a necessity in order to get Muslims off their arses and onto the streets to voice their disapproval. Sure, there will always be some figurehead from the Anglican Church speaking at a march, but the inevitable feeling is that he's just there to keep the crowd believing that 'even other religions are with us'. With Ronnie Kasrils and the Pahad brothers no longer in government, the Palestinian lobby groups in South Africa would do well to rebrand the Palestinian issue and its Boycott Divestment and Sanctions (BDS) campaign as a human-rights issue, steering clear of religion as much as possible. Though they have been engaging the labour confederation Cosatu, the ANC Youth League and various human-rights organizations to garner mass support, they have yet to capture the imagination of the public and push for a more radical South African government position on the issue.

To consider it in another light, you don't hear many South African Muslims talking about the injustices in Myanmar or Sri Lanka or Zimbabwe (unless they have a business there). They aren't usually interested in the rights of informal traders in the city centre or shack dwellers across the street but they have a fat load to say about abuse to home and property in Palestine or Kashmir. Of course, asking them to stand up for gay-and-lesbian rights would be too much to ask from most homophobic Muslims, because the fact is that most of my brethren aren't really interested in human rights; they are mostly interested in Muslim rights.

Of course, stalwarts of the cause will disagree with this analysis, and will go on to cite a hundred sources to prove that the South African pro-Palestine struggle on the ground is multi-faith and non-racialized. But, sadly, this is not the case. For me, the hijacking of the Palestinian cause by Muslims in South Africa and elsewhere as well as the fact that Muslims are not overtly interested in causes or histories that do not pull at their Muslim sensibilities (like the Armenians in Turkey or Sri Lankan maids in Saudi Arabia) undermines the moral basis of their discontent. Muslims ought to be more generous with their politicking and lobbying for all disenfranchised people. But the inequity is pretty well spread; even Shiah Muslims in Bahrain battle to win an audience with Sunnis mostly obsessed with promulgating their version of heaven worldwide.

Juxtaposed with this cherry-picking activism is the insistence of Muslims to fall over each other in protesting silly cartoons, arguing over the permissibility of female voices on radio, or (and also a personal favourite) debating whether pygmies could ever be halaal. Meanwhile, the Zionist propaganda machine rolls on, sponsoring journalists to check out Israel's perspective on a first-hand basis and explore the various Israel–Arab reconciliatory centres before returning home to tell a tale of a blooming benevolence. Thus, while an entire Israeli media juggernaut is at work, repairing damaged reputations and building new sympathies through effective, innovative (if cheesy) media campaigns, the Palestine solidarity movement, on the other hand, must deal with Hamas banning women's underwear from shop windows.

Of course, all this hyperbole distracts from the real issue at hand and some activists would say that renewed talks, negotiations and the official bid for a Palestinian state are further diversions. Rather, the emphasis should be on rights, not statehood, and that action is long overdue. The gallery, sitting on the periphery, wishes the whole issue would just go away.

But it does feel like an issue battling to regain traction – a political economy burning slowly with occasional crackles, sparks and burnt crusts.

One just gets the feeling that the level of romanticism, religious fanaticism and outside interference will make this quite a mountain to climb, even for cousins.

Shape without drape: Muslim fashion du jour

Tens of thousands of Muslims marched through the streets of Paris yesterday to bid farewell to the burqa, the famed fashion accessory that is due to bow out of French society just in time for Summer 2010. Demonstrators cried, sang victory songs and waved an array of banners, from the heartfelt FREE AT LAST! and THANK YOU SARKOZY to the more obscure MUM, I'M ON TV and KILL THE BOER.

Capturing the spirit of the day, head fashion guru of Paris Fashion Week, Simin Leveque, encouraged the boisterous crowd. 'We are here to demonstrate that while the burqa might be out, pumps are still in!' she cried over the loudspeaker.

It was a scene of extraordinary festivity as hip-and-happening Muslim women from all over France and Belgium united in a cacophony of 'naughty noor'. Confessing to be slaves to fashion, the demonstrating women were all (voluntarily) dressed in the current trend uniform of movement-constricting skinny jeans and slinky t-shirts, boldly accessorized with pink hijabs and lemon-yellow pumps. Across their well-proportioned chests the words *ADIEU À LA BURQA* were proudly born, and the look was completed with this season's must-have *mahrams*. *'Liberté, égalité, fraternité!'* the crowd chanted in unison. Fashion insiders professed it to be the biggest movement since the French Revolution.

The month before, the burqa, a type of face-and-bodygear ensemble created in pre-Islamic times to protect women from sandstorms and kidnapping during tribal wars, was banned in Belgium. Now moves were in place to ban it in France in time for the year's Paris Fashion Week.

'Look,' said Fatima Mumkhin, a construction worker from Brussels who hitchhiked for a day and a half to get to Paris, 'Europe has cobbled streets now and eastern European women are the only ones being trafficked these days. Muslim women are no longer under threat. Can't say the same about Romanians though . . .'

Organizers of the commemoration, a collaborative effort between Paris Fashion Week and Free The Women (FTW), a gender consultancy firm based in almost-important Colmar, explained that they wanted to give the burqa 'a flamboyant, post-modern sendoff befitting an antiquity destined for the museum'.

Laughed Leveque: 'It belongs to the Louvre – not on people's faces!'

The esteemed fashionista noted that the response of Muslim women had been overwhelming. 'The thirty or so women who once wore the burqa in Belgium are all here and they are thrilled to be blending into the crowd in their new skinny jeans and tank tops. The boys love them!'

Of course, there are far more than thirty burqa wearers in France. It is estimated that of a French Muslim population of around five million people, nearly 2,000 women make use of it in public – an astounding 0.04 per cent.

Radwa el-Sherbini, originally from Egypt, said that she was ecstatic that the new law was about to be instituted, as living in a tent had often brought stares from pensioners, children and stray dogs. 'The mutts used to snigger and bark at me. Damn those Western imperialist dogs!' she exclaimed.

El-Sherbini explained that living in Europe as an economic migrant had given her the freedom to work, unlike millions of women denied this basic right in the Muslim world. 'I work sixteen hours a day here, cleaning toilets in people's houses. I've never had opportunities like this before,' she said with a smile. 'It's just wonderful.'

But el-Sherbini – no relative of Marwa el-Sherbini, the woman killed in a court in Germany the year before as a result of her fashion sense – says that Muslims need to understand that if they abide by the rules it is relatively easy to live in Europe. 'Europeans are tolerant and open-minded. As long as you never say anything about the Holocaust, you are safe in this place.'

Another woman, Almas Rafiki, from Morocco, married to an Algerian and living in Antwerp, says she couldn't understand why the Muslim world was upset about the ban. 'Here in Europe, men appreciate our bodies more,' she says. 'I love being a sex symbol.'

Afreen Athiyabaushna, a born-and-bred French national of Iranian descent, was filled with patriotic pride as she proclaimed how the French government went into painstaking detail to establish whether the ban should be implemented. 'They went to each and every Muslim woman in this country and asked us if we were forced to wear the burqa,' she said, claiming that the impending legislation did not mirror a steady shift to the right in Europe. 'Today they tell us to get rid of the burqa; tomorrow they will make us remove our scarves; then they will tell us to change our names. And then we will finally be Europeans,' she beamed.

The unusual commemoration rounded the Champs-Élysées and ended with a rock concert featuring Bono, Ricky Martin and Sami Yusuf, thus completing an extraordinary day in French history that was celebrated by many.

But right-wing sources have claimed that the festivities have sent shock waves across the continent. According to unconfirmed reports, there is growing concern that French president Nicholas Sarkozy's fixation on emancipating Muslim women from the clutches of their uncivilized male oppressors may set an unhealthy precedent.

Jean le Marc, a member of radical group Merde Mossalman, fears the new law banning the burqa could fundamentally shift the social structure of French society. 'I am not sure if the economy can handle a sudden rush of free Muslim women in the job market,' said Le Marc. 'People think they are uneducated, socially inept and only good for making babies, but we know for a fact that most of them have read *The Kite Runner*.'

Le Marc is not the only one who believes Europeans may be getting more than they had bargained for by promulgating this law. The domestic violence desk outside the Gare de l'Est train station in Paris stands to lose its purpose now that the burqa is on its way out.

'The burqa kept us in business,' says chap-in-charge Rene Durand. 'We will be suing the French government for damages and loss of income.'

Alberto Mattarazzi, a medico-anthro-sociologist in Rome, concurs that there needs to be some regulation in the removal of the scarf or veil, for the safety of both the women involved and society at large.

'First, we don't know what we will find under those veils,' said Mattarazzi. 'There are possible health risks. And second, I think that we need to emancipate these women in batches just to keep things under control.'

He warns that there could be a dangerous face-off with French society if these women did not experience some sort of rehabilitation and orientation.

'To suddenly be judged by your shape and physical appearance rather than on your intellect and ability can be quite a traumatizing process. We want them to enjoy European culture, not rebel against it.'

Meanwhile, fashion guru Leveque said that the success of this commemoration signals the need to spread the love. Further events were planned for Brussels, Berlin and Rome later in the month.

'Ultimately, I want to take this roadshow to downtown Kabul to show them what European life is all about,' she said. 'I would die for an opportunity like that.'

POSTSCRIPT

At is stands, both France and Belgium have officially banned the wearing of the burqa in public, while Spain, Germany and Australia have signalled signs of following suit.

I have to concede that I don't like the burqa (the full tent) or the niqab (the tent with cutout for the eyes) – they represent a type of Islam that I cannot identify with. They are reclusive, isolating and supposedly burdened with the literal interpretation of religious texts and practice. I understand the rules. I just think everything comes with a sense of humour.

And while most Islamic scholars agree that the burqa is not strictly necessary – as compared to the hijab (the headscarf), which is – it is also easy to argue that the historical context that made it a practical garment once upon a time no longer exists in a modern secular country like France. In other words, the burqa may have made sense five hundred years ago when it deflected dust and pervy male stares, but it doesn't today on the nicely paved streets of twenty-first-century Paris, where every woman has more rights than God (and likely owns a vacuum cleaner). In fact, it achieves the opposite effect today: it brings unwanted attention to the wearer.

In a typically secular environment, the burqa certainly takes some getting used to. It is hardly a flattering garment; it's not meant to be. It spawns alienation, it kills conversation before it even starts, it screams 'patriarchy', 'abuse' and 'secrecy' – all modern warning signs to incite the feminist police. Factor in years of stock imagery from poorly conveyed Orientalist subtext in paintings, writings, movies and CNN broadcasts – which have grossly misrepresented the position of women in Islam – and the burqa itself turns into 'an act of violence'.

With all the horror stories from faraway places like Afghanistan and Pakistan feeding our collective imagination, there seems to have been a wide acceptance of the oppression of the Muslim woman. So it doesn't matter if she has fought to wear the burqa, believes it will take her closer to her God and wants no contact with men other than her father, husband, siblings and close family – because we have already decided that her wearing of the burqa is the ultimate symbol of female oppression. In the European context, it is treated as a stubborn demonic relic that is thwarting integration, modernization and free thought.

Please note that I am not simply describing what I believe to be the Western interpretation of the burqa. I am Muslim, but even *I* get nervous when in the (rare) company of a burqa-chick: in the queue at Pick n Pay, for example, or at the Butcher Boys, where she will try to surreptitiously slip pieces of sirloin steak between the cloth without anyone seeing her puffy lips. Truth is, I often don't know how to act around a woman in such attire because no one teaches you what etiquette to follow when someone pitches a tent around her body and then stands next to you. Should you greet her? Should you ignore her? Should you lower your gaze and dare to check out her Nik-Nak-shaped toes? Even non-burqa-wearing Muslim women – in headscarves or without – can feel uncomfortable around their swathed sisters. A troop of ninjas looking down with (supposed) disdain at regular Muslim women in hipsters and short-sleeve tops can be quite terrifying.

The obvious conclusion here is that if fellow Muslims struggle to deal with the burqa, it's almost impossible to expect non-Muslims, burdened already with enough propaganda and misconception, not to feel some discomfort or, at the very least, hold a jaundiced opinion on the matter. I can't help but agree, for reasons mentioned, that the burqa appears to be incompatible with modern settings.

But, hold on. Who am I to waltz in with my fancy education, torn jeans and funky All Stars and conclude that an item of religious clothing should be banned because of a 'discomfort' with it? Or because 'it doesn't make sense'? This isn't female mutilation or child brides or honour killings. We're talking about a piece of cloth that has become a battleground for opposing ideologies.

I don't like the burqa. Europe doesn't like the burqa. But so what?

The obvious satire of this particular piece was (mostly) well received by my blog readers. What they possibly weren't aware of was that most of the facts weren't made up. There really are just thirty or so women in Belgium who wear (or wore?) the burqa, and fewer than 2,000 women in France who do likewise, out of a Muslim population of three to five million. These are less than arbitrary figures; there are probably more than 2,000 transvestite hookers in Paris alone! It is not as if a new trend has arisen in which every second Muslim bedecks herself from head to toe, signifying a new global jihad against European liberty.

The truth is that Europe's so-called concern for Muslim women makes far too many assumptions about the veil and its negative influence on integration in European society. How will a ban catalyse integration or deter the ghettoization of Muslim communities in Europe when so few wear it in the first place? How will it halt abuse in households or usher Muslim women into the workplace? How will it solve any of the social problems European governments claim to be trying to address?

In my view, the insistence on removing the burqa from the 'oppressed Muslim woman' is nothing more than contrived spin designed to protect a

'European' environment from the (perceived) oncoming Islamic armada. It is a rallying point in a larger power struggle which lacks credibility; it is a quest for assimilation, not integration.

In reality, this controversy is taking place in Europe, not the Middle East. And by definition, Europeans can do what they like about it. But banning the burqa would turn it into a sacred relic, and a new mythology of institutionalized oppression will emerge – which would simply be counterproductive.

Yes, there are women forced into wearing the burqa and the hijab. Some are even forced to wear underwear. At the same time there are those who voluntarily and wholeheartedly accept it as a religious obligation. How can a government or an individual, from a judgemental distance, distinguish between those on whom the burqa is being forced and those wearing it freely?

It may sound foolish, even disingenuous, to defend a symbol that so obviously places women behind men, that so clearly demarcates farcical boundaries between the sexes. But I think it would be even more naïve to believe that conservative European governments can be trusted with 'the emancipation of the Muslim woman'.

Just how moronic do they think these terrorists are?

I am standing behind all shapes, sizes, colours and nationalities at Dubai International Mall, otherwise known as Dubai International Airport, waiting to surrender my boarding pass at the gate so I can catch my flight to Frankfurt. In front of me is an old woman flanked by her two sons. The woman wears a black hijab, which covers her hair and arms but reveals her face. The elder of the two boys, a tall, skinny lad of no more than eighteen years, handles the passports and boarding passes as they approach one of the attendants at the gate. Remember, this is the final step in the boarding process; the visas have been issued, they've passed through security, their luggage is already checked in and they are simply in the process of moving from one plane to another, having arrived from some other place. But the woman accepting boarding passes and wishing travellers a pleasant journey ignores this fact; she gives the small family's passports a once-over and begins the second-longest inquisition of modern times:

GATE ATTENDANT: Where are you going?

BOY: To Frankfurt.

GATE ATTENDANT: Okay. Why are you going to Frankfurt?

BOY: To visit my father.

GATE ATTENDANT: What is he doing there?

BOY: He is working there.

GATE ATTENDANT (looking at boy's passport): Okay. What is your father's name?

BOY (mostly inaudible, but something along the lines of): Abdul Mohamed Jamal Mustapha . . .

GATE ATTENDANT: According to this passport, you missed one name.

The boy quietly clarifies the problem, pointing to something on the passport. I can't make out the details.

GATE ATTENDANT: So when did you last visit your father?

BOY: About nine years ago.

GATE ATTENDANT: Why so long ago?

BOY: Because . . .

It continues like this for some time, and while I am watching the circus act play out, wondering when the boy will lose his patience and scream out something randomly damning ('Okay! Okay! I like watching granny porn!'), I am called to the other counter by another attendant to board the flight. As I pass by the family, I glance at their passports. Pakistanis. Naturally. My eyes wander to the name badge of the woman-hound at the counter – who suspiciously looks like my Aunt Katie back home and resembles the average Savitri from Bangalore – and it reveals, unsurprisingly, that she is 'Gayatri'.

I squirm at the fair assumption that Gayatri, like thousands of other migrant workers in the UAE, is really an Indian national taking her national prestige and honour – already far up her rectum – to a whole new level of perversity as she takes the Mickey out of this little Pakistani family trying to get to Europe. Of course, whether she is Indian, Sri Lankan or even Taiwanese is hardly the point.

First, Gayatri is really just an airline employee and not an immigration officer. Second, the boy who can't remember his father's fifteenth name is not some indentured labourer hitchhiking through the galaxy; he isn't even on the first leg of his journey, which would at least give more justification to such a frenetic check-up. He is already in Dubai International, about to board a connecting flight to Frankfurt, meaning that the million necessary check-ups were already completed half a day ago. Granted that airlines have to check that visas are in order (that is, issued) to protect themselves from having to fly miscreants back to the place of departure at their own cost, but this woman has clearly overstepped the mark. Asking the boy why he hasn't seen his father for nine years is hardly bound to reconfirm the legitimacy of his visa.

Nevertheless, our tall Pakistani friend continues bravely, dealing superfluously with the entire air-travel-soaked-in-terrorism rhetoric that makes him a beggar at every airport he ventures into and turns his admission onto every flight he takes into an act of (paid-for-in-full) charity. In theory, because he's the customer, he could tell Gayatri that he's going via Frankfurt to visit her whoring sister at Bob's Youth Hostel on 92 Voorbergval Street in Amsterdam. In reality though, he has to talk to Gayatri with his eyes to the floor until she deigns to allow him access to the plane that will take him to the much-fabled land of Europe. Rather than raising the alarm about her clearly prejudiced questions, he treats his obstacle course like a champion dervish would when seeking the highest levels of tolerance, patience and spirituality.

But what choice does he have? He is brown: strike one. He is Muslim: strike two. If he were to open his mouth without thinking, to act a little too smart, it would be strike three – 'out'.

It seems peculiar that airlines can be the vanguard of human mobility and movement, leaders in the creation of the global village – yet they remain unequivocally tied to the state with fermenting umbilical cords, simultaneously discrediting national boundaries and suckling the powers that be. Sure, we all remember 9/11 and London and Madrid and Hiroshima and Nagasaki, but is it really acceptable that racial profiling has become fair discrimination – universally – because of an overwhelmingly stronger terrorism concern?

With this in mind, it was almost funny to hear Barack Obama thrilling us with his Qur'anic quotes and earnest ideologies during his address to the Muslim world in Cairo back in June 2009, as he regaled us with clash-of-civilizations anecdotes and called for an end to inter-faith mistrust. Because the sad fact is that the nature of travel and mobility today suggests it will take decades or more, or perhaps a global threat to mankind – such as our imminent destruction by the Decepticons – to thwart years of strong Islamophobic propaganda.

Obama also proposed that we work towards improving exchange programmes and building online communities where youngsters in Kansas can flirt with youngsters in Cairo as a means to facilitate positive intercultural dialogue. But the online and real worlds, as our Kansan-Cairene couple will surely find out on the day they decide to move their relationship beyond cybersex, are literally worlds apart. Put simply: how long do we wait before North Africans or South Asians or Arab-looking travellers are no longer treated like lepers with suicide-bomber tendencies at airports en route to the Western World?

And if this is the route we're taking – if, based on recent history, we really believe that brown-skinned Moslems are more likely to blow themselves up – why not ask every black man for a police-clearance certificate and every white man for proof they aren't racist twats? Since these are the essential archetypes of our times, why not institutionalize them all? Oh wait, they *were* institutionalized: it was called apartheid.

Put into perspective, being consistently profiled could never be as bad as being shelled in Baghdad while out walking your goat, or having rockets light up your fields in Peshawar while bringing in the opium harvest, or sitting up with your suffering children because of the after effects of white phosphorous in Gaza. Of course, demeaning and embarrassing yourself or having cheeky security personnel check out your anus simply because of a flawed classification system can never be as terrible as the horrors of war. Forgive me, then, for being petty in my attempt to reclaim my dignity. But one thing is for sure: I am no longer comfortable continuously pulling out my anti-terrorist kit every time I travel.

For someone who hates shaving – since my clean-shaven face resembles a scratchy stick of asparagus that no one wants to dip into their soup – I have to first pull out the razor blades and take a haircut. Then it is my vocabulary that must be tied up. Since 'bomb' is a word that's pretty much a part of every Muslim's lexicon these days, I need to discipline myself not to shout out 'I will bomb this place!' as a kneejerk reaction to all things we Muslims don't like. Then it's my luggage. Instead of spraying my bags with religious phrases asking God to protect my travel, I spray my bag with Rough Rider condoms. Finally, it's my image. I switch into the typically undernourished journo mode, strutting around in slightly torn cargos, takkies and a hoodie while blatantly boasting the latest iPod in an effort to look too scruffy to be a fresh puppy out of a madrasah *aus* Kandahar and too stupid to be a polished undercover pilot in an Armani suit. Finally, I cease all contentious behaviour within a five-kilometre radius of all airports and I assume I'll be fine . . .

And it works. No one bothers me.

The only trick is that all parts must function in unison. For example, the last time I was in Europe I decided not to shave before catching my return flight out of Amsterdam. Call it a slightly demented social experiment, if you will, but mainly it was because shaving during a European winter is like scraping your balls with a heated metal grater. Needless to say, I paid the price.

I had flown out of Europe three times in the three years prior to this trip, and I had never experienced any incidents. As a result, my passport was laced with German study visas (attaining the visas generally made the studying itself feel like child's play), each one further emphasizing my legitimate travel credentials, which is what frequent travel is supposed to infer. Of course, a brown Muslim travelling to Europe many times achieves quite the opposite. And the one time I chose not to shave my six-day unkempt beard I was – naturally – picked out like Ahmed the plump chicken terrorist asking to be slaughtered. I might as well have used the grater.

The concept of security profiling is painfully comical when you realize the process has little to do with real safety and is instead about creating a superficial sense of control/security. Because, of course, terrorists are aware that airport security is keeping a lookout for a big, bearded guy with a towel on his head and a bomb strapped to his nuts. Any vaguely competent fundamentalist is aware he needs to shave. Yet airport security acts as if terrorists are all retarded blokes who look like caricatures of themselves.

Real security would not be based on skin colour, facial hair, kurtas or shiny suits. Real security would check everyone equally. The world is so much smaller these days, and so diluted, that identity and ideology literally transcend the stereotypes of the past. In short, there is no place for profiling.

Except that checking everyone equally would take too much time and money. So let's pick out the bearded brown man with an Arabic name who is quite obviously more dangerous than the clean-shaven brown man with an Arabic name. This is called deductive reasoning . . .

So, having foolishly attempted to catch a flight while sporting several days' growth of facial hair, my bags were turned upside down, my passport put into some CIA-type gadget to verify authenticity, and a multitude of questions that bordered on the insane were thrown at me. Meanwhile, ordinary law-abiding Europeans did their bit by pointing at me and explaining to their little Heidis, Heinrichs and Hannahs why the queue resembled a lunch-time traffic jam.

Some airlines, however, take profiling a disingenuous step further than this. A blonde American professor at Berkeley explained to me recently that since 9/11 she has been continuously singled out for extra security checks every time she travels abroad. After finding it peculiar that she was regularly being singled out despite not fitting into any conceivable threatening profile, she realized she wasn't really being searched. It was just a façade. She deduced that she kept falling prey to a systematic attempt to create the feeling that profiling wasn't taking place. After all, drug mules and suicide bombers are hardly ever middle-aged female professors at Ivy League schools, are they? But here was 'proof', if ever some idiot like me raised questions, that unfair profiling didn't exist.

Of course, I am South African, so any airport checks I must endure are generally less terrorist-oriented and more concerned with the search for curry powder laced with marijuana. The possibility of being a dangerous radical is close to minuscule since the local Jamiatul Ulama is just a bunch of impotent clerics, not some Interpol-referenced terrorist movement claiming Fordsburg in Gauteng as an autonomous Muslim state. But still the little week-long beard can twist the mood of your travel experience, even if every other aspect of your anti-terrorism kit is in order.

In contrast, if you're coming from Pakistan, a nation confused for a country and now in some sort of chaos, you might have to prove you are a homosexual seeking asylum in Europe, since your nationality makes all attempts to clean up your image null and void. And even if you do get the visa, you still need to prove you actually plan on returning home alive rather than as a burnt-out firecracker. In other words, the whole world is really against you.

Predictably, the Pakistani boy I observed in Dubai International Airport continued answering the trigger-happy airline employee's questions as meekly as possible, and I continued to wonder how much longer he could hold out before he mentioned the porn. But he didn't buckle and eventually his family was allowed to proceed; in these times patience for the brown man is a crucial survival tool, and he was well aware of this. It was a lesson I had learnt two years earlier when I had an altercation with an employee of the low-cost Condor airline at the Frankfurt airport.

What started as a mere request for a form on my part, suddenly became a nasty incident when I threatened to report the attendant to his company for barking at me like a rabid animal. He dropped the aggression, changed his tone and moved close to my face, purposefully popping that precious space bubble as he slowly and deliberately opened my passport.

'Mohamed. Azad. Ebrahim. Essa,' he whispered coldly, emphasizing each vowel meticulously. 'Are you really sure you want to fly?'

Being a slow sod, it took me a whole five seconds to realize what was going on here, and when I did I blinked and stepped back, feeling a fire rage through my lungs and the veins on my forehead tense so tautly that they beckoned me to scream. But it quickly simmered into a defeatist subcontinental nod, complete with dented smile and Indian accent.

'Okay,' I said. 'I understand. I understand completely.'

The man had my passport in his hands, after all, and I had an important flight to catch – more important, evidently, than my dignity. My words had appeased him and he consented to allow me to go on my way. I secured my passport, thanked him for his time very politely and walked away, pensively biting my lip as flames of fury lit my path. Then, not able to bottle it up any longer, I turned around, called out his name and unceremoniously showed him the finger. I didn't turn back to see his response, though I remember thinking special paratroopers would surely break through the airport windows in an instant and whisk me away, *Minority Report* style. But none of it happened.

The Condor employee was a prick; even the average neo-Nazi would battle to be such a goon as he so easily was born to be. I should have reported him. But I didn't have any proof, or any real argument. What was I going to say exactly?

I was young and naïve. But just let that happen today. I would get his full name, blog about it violently and send the link to his mother.

I wasn't born to scream Islamophobia

There are those sick of hearing that colonization turned Africa into a cuckoo's nest and every new African leader into a darker version of crazy Jack Nicholson. There are those equally tired of hearing non-white individuals cry wolf every time they're treated with disdain at work or at the mall or in the bedroom. People don't just treat each other badly because they are racist; they also do it because they're assholes and imbeciles whose mothers never loved them. Of course, this truth doesn't mean that racism is imaginary. And it doesn't mean that Africa is still not feeling the calamitous aftershocks from centuries of outsider control.

A pet hate of mine is listening to the imam screaming 'Islamophobia' at the mosque, or politicians doing likewise on television, or the local Muslim population doing the same at the neighbourhood grocery store, where people gather in the veggie section to talk about the grand conspiracy against Islam created by the Freemasons, propagated by CNN and sold in booty-shaped Coke bottles. I normally prefer the political opinions of those with the least to gain and perhaps the most to lose when confronting discrimination or unfair practices. So I would prefer hearing the Pope say that gays and lesbians are treated unfairly, or a Chinese academic say that his government has made chopsuey out of monk meat. In short, there is often little point in hearing from our free-love brothers and sisters that they're having a hard time – because, of course, they're going to say that.

But, then, does this approach mean that we have to ignore people who tell us their own stories of personal subjugation? Do we need an anthropologist from Belgium to explain his country's brutal occupation of Congo in order for us to take colonialist crimes seriously? Likewise, do we need Germans to concur that the Holocaust did happen as brutally as the Jewish people (or their representatives) suggest, or do we need Iranian president Mahmoud Ahmadinejad to trample over protestors in Tehran and deny the Holocaust to realize that the issue really deserves some sensitivity?

I don't think so.

If people are screaming at the top of their voices, spinning on their heads, swinging on vines between skyscrapers, or throwing their toys out of their cots, even if it is to exhort a shrilling accusation of ill-treatment, they deserve to be heard and their cause and story considered – briefly, at least.

Black kids don't lose their umbilical cords and then tout 'racism' as their first word. Jewish families don't talk about their grandfathers being force-fed currywurst in Auschwitz every night at the supper table. And Jehovah's Witnesses don't talk about how Hollywood bastardizes their religion every time they go to the movies. In other words, people don't enjoy crying wolf. There is no joy in being a victim, in saying 'I was robbed of my dignity' every day of your life. Such protestations don't get you laid. So perhaps they should be taken a little more seriously than they are.

Having just spent almost two months in Germany, living a daily life with friends in local circles far from the tourist charades, I discovered a world far removed from the Germany (and Europe) I believed existed: a far less tolerant place than I had first explored as a student five years ago. Stories of racism, xenophobia and Islamophobia seemed more normalized, etched into the psyche of non-native Europeans' daily lives more than ever. I have witnessed and been involved in some needlessly ugly experiences. And having detailed my experiences, I found that the reader's assumption was often that I, like millions of Muslim brats worldwide, have been brainwashed during early morning whipping sessions at the local madrasah into always defending the Islamic religion, no matter how many times I disagree with its policies or actions. I am Muslim. I am supposed to scream 'victim'. I am supposed to burn embassies. I am supposed to kill my sister's boyfriend. And as many of the responses to my blog post 'Just how moronic do they think these terrorists are?' suggested, even Thought Leader readers would prefer to read about racial profiling and Islamophobia from an atheist, an Aussie, a Japanese kamikaze pilot – anybody but me.

Right?

But I really wasn't born to scream Islamophobia.

Thing is, the stories of Muslims being discriminated against never ceased during my trip, and my involuntary exposure to the issues and the denial thereof slowly became impossible to ignore. The silence began to overwhelm me. It was a chilly evening in Munich, with three policemen in plainclothes surrounding me and telling me to take my hands out my pockets as they went about checking if I was on one of those terror lists, when I realized enough was enough. It was a particularly nasty experience. And it was time to stop worrying about sounding like a victim and confront the issue head on.

There is a startling fear of Muslims and Islam that seems to be increasing exponentially, a thing called Islamophobia – and it is not going away.

In spite of being Muslim, and therefore naturally biased in any non-Muslim's eyes, I should be entitled to scream Islamophobia from the rooftops when I encounter it, and I should be able to talk about it in an open forum without sounding like an evil, brainwashed caricature from a bad movie throwing a jihadist tantrum.

Is that too much to ask?

THE RESTLESS GENERATION

Remember 100 days before we were screwed over

I don't like press conferences. Stage-managed to propagate nothing more than a prearranged message, press conferences are events where real questions are rarely asked because real answers are never forthcoming. Everything is pre-empted and rehearsed. Answers are a performed act choreographed by media spin doctors and public-relations advisers.

Everyone knows that real answers to probing questions are found in the unlikeliest of places: in the bar, on the golf course, in someone else's bed. The journalists who are forced to patronize press conferences merely rotate old rhetoric on new paper before they go outside to cuss and light a smoke.

'He didn't answer anyone's questions properly', 'Another pointless exercise' and 'This is such bullshit' are the types of comments that loop through the corridors like broken memory sticks.

All journalists know this, so any of us at the recent '100 days to the World Cup' press conference who expected to receive substantial answers from Fifa's big boys or representatives of the South African government – rather than watching the old geezers masturbate to the sounds of their own voices – should have hit the beach instead.

I know I should have.

The event was held at the sparkling new Moses Mabhida stadium in Durban, where Sepp Blatter did his usual thing and gave us some neatly packaged rhetoric about 'Fifa giving back to Africa', while deputy president Kgalema Mothlanthe tried gamely to charm us all as he smiled about wanting to put on his 'boots and run on the pitch'.

To be fair, this was a euphoric occasion, one that celebrated the winding route of a journey that started about 2,000 days ago when South Africa first won the bid to host the event. The road has been long and filled with all sorts of scepticism, talk of an imminent plan B or even C, long, hard work in constructing various new stadiums and upgrading roads, transport systems and stadium precincts – so yes, it made sense to mark the 100-day milestone.

But the World Cup was not sold on the back of a logic that simply promised to make us feel good about ourselves.

Unfortunately – while dignitaries eloquently answered all the typically over-asked questions about what this World Cup will mean to the people of South Africa and the rest of Africa in terms of nation building, self-esteem, pride and all that – there was little attempt to address the legitimate concerns posed by those journalists interested in more than the glitz and glam. A plethora of unanswered questions regarding what this event would actually *accomplish* for the people of South Africa hung in the air like a bad odour.

A question posed about the thousands of construction workers who have lost their jobs following the completion of the stadiums turned our beaming deputy president into a fumbling comedian, mumbling on about how the construction industry was the only sector that saw growth during the recession. A question asking what percentage of revenue made by Fifa during the World Cup would be put back into South African football saw a Fifa representative admitting that it was difficult to answer – but then performing a U-turn and assuring us that Fifa's financial statements were completely transparent.

And when asked about the continued lack of professionalism in African football, which has seen so many World Cup-bound African teams replace their managers at the last minute, and how this might affect Africa's chances of performing during the competition, the South African Football Association (Safa) president Kirsten

Nematandani let fire a misdirected rant about how immensely prepared Bafana Bafana will be under Alberto Carlos Parreira.

Journalists glanced at each other with wry smiles while I looked on like a gobsmacked child at the spectacle: there was eThekwini mayor Obed Mlaba looking rounder than usual (perhaps he was constipated); and KwaZulu-Natal (KZN) premier Zweli Mkhize seeming disinterested; and Local Organizing Committee chairperson, Irvin Khoza, appearing pensive . . . And as the show rolled on, the dignitaries collectively toed the press-conference line, sticking to singing school hymns about the World Cup taking us closer to Jesus (and some utopian economic prosperity), rather than addressing the specific concerns of the ordinary.

For a country that was sold the World Cup based on the positive spin-offs the event would supposedly have on the economy and South African society, it was embarrassing to listen to South African leaders mumble awkwardly when it came to just about any question that posed half a challenge about such tangible effects. They were unwilling to answer with any conviction and looked, dare I say it, wholly under-prepared. Maybe this was because they knew that no proof exists to support the claim that mega-sporting events catalyse growth in local economies. Yes, unfortunately, this is the sad fact: there is no proof that the economies of South Korea, Japan or Germany grew dramatically after hosting their respective World Cups.

So it was perhaps no surprise that, on the other side of town, the World Class Cities for All (WCCA) campaign was issuing its own press statements commemorating 100 days before kickoff with exactly these concerns on its mind. Whereas Blatter described the World Cup as a grand wedding ceremony that would consummate the splendid love affair between Fifa and South Africa that began many years back, the focus of WCCA rested on how the event would affect the urban poor, especially those whose lives have changed for the worse as a result of the World Cup coming to our shores.

'With 100 days to go before the games open, official action towards the urban poor fails to meet any standard of fair play,' said StreetNet International coordinator Pat Horn in a statement. 'We want to see African street culture, music and indigenous food, the *shisa nyama*, and informal traders as integral part of a visitor's experience of South Africa.'

'However, the opposite is happening,' she continued. 'The host-city by-laws ensure there is no trading near the stadiums and Fifa copyright and agreements are firmly in the hands of big businesses. Worse still, in some of the fan parks, such as Cape Town, the livelihood of informal traders is under threat, as existing trading sites will be taken over by official Fifa concessions.'

According to the WCCA, informal traders have been told to buzz off from the Parade and Greenmarket Squares, both popular tourist spots that have been declared official fan parks. The WCCA further claimed that in Nelspruit (now Mbombela), a tangible commitment to rebuild schools that were destroyed to make way for the R1.3 billion stadium was yet to be made.

With more than 900,000 jobs lost in 2009, and with economic recovery yet to initiate a positive ripple effect to the lowest economic strata, the informal economy is still the respite of most unemployed South Africans seeking work. The WCCA believes the World Cup will do little for this segment of society; instead it will result in the removal of 'undesirables' and create further impediments to their ability to earn a living.

The irony of the press conference held at the Moses Mabhida stadium was that the harder the dignitaries tried to elucidate the point that the 'time for scepticism had passed', that 'this really was Africa's moment', that we would be witnessing 'football for hope, development and good health', the further they seemed to deflect from the real issues. Instead, Fifa and our government continued to brand this event as the ultimate intervention towards ending international pessimism about Africa. An integral part of this branding, of course, is the showcasing of images of the 'other Africa' to the multibillion-strong television audience. So we were shown plush stadiums, revamped airports, shiny shopping malls and the inevitable shots of pretty animals gamboling in the Kruger National Park. No mention of the 'poor blacks'.

It is highly unlikely that there will be an iconic '100 days after Fifa fucked us over' press conference. But I'm guessing we'll only be able to think straight once Fifa detaches its leech-like sucking self from our backsides.

That said, even amid the Fifa-formulated madness of the past three years, while pandering to every rule and regulation in their book, we knew all along that we were building grand stadiums when TB medication was running low in our hospitals. We knew when the Fifa lights came up on Dr Pixley KaSeme Street (West Street) and we couldn't see any of the street children we might expect to find there, that they must have been dumped somewhere outside the city. And we knew that our lavish airports and stadiums and fan walks were being designed and built while millions of South Africans on the bread line still waited for simple homes.

One hundred days before the greatest show on earth reached our land, our politicians dusted off the real issues and pretended not to hear. The ugly truth is that we, along with our government officials and leaders, were too consumed with the 'I was there!' chant to be really honest with ourselves. It will take years for the country to recover, though I am guessing it will take less than 100 days to figure this out.

My World Cup washout

I

It's a chilly afternoon in Durban. After the early morning promise of warm blue skies, the midday breeze has treacherously ushered in a deposit of dark clouds, a reminder that the sunny days we've been blessed with over the past month have now passed. It is winter after all, and even Durban can't escape the compelling cold front that has marched across the country.

But it doesn't matter. Tonight is 11 July 2010. The World Cup final.

The city, so often the poorer cousin of cosmopolitan Cape Town and intense Johannesburg, has unexpectedly been heralded as having the neatest fan park *in the world*. According to estimates, Durban's fan parks have been among the most successful, with more than a million people frequenting the beach Fan Fest over the preceding month of soccer sensation. While many South Africans (including me) have travelled to different cities to watch the matches live, some folk have flown to Durban just to experience the fan parks across the city – that's how good they've been.

It's been an extraordinary mix of sand, surf and warm weather, and the weird melting pot of local characters has made Durban too spicy to simply digest; tourists have been reluctant to leave. I suppose there is a certain thrill to walking around in shorts in the middle of winter and digging your toes into beach sand while watching world-class soccer on a huge screen between thousands of fans all stinking of beaver piss (aka Budweiser beer) . . .

Of course, watching the World Cup final at Soccer City would have been the ultimate, but the prospect of closing the World Cup at the Durban beach Fan Fest will more than suffice for me. It is, after all, the same place where my World Cup began; where the earth shook in jubilation when Siphiwe Tshabalala's thunderous goal in the opening game against Mexico sent tremors up all our spines, turning strangers into long-lost brethren and abstemious Bafana supporters into raging patriotic lunatics; where champagne bottles sprayed exhilarating scents that sent us all into one collective nirvana.

II

While sitting on one of the concrete blocks along the promenade opposite the giant Coca-Cola dome, obliviously soaking in the pre-match vibe, my bag is nicked. No shuffle, no scuffle – just nicked. Gone like a zephyr. Inside was my neatly packed Nikon D60 SLR camera and 55–300 mm Tamron lens: elementary gear for every friendly journalist and stalker. Gone. Gone, too, are my bank cards, driver's licence and Pink Lady apples, which I'd spent a whole ten minutes carefully selecting at the local Pick n Pay. (I have a fetish for anything pink, in case you're speculating.)

In that dizzy rush to the head that immerses all my senses once I realize my bag is gone, I stand on the concrete block and scan the promenade for the evil soul rushing off with my booty among the thousands of milling football fans. My vision pixellates into a complete blur of blue, red and orange; the horizon made by a dark ocean tells of a coming storm. I feel light-headed as I scan haplessly. In my slippery chappals, made exclusively for walking from bedroom to loo three times a day, I jump onto the cement floor and dash, bolt, trip and halt in different directions, not knowing who to ask for help. That was my beloved camera loaded with my *entire* World Cup experience, not to mention my cousin's wedding and various documented memorabilia designed to bolster the imagination. The angles were my stories, the visuals my ambience and people's captured body language my inspiration. Gone. I begin to feel giddy.

I run over to an MTN promoter, dressed in bright yellow, lip gloss glistening with airtime on her pout. I ask her where I should report a crime. She replies with something that sounds like *Ayoba*! I want to strangle her.

I turn and continue scampering through the tumultuous crowd like a lost kid looking for his mother. I bump into a policeman and explain what happened. I ask him to radio the fan-park security and keep an eye out for someone running with a dark-blue-and-black backpack. There are only three entrances, all under a tight loop. If the bastard is heading out he could be apprehended, I figure.

'Listen, I have a journalist here, who says his bag got stolen,' says the cop into his radio. 'What's the procedure?'

I look at him aghast. *What's the procedure?* Is this guy really a policeman or just some punk dressed for a Halloween party?

He tells me it must be one of the street kids who nicked my bag and suggests I go to the South Beach police station at the other entrance to file a report. I hurry away, the hems of my torn jeans dragging along the floor as I cut in and out of the manic crowd high on vuvuzelas, alcohol and mass hysteria – and clearly oblivious to my crisis. Jealousy skulks down my spine.

I know this whole crisis is my fault. Normally, that bag would be like the hair on my back; you'd have to apply hot wax and tear it off to get it from me. Not to mention that this is Durban, not a cocktail party outside the Porsche museum in Stuttgart; you don't hang even your cheapest possessions out to air in this town if you plan on taking them home with you. There may be some collective euphoria doing the rounds, but it is still the same beach that I wouldn't visit with any valuables on me just six weeks ago because of the rampant theft on the shore. What business did I have leaving my bag unwatched? It was careless, complacent, irresponsible and just downright daft. (Yes, we live in a time and place when having something stolen can be as much your own fault as the thief's.)

I cross the promenade and spot two barefoot kids with dirty

clothes and stuffy noses trying to eat a vuvuzela. They must be street kids. I thought Michael Sutcliffe, our over eager city manager, had loaded these little buggers into a van and dropped them a couple of hundred kilometres somewhere past Richards Bay. But that was a while ago, so I guess they must have walked back.

Approaching them, I hope they aren't kids from the Zulu royal family just having a random day at the beach, and go on to tell them about my stolen bag and that I will pay for their education if they retrieve it. They nod their understanding and race away back towards the Coca-Cola dome, with me following. Circling the tent slowly, they peer over the fence, suggesting a possible hiding place for swag. Two more cops appear nearby and I explain my story to them. They recommend I report the theft at the station next to the uShaka Beach entrance, about a hundred metres away. Meanwhile, the kids tell me they are going to go speak to their mates who may know about the missing bag. I give them ten minutes.

As I pace back and forth awaiting my midget agents' return, I reflect on a conversation I had had with my dad at the very same spot, just yesterday. So impressed was I with the wide open spaces of the promenade and the atmosphere that has turned the beach into a celebrated public space, that I asked if he thought the city would be able to maintain the buzz. We could keep the big screens for cricket and football matches, use the concert platforms to promote local acts and maintain a police presence to keep the place nice and tidy, I suggested.

'Sure, why not?' said my father, without the hint of cynicism that would normally accompany any plans concerning the city.

But could it really work – creating a year-round festive buzz?

Of course, we both knew that the city had subcontracted various responsibilities to private companies and that a company called Black Pepper was managing this particular Fan Fest precinct. Whereas a hobo could usually take a dump in one of the sand sculptures at night without city officials ever catching a whiff, you couldn't even hand out a flyer in the area during the World Cup without the company-sponsored Gestapo on your case. Fact is, this wasn't a public space after all, but since us middle-class families weren't likely to peddle trinkets and vegetables or hand out pamphlets on the promenade, we didn't go on to discuss the injustice of it all.

Nevertheless, and whether I liked it or not, the revitalization of the promenade did signal a shift in the way I viewed my city. It was suddenly possible to imagine Durban differently; it could be more than just a crime-ravaged metropolis with faulty traffic lights and new street names that nobody could pronounce. It felt like the city could truly reinvent itself; that it could weave a new texture in our lives by stitching out the bits that made its residents feel fearful of walking its streets and patronizing its beaches (and that ultimately forced them to trek to the malls instead).

That said, I am well aware that crime has not abated in the suburbs or townships during the World Cup fanfare. In lowly Clare Estate, a former 'Indian suburb' where I live, the crooks have been having a festival of their own. At least two convenience stores I know of have been robbed at gunpoint during this time, and I personally witnessed some street justice from my window at 3 o'clock one morning when locals on their way home from their late-night binge session finally nabbed our regular cable thieves. The list goes on, of course. Meanwhile, doctor friends of mine report on the nightmarish emergency wards that match nights have inevitably presented, as fans have gone on brutal sprees resulting in axed-in heads and broken beer bottles lodged up in arses and the like – typical alcohol-related violence.

And yet, despite these and other downbeat setbacks that have been documented during the World Cup, I have still succumbed to the intoxicating *Ayoba!* stupor and imagined that the city could be something else.

Up until now, perhaps. Because here I am killing that dream by allowing myself to be robbed like a little blind girl.

I try to imagine what I would do if I had stolen a bag in such a huge crowd. It's difficult, since I grew up in a nice house surrounded by mango and mulberry trees. The worst thing I ever did was pinch porn mags from the local news agent as an adolescent. How the hell would I know where to go and what to do with a stolen bag filled with apples, a camera and bank cards?

I look around. I figure a plausible option would be to run to one of the mobile toilets deep into the centre of the labyrinth of plastic piss-stops to rummage through the contents of the bag behind a locked door. I visualize the brat sitting on a warmed toilet seat and checking out my cousin's wedding photos, swinging his legs as he munches an apple.

Just then one of my spy kids returns and saves my imagination the misery of living out its vague proposal to inspect every Portaloo in a half-kilometre radius. He tells me there's no sign of the bag. I wince. I reiterate that he would be a rich little poor kid if he could track it down, but he is steadfast. 'I'll let you know, man,' he pipes. I shake my head. What next? Is he going to present me with a business card? Direct me to lost and found? For all I know, Philemon Fagin emerged from behind one of the sand castles, took a stealthy peep at the stolen camera and told Oliver-Bongani Twist to come give me the bad news before he set off for the local pawn shop.

I race off in the general direction of the police station, where I speak to yet another policeman about the theft, hoping that the information will spread among the doughnut-munchers. He tells me that I can't report the crime on the beachfront and refers me to the Point police station instead. I protest that there are enough cops in this area to make the Lesotho army jealous, and that surely there is no need to go all the way to another police station. I still need to head home to cancel my bank cards before these guys start buying overpriced Fifa memorabilia for their Nigerian friends to resell on West Street. He grunts and we part ways.

Almost immediately I bump into two more policemen, who assure me that I needn't go all the way to the Point station. That last cop was just a chop, they say. I exit the fan park one last time, walk under those McDonald's-like arches and head past yet more policemen. These guys are heavy-duty cops, with darker uniforms and better physiques; they look like the well-hung Colin Farrell and his specialized SWAT team from the movie of the same name, except that they are all black. Turns out they can't help me either.

III

I enter the South Beach police station and their Masonic one-eyed security guard takes me to their leader. Escorted to the makeshift security control room for the World Cup, I enter the unit and see policemen sitting around in merry repose, their legs stretched as they chat in a circle. A few sit at computer screens exchanging hearty conversations, while the cop at the entrance plays solitaire. I am told to go back outside.

A man comes out and identifies himself as the *induna* of the joint. He informs me that they 'can't open a case because we are not here to do admin work, we're here to stop crime'. I smile and mumble a 'stop-crime-eh?' response. He pretends to hear and we both go on to chuckle and pretend to find it funny.

I did find it funny – in a let-me-reach-for-a-revolver-and-blow-my-brains-out kind of way, and I laugh because this is the precise bullshit ordinary people endure every single time they need police assistance in the country. Yes, I shouldn't have allowed myself to be robbed of my candy, but *surely*, after a month of protecting tourists in every nook and cranny of the country, it wouldn't be such a mind-job to report a crime at the biggest Fifa fan festival on the planet?

I walk out of the police station and look out at the throngs of people waiting in anticipation for the big match. It begins to rain.

Kicking off my sandals, I run the few hundred metres towards my car barefoot, tiptoeing around all sorts of podiatric hazards along the way. Onlookers peer at the imbecile running by, flinching after encountering every stone or unidentifiable gooey substance on the ground. I jump into the car and look one last time in earnest for my camera bag, hoping that it's all been just a bad dream. No such luck.

I make my way along Brickhill Road, which soon becomes

Mahatma Gandhi Road (Point Road), my wipers clearing the windscreen of the now persistent drizzle. The route is clogged, as are the connecting side roads. Cars teeter dangerously across tight gaps, their horns blaring alongside buzzing vuvuzela-blowing pedestrians, as they combine to create a truly dizzying ambience. It really is mayhem.

It's less than two hours before the kickoff of the World Cup final and here I am rushing to a fucking police station.

By now my BlackBerry is going bezerk as the multiple rings, bleeps and blurps vibrate from the passenger seat. For once I ignore their entreaties, but I feel *skaam* that I've ditched mates who I promised I'd 'go apeshit' with during what will be one of Africa's greatest moments. I punch the steering wheel, frustrated, and curse my predicament.

Further down MG Road the racket dwindles and it suddenly becomes darker, feels more remote. The large warehouses and shady-looking auto shops feel ominous in the twilight. This is one of the dodgier areas of the central business district (CBD). Most Durbanites think it would be a fair idea to necklace city manager Mike Sutcliffe for renaming this notorious drug and high-heeled-whorehouse district after the Mahatma. On my right, junkies fiddle with each other at a street corner. To my left, gawdy characters emerge from cheap hotels and lowly lit bars. Ahead, I watch illegally parked cars being loaded on to tow-trucks by Metro Police doing their best to ruin at least a few fans' nights.

There are suddenly no vuvuzelas, no random World Cup chants. African foreigners, identified by their boldly printed garb, deeply sunken features and glamorous East African hijabs, wander by. I notice that the streetlights aren't working; the already dodgy district is cast in a darker shade of itself.

I finally find the police station, identified by a string of police vehicles rather than an actual sign on the building, which turns out to be a bleak Soviet-reminiscent structure. The place smells empty, but I find a handful of cops inside chatting with each other. My appearance is clearly an intrusion and my inquiry is met with a curt

'The shift is changing. You must wait for the evening chief to come in.'

'But why can't you do it? You are here?' I ask–state.

'You must be patient,' is the reply.

Again, I remind myself that this entire drama is my fault. So I wait.

As I stand behind the counter, a white couple shuffle into the station. The woman is huge, hardly fits through the door, while her (presumed) husband is laughably slender next to her. 'We have no place to stay tonight,' she says in an Afrikans accent. 'Last night we stayed at Durban station, but they said no for tonight. The streets are dangerous. Can we stay here?'

An off-duty policeman stops chatting with an alluring policewoman and replies that they can sit outside on the leather bench. She thanks them and they disappear. The policemen and women continue their conversation just as a tall white cop strides in with a typically puny Indian boy in tow; he's no older than seventeen, and in handcuffs. The cop hands over the young rascal and announces his arrival: 'It's been years since I have been here, eh.' No one responds. Perhaps the last time was before 1994. An officer drags the boy to the holding cell while another scoffs, 'Why is he acting like he doesn't know where to go; this is the boy's second home.'

Just then my phone beeps: a text message from my father informing me that my sister's flight to Johannesburg, which was meant to take off at 3 p.m., has for various reasons still not departed. It's now 7 p.m., and he's not amused. A couple of days ago, on the day of the semi-final fixture in Durban, the King Shaka International airport was plunged into chaos because private jets took up all the parking spaces. Hundreds of ordinary passengers arriving from other cities missed the game because aeroplanes couldn't land. (Another epic failure.) Dad enquires about my whereabouts and obviously wants me to thrill him with some anecdote from the fabulous fan park. I don't reply.

I am finally helped by a friendly policewoman who can barely speak, spell or hear. She has a neat handwriting, but doesn't believe the digits of my postal code. I dictate my story, fill in the forms and leave the 'race' section blank. She reminds me to fill it in. I can't understand why I need to.

I ask her and another officer hanging about if there have been many crimes at the fan park. 'I don't know,' is the response.

Is there any chance of my stolen goods being retrieved? 'No.' They both shake their heads wisely.

Eventually, exiting through the station doors, I find the Afrikaner couple sitting on the cold bench outside. The woman is crying now; the man is looking the other way. I walk slowly to my car, defeated, exhausted – but strangely relieved. I look around at the darkness one last time and wonder if the World Cup has been but a dream, a figment of our imagination as we endeavoured to escape the daily horrors of a warped existence. It feels to me as if real life has already made a staggering comeback just as I thought we might have trounced it.

I now have to get home, dig up my documents, cancel the bank cards and arrange my paperwork for the inevitable bureaucracy to follow. I will watch the final at home, in silence.

POSTSCRIPT

The truth is I'd enjoyed the SWC to this point. I'd watched three games live in Durban and squeezed in a quarterfinal in Cape Town. I'd followed the progress of Bafana Bafana (while it lasted) and then the German team, and salivated at the prospect of watching Germany play Argentina (my preferred final). I'd got caught up in the emotion of it all, and I have a broken bed to prove it (jiving to K'naan's flag waving). It was hardly possible not to – if you were well off enough, that is.

Since the angry cynicism of my previous post ('Remember 100 days before we were screwed over', p. 37) I'd almost been won over by the mass hysteria surrounding the fixtures, the flags on the cars, the awestruck tourists and the palatable magic that lifted us way above our daily disappointments. This sour end note was the sudden return to reality that was, at some stage or other, inevitable.

The country – or most of it – had given in to the madness and loved every minute of the World Cup. Which was great. But it will make our collective return to earth in the coming months and years – as our flash stadiums loom over us, underused and running up debts, and the starving poor remain starving and poor – that much more painful. After the World Cup, Durban started pimping out itself for the 2020 Summer Olympic bid. Thank goodness, the city's officials stopped the drugs and withdrew their intention to bid just days before the cut-off date.

Hosting the soccer World Cup is one thing, but shifting the skyline, uprooting people and selling optimism yet again for another sporting event – especially one with an even more dubious financial rewards – would have been disastrous; there is only that much opium one can pump into a restless generation still looking for the meaning of the word 'freedom'.

Was Eugène Terror Blanche a Muslim?

As racial tensions continued to rise in the aftermath of the murder of the white supremacist leader Eugène Terre'Blanche, and concerns about the ability of black people to host thousands of visiting white people for the Word Cup flourished, the South African Muslim and Halaal Association (Samha) reported that it has been inundated with calls from foreigners asking whether Terre'Blanche was, in fact, a Muslim.

Speaking at a press conference on Easter Monday, Samha spokesperson Abu Is'a Vanker said, 'The suggestion that Mr Terror Blanche was a Muslim is outrageous.'

When pressed for further comment, he remarked, 'Look, just because he had a long beard, treated workers badly and attacked the World Trade Centre, that doesn't mean he was Muslim, okay?'

Vanker was referring to Terre'Blanche's infamous attack on the South African version of the World Trade Centre in Kempton Park back in 1993, when he stormed the building with 3,000 of his followers, who ended up spraying slogans on the walls and urinating on the furniture. It was widely believed that Terre'Blanche had initially planned to fly a crop duster into the two-storey building in the hope of disrupting the multi-party end-of-apartheid negotiations that were taking place at the venue.

'We would expect people to give Muslims more credit than that,' said Vanker, shaking his head, before noting that Samha officials were surprised to be inundated with these queries, considering they were not a theological association who kept a conversion register. 'We are only interested in certifying the slaughter of animals on farms.'

He added that the organization was non-partisan and merely in the business of verifying the halaal status of food, drink and toothpicks for Muslim consumption. 'But we don't mind. You know what they say: earning interest may be *haraam*, but any publicity is good publicity,' he chuckled.

Nevertheless, industry insiders believe there may be more than meets the eye in this Muslim–TerréBlanche business. It is public knowledge that, despite private scorn for Zuma's infidelity and links to countless corruption scandals, Muslim businesses were quick to throw their chips into Zuma's election campaign. Sources say that Muslim big businesses will likely suffer dramatic losses if rumours of a beefy right-wing liaison with the Muslim community surface.

'There is talk about minorities working behind our backs in the meat industry,' said one African National Congress (ANC) member who refused to be named. 'It is most distressing.'

This was a topic that dominated the Samha press conference, as top-level and well-paid journalists from some of the Muslim community's finest Durban-based investigative publications dug into the association's business relationship with Terre'Blanche. But Vanker steadfastly refuted all claims of an existing business liaison.

'Mr Terror Blanche did approach us as a potential meat supplier, assuring us that one of his slaves . . . er . . . labourers was a practising Muslim, but we were not able to reach any agreement,' he said, before noting that Samha officials were not happy with the working environment they witnessed during their inspection.

When asked if conditions of employment for Terre'Blanche's labourers had put them off dealing with him, Vanker said it was nothing of the sort. 'Samha is not concerned with labour practice . . . We observed that the black workers were living next to the swines and decided it was not worth the risk of contamination. We can't have anything at all to do with P-I-G-s, you see.'

But a leading Islamic history scholar, Professor Alshyma Omarjee at the University of the Rudwa Islamic Business School (RIBS), an all-girls finishing school based in Durban, said it was plausible that the right-wing leader experimented with Islam after being convicted of manslaughter in the mid-1990s.

'Influential leaders tend to search for spiritual guidance when incarcerated. Think about Malcolm X and how he returned to emancipate the African Americans,' explained Professor Omarjee. 'This might be why ET wanted his meat to be halaal.'

Omarjee warned that the spate of ambiguity regarding the halaal status of Rainbow Chicken, Woolworths croissants and Cadbury Whispers had already made many Muslims deeply resentful towards the halaal authorities, and another dilemma would signal an irreconcilable crisis for the community. 'The media needs to be responsible. We don't need any more ambiguity. Besides, my husband loves his meat,' the professor blushed.

Commenting on the possible connection between Julius Malema's '*Kill the Boer*' song and the murder of the biggest Boer of them all, Terre'Blanche, esteemed Muslim cleric Mufti Adam al Jamali from East London said that all music ought to be banned anyway.

'Look, whether it is instruments or beatboxing, all such manipulations of sound are categorically haraam and must be condemned. What does *shaytaani* Beyon-che mean when she sings 'All the single ladies, all the single ladies'?' he said, gesticulating. 'Treating workers badly is one thing. But why do we have all these single ladies? Music encourages homosexuality as well!'

On whether Terre'Blanche was Muslim, Mufti al Jamali noted that an autopsy wouldn't reveal much. 'Even an autopsy wouldn't indicate if he is Deobandhi, Salafi, Sufi . . .' he said. 'And it would kill our morale if we were to somehow find out that he was a Shia. Of course, Shias might be the future, but it might also be insensitive to reveal such a thing at this point.'

The Mufti also said that it was not the policy of the local Muslims to alienate any group in business, but it would not be wise to mess with the ruling party. 'So I honestly doubt that the Muslim community would dare have such strong links with Terre'Blanche,' he concluded. 'Besides, as it is we have this "terrorist" cloud hanging over us, so to be labelled as right-wing allies just because a couple of Malays speak Afrikans and this crazy ET had a big beard – well, that would be just too much.'

A delegation of Muslim clerics and prominent businesspeople was due to meet the ANC early on Tuesday morning to clarify the situation.

POSTSCRIPT

Some weeks before the 2009 general elections, news broke of prominent Muslim businessmen gifting Jacob Zuma large hoards of cash as an early Eid present at a glittering ceremony in Durban. I was initially pissed at the hypocrisy of my community, knowing what they thought about the man behind the scenes. But after sitting in the dark through yet another Eskom outage and being forced to think about it more clearly, I was secretly thrilled – because with all the political ambiguity following Polokwane, the recalling of Thabo Mbeki, the proposed disbanding of the Scorpions, the ominous 'Kill for Zuma' charades, traffic jammed between broken traffic lights, load-shedding and rising paranoia among ordinary folk, I realized that if the shit had to hit the democratic fan, my uncles had strategically bought us Muslims some extra time in the republic. 'Don't kill the mullahs, they gave Msholozi lots of moolah . . . And ay, remember Schabir Sheik – a good man!' I could hear them saying.

Of course, in reality, my uncles were just cementing their PTO (Prioritization of Tender Opportunities) credentials for the next five years of Zuma's presidency. There was some talk about the community also getting in bed with the main opposition, the Democratic Alliance, because 'we need some fucking law and order in this place'. Chances are it's probably true. Although I didn't hear who the Hindu community were angling for. It's highly unlikely that it was the late Amichand Rajbansi . . . may he and his toupee rest in peace.

Meanwhile, Eugène Terre'Blanche's murder scared South Africa. Here was the very symbol of Afrikaner separatism, nationalism and racism bludgeoned to death on his farm by two black employees. 'Oh my god, it's Zimbabwe all over again' was the widely heard refrain. It didn't help that Julius Malema was actually in Zimbabwe at the time, dressed in Zanu-PF apparel and singing the real Zulu version of *'Kill the Boer'*. Even the brown liberals were shitting themselves.

I know I almost did.

But then it became clear that this murder was, in fact, about a wage dispute that turned into a hacking session, so we all calmed down. The liberals breathed a sigh of relief, returned their one-way tickets to Australia to their Flight Centre agents and compensated for their lack of faith in the country by vehemently lobbying for the end of farm-worker abuse and poor working standards.

Anyway, just as we were getting used to singing the 'Save the black farmer from the white farmers in khaki' hymn, news broke of the Terre'Blanche saga being a possible hate–sex crime. The psychologists popped out of the woodwork to explain how white supremacy and homophobia could morph into a perverted thrill designed to disgrace the black boy by lacing him. It is often the case that homophobes are simply gay folk in denial, and to rape a black boy would be the ultimate expression of self-hate – which in turn could lead to revenge murder by said black boy . . . Well, it made some sort of media sense at the time, so sodomy, blood and the misplaced condom hit the headlines.

But alas, the condom didn't fit and apparently there had been no gay sex. Which makes me strongly suspect that Terre'Blanche was indeed a Muslim, after all. Because Muslims are *not* gay. Ever.

Like never.

Slip on those heels and grow a penis

When my friend Sara joined a reputable graduate programme in Johannesburg, she was assured that even though the company kills people for a living (they manufacture cigarettes) the organizational culture at work would be categorically awesome. She was promised an informal atmosphere in which personal development mixed with out-of-the-box thinking would reign supreme over egos, hierarchy and the phoney baloney of antiquated staffing models. And she wasn't disappointed. With great enthusiasm, she entered a jet-setting lifestyle of privilege and concession, turning her butt into the envy of every unemployed South African graduate.

But now Sara has the audacity to complain. She says that despite all the goodies and perky puddings offered by the corporate world to make her time, experience and conscience as jelly-cool as possible, she has a problem. Turns out she just can't handle all the sex talk in the workplace.

My friend tells me that though she loves her work she is quickly realizing that the precious 'informal atmosphere' she was promised was really an euphemism to allow her manager to 'talk about sex all the time'. Between work, during breaks, on the road – just about anywhere and at any time. So during her coffee breaks, Sara's boss now informs her how nifty Viagra can be with the missus, or how his daughter is approaching that 'pumpable' age, or how prolifically he scored dressed as Wolverine at a fancy-dress party some years back.

And Sara just stands there laughing at his manliness, feigning hysteria when she actually feels like puking. It's beginning to needle her in ways that only freaks, stalkers and the neighbour's wet dog ought to. But I know Sara. She may be cute and coy, and she may come across all Santa Maria-like, but there's no doubt she is quite capable of handling it. In fact, I know she enjoys a good bit of banter.

The thing is, her manager is no Brad or Jude. Just the opposite actually. He's more clown than Clooney. He is the married antithesis of the young, sexy commanding officer whose gruff voice and strong arms would have otherwise sent vibrations through the petite young woman trying to make it up the corporate pole. In short, this man is thoroughly unattractive. Hell, he could even be her father.

No, she insists, it's not because he isn't hot.

Lies, I say, of course it is.

That's just sick thinking, she protests, going on to explain that she's no prude but she doesn't want to be forced to listen to his sexist rubbish and be all polite just because he is her boss and she doesn't want to offend him.

But then what does she think the corporate world is? I ask. A place where diverse cultures, opinions and methods work side by side in perfect harmony to further the goals of the organization? Did she imagine her sense of propriety would remain intact simply because everyone looked so good, drove such nice cars and didn't live in a township? And wait, I demand, does she really think she was hired because she's special and unique? Or rather because 'they' (yes, the same ones who are watching you) figured her cute ass would fit into the blithely mithely tithely world of the corporate shebang? Doesn't she know, I press on, that the corporate world is nothing but the big stage, an overt demonstration of power, where the goal is an insatiable, endless and maddening urge to grow bigger and outwit and outlast the competition? That it is irrepressibly macho – as well as insecure, moody, risky, philandering, exhibitionist and praise-seeking? That the corporate world is precisely some organ just *waiting* for something to happen? And, most importantly, that her work environment requires constant gardening, stroking and banter for her to progress?

Doesn't she know, I continue relentlessly, that the modern corporate is really just a man's penis, and that to survive, thrive and truly advance, you have to grow one?

Say what? she gapes.

And that when you grow one, I expound inexorably, the minefield of contemptuous egos becomes permanent; differing sexualities fade away; men and women morph into one despicable corporate macho prototype? That the perversion invariably becomes so ingrained that women are often forced into replacing their culturally inherent femininity with a manufactured corporate manly identity?

Cracking the glass ceiling becomes farcical, I conclude triumphantly, and women may as well be wearing strap-on dildos!

When I eventually calm down, Sara inquires politely as to what, exactly, my rant has to do with her.

Well, it's about her options, I tell her. She could, as a first course of action, be old-fashioned about it and talk to him the way most women did before the advent of email. She could explain how his wild sex talk turns her into a scornful dyke with a penchant to shred the tools of boastful men into chicken feed. This could work, possibly, but I warn that the news will spread very fast indeed that she is the scary-prude-virgin-from-planet-uptight who won't stand for any rude jokes.

Sara's second option is to report the problem to the divisional head or whoever else seems to be the resident in-house feminist. But with all the sex talk being random sex talk, and with no tangible pass made or bum pinched, the complaint would likely pale and instead just sabotage the otherwise good working relationship she has with the (ugly) hero.

And then there's option three. She could go and discuss the issue with another woman, who clearly doesn't seem to be too flustered by the random sexualized comments directed within earshot. But we know what advice she is bound to find there: develop a thick skin, slip on those heels and grow a penis.

So I need to adapt then, she questions–states–concludes. But I really don't think she ought to.

POSTSCRIPT

Even though readers of my blog encouraged Sara to knee her moron boss in the balls, Sara decided to bide her time and wait for a transfer. She says she feels like a cop-out for not addressing the situation, but she reckons it wasn't the time for a messy confrontation. The good news is that, despite sinking deeper into the corporate world, she has avoided having to strap on a dildo – which is probably a good thing.

INGLORIOUS BASTARDS

Fore! I smell the blood of a Schabir Shaikman

In 2005, a powerful South African businessman named Schabir Shaik was found guilty of having a corrupt relationship with Jacob Zuma, the then deputy president of South Africa. The judge concluded that Shaik, a former financial adviser to Zuma and a fervent supporter of the ANC during the bad old days, had advanced his business interests through his association with Zuma. The nation erupted in righteous indignation, Shaik was sentenced to fifteen years in prison and President Thabo Mbeki went on to dismiss Zuma from office. At the heart of the scandal was the infamous multi-million-rand arms deal that is well known to have fattened the pockets of a bevy of South African politicians. Zuma's political career was imperilled but he conscientiously maintained his innocence. While Zuma sang and danced his way over the legal hurdles strewn in his path, liberals in every corner of the country spoke of a Zuma presidency with the fear and loathing usually reserved for Doomsday. Word on the street was that the case against Zuma had been concocted in the production cycle of political conspiracies to prevent him from running for elections in 2008. When Zuma later went to court, the case was thrown out after evidence surfaced of political interference during the investigation. The decision paved the way for Zuma to run in the next presidential elections – an election which he won emphatically. Shaik, meanwhile, had become the pin-up boy for corrupt government groupies. He was abhorred by the South African public as a symbol of corruption – emblematic of everything that was wrong with the ANC. Here was a man who supported the ANC when it held little promise for profit or personal gain. Yet like so many other ANC personalities, he had acquired a taste for sleaze and had morphed into a greedy fraudster obsessed with ostentatious displays of his wealth. His metamorphosis however was not yet complete. Following his conviction, Shaik turned from a cocky millionaire into an iconic political buffoon, played like a spastic kid in a playground.

And like all good stories, it gets better.

Shaik, through his astounding medley of well-placed contacts and strategic influences, hardly spent time behind bars. Doctors concocted illness after illness to ensure he would never have to endure his jail cell for too long. Instead, he convalesced in the comfort of a hospital bed. He had dangerously high blood pressure, we were told. Parole officers were informed he was terminally ill – hypertension had apparently turned him into a man on his death bed . . . and so with these health considerations in mind, Shaik was subsequently released on medical parole. He had served just two years and four months of his sentence. As soon as he made his escape, he issued an urgent application for a presidential pardon from the newly inaugurated President Zuma.

Or as he put it, he wanted a 'fucking pardon'.

Shaik, however, was soon to realize that things were going to be much harder than he had expected. This was a man well used to things working out his way, by hook or by crook. Shaik faced the undiluted wrath of a hostile media baying for his blood and he would have to face that hostility alone. Zuma's aides had strongly advised him to have nothing to do with Shaik. Shortly after Zuma's inauguration, Shaik would never hear from Zuma again. Having lost most of his wealth, his assets, estranged from his wife, abandoned by Zuma and perennially hounded by Opposition parties and the media, Shaik became a very bitter man.

This was a man who once had an empire that had secured multi-million-dollar arms deals, and now he was reduced to the ignominy of a disgraced hound on a leash. Languishing under house arrest (with occasional trips to holiday resorts and shopping malls), Shaik's frustration culminated in his friends and 'associates' to search for ways to tell his side of the story . . .

The Papwa Sewgolum Golf Course seems like a perfect place to carry out a quiet assassination.

Here, between the silent, overburdened mango trees and rotting shacks, old Indian men dressed in skinny golf shirts, bomber-taupe golf shoes and biscuit-coloured shorts indulge in their colonial fetish for nine irons and black caddies.

The course is named after the great Sewsunker 'Papwa' Sewgolum, who kicked Gary Player's butt back in the sixties.

It's a glory still talked about with some fondness over pints of Castle in the clubhouse. But far from the luscious greens of an Augusta, the Papwa Sewgolum Golf Course sits uncomfortably like a dampened oasis in a swamp of discontent, prejudice and municipal neglect.

There aren't many golf courses that can boast a crematorium and squatter camp as neighbours. Little wonder then, if you are an old Indian man with golf clubs and enough under the mattress, you come here to Papwa, to die.

This might explain the spooks about the course.

So, it is with a mixture of trepidation and fascination that I agreed to meet Krish Dhudraj in the parking lot of Papwa Sewgolum. I imagine a scream muffled under a duffel bag would pass for an irreverent cry of a passing hadeda.

The previous day, Dhudraj had called me from a private number and introduced himself as an associate of Schabir Shaik. He'd read about me in the *Sunday Times* as a 'rockstar political blogger', or so he said.

'I have a story for you. Meet me in the parking lot of Papwa Sewgolum,' he instructed me.

Krish rocked up in a BMW. I don't remember the colour, but I'm guessing it was black (it would suit him).

He climbed out of the car, his long hair glistening in the April sun. I readied myself. His dramatically faded jeans and steel-toed boots made him look more like a cowboy than an empowerment groupie. He tapped his cigarette pack and bit on to one with the grittiness of a Texan in a black-and-white Western about to describe a righteous kill.

He offered me a cigarette. I could have done with a drink.

I declined. He leaned slightly against the bonnet of the car and looked me up. And then down.

'You are the writer then,' he began.

He seemed sceptical; people usually are. I don't know why readers imagine me to be older, taller and my pen a blood-stained machete. I tried hard to narrow my eyes to a squint, hoping my forehead creased in thoughtful intensity.

He then got down to business. Pulling out news clippings inserted in plastic sleeves that proved his close relationship to Shaik, he went on to give me a snappy summary of the political conspiracy at play. Shaik, it seemed, was promised a political pardon if he took the fall for Zuma, but with the president already in power for a year and controversy after controversy dogging his heels, the prospect of a presidential pardon was fast becoming a distinct impossibility.

Public sentiment had already dramatically dived against Zuma after it was revealed that he had fathered another child, this time with South African football boss Irvin Khoza's daughter.

'Shaik is becoming impatient with his situation,' he said. 'What about his health?' I ask.

He went on to fill me in on Shaik's 'good health'; about how the media was operating in a separate universe, dislocated from the actual political reality; that blaming Shaik, who he insisted was not guilty of any crime, was the easy way out.

'Shaik's side of the story needs to be told . . . it's taking a strain on the family, and as his friends, we think it's time,' he told me.

I disagreed that the media would be against publishing his side of the story. I had already received a go-ahead from the weekly *City Press* newspaper for a large *Vanity Fair*-type profile of Shaik before I had even met Dhudraj. But I did agree with Dhudraj that however battered to death the story had been in the local media, it did feel rather incomplete. That is why I'd agreed to look into it. But I needed proof and I would not, I clarified to Dhudraj, be anyone's political mouthpiece.

At his disposal, he said, was evidence that would exonerate Shaik of any wrongdoing, specific things related to the relationship between former president Thabo Mbeki and Jacob Zuma, information he reckoned 'could result in a civil war'.

I was suddenly excited at what I thought for a few seconds would be the biggest scoop in recent South African media history. But the deep humming from funeral rites being recited at the neighbouring crematorium interrupted my free fall into self-importance. I made a request to meet Shaik before I took the story seriously. For all I knew, Dhudraj could well be a delusional lover Shaik had made promises to in St Augustine's Hospital the last time he hung out there. I wanted a meeting with Corleone to know if any of this was true.

Dhudraj puffed a little more smoke into my face and said he needed to meet me a few times, 'sift you out' as he so delicately put it, and would then get the ball rolling with Shaik. But I needed to understand that, as a convicted criminal, Shaik was not quotable and that he would have to give the green light that a campaign of sorts be started to clear his name, before 'anything could be published'.

'So nothing must be written just yet . . . remember, we run this city . . . the police, everything, so don't write anything until I tell you,' he warned.

'Is that . . . a kind of . . . threat?' My reply was punctuated with a nervous giggle.

'No . . . it's not a threat,' he replied sheepishly, expecting me to have understood. His cigarette quickly burned away as the awkward moment passed.

'So I will speak to Schabir and tell him about you, and then we shall talk,' he said.

I drove off, wondering if he had noted my car's licence plate.

We exchanged a few text messages after the meeting. They were mostly acts of deference; meeting Shaik was still off-limits.

When Dhudraj's name popped up on my phone some weeks later, I had relocated to a different postal code.

POSTSCRIPT

I didn't recognize him at first. I can't say he looked thinner, or healthier. I had never seen him before, not in real life at least. And while newspaper clippings are my only reference, those eyes are hard to forget. Schabir Shaik, flanked by his four-year-old son, walks hurriedly past my table at the pre-launch signing of my first book, *Zuma's Bastard*, at Gateway's Exclusive Books. I am in mid-sentence with another would-be customer when Shaik, obviously enticed by the curious bold yellow font screaming 'Zuma's Bastard' stops in his tracks, turns and approaches the table. He picks up a book.

'What's this about?' he asks me, fondling the cover curiously.

'It plays with Zuma's infidelities to tell a story of an illegitimate child of the democracy.'

'Yes, maybe I should have just let the Zulus kill the Indians and the whites, back then,' he interrupts my answer, putting the book down onto the table, with clear annoyance. 'It seems I wasted my time going to jail and negotiating – and should have just allowed them to get rid of all . . .'

'Look,' I reply, trying to manage a smile in an attempt to feign control over a discussion, 'The book is not anti-Zuma . . . It is a take on South African society, and it goes after everyone, it even goes after the Indian community's hypocrisy and racism, even local Muslims.'

'And you know this Ferial Haffajee,' he continues smugly, pointing to the 'Foreword by Ferial Haffajee' on the book's cover. 'She knows nothing about politics.'

'But okay,' he turns, a faint smile playing on his lips, 'I will come get a copy . . . and keep on being critical.'

He walks off, his little boy in tow and from across the railings, I watch him amble into the Body Shop, never to return.

That was just six months after my meeting with Dhudraj in that God-forsaken parking lot. Little did the don know I may have been the guy to have told his side of the story . . .

The JZ roller coaster

I

It was June 2008 and Jacob Zuma was under a cloud of corruption charges. Certain middle-class liberal South Africans – so used to patronizing the affirmative-action candidate at work, and beaming at Castle Lager Rainbow Nation ads at home – were outraged beyond belief when Julius Malema entered their living rooms one night screaming from the flat screen that he would kill for Zuma.

It was shocking for even the most ardent disbelievers among us, considering we had just suffered the dreadful 'xenophobic attacks' that left scores dead and thousands homeless. In the following weeks, the accompanying visuals of pro-Zuma supporters lapping up Malema's outrageous utterances were beginning to resemble a bad Hollywood film about some random banana republic in deepest Africa, featuring despicable gold-encrusted army generals bearing AK-47s and brash accents. It was ironic in-house Afro-phobia in the making as our worst nightmares seemed about to be realized.

Malema's comments scared us; we knew there was destructive fire in his potbelly and it was worrying that someone so close to the ANC leadership could get away with such drivel. But it was when Cosatu's general secretary Zwelinzima Vavi added to the 'kill for Zuma' chorus that it occurred to me there was a deeper set of issues at play here.

Many were surprised when Jacob Zuma chose not to condemn such talk or request that it at least be quarantined to the private shower. But I had my own theory about the violent talk and what it really meant.

Julius Malema's recent 'kill for Zuma' comments have managed to turn yawns into wide-mouthed alarm for even the most jaded among us. With Mugabe continuing his personal terrorism north of the border, and the rampage against foreign African nationals (aka xenophobic attacks) still fresh in our minds, the comments seem rather callous, to say the least.

The book – not the Bible, rather the Constitution – has been thrown at him; the Human Rights Commission (HRC) has issued ultimatum after ultimatum in search of an apology; Helen Zille's Democratic Alliance (DA) party has tried to capitalize, believing this could be the political trump card they've been fantasizing about; and upstanding (but gullible) citizens have gathered publicly, disgusted by the violence-stirring rhetoric. Comments ranging from 'Malema should focus on real issues' and 'He should stop trying to be a brainless revolutionary' to 'Malema embodies all that is rotten about the ANC' have poured unceremoniously into all major newspapers.

But whether we like it or not, Malema's utterances have cemented his place in the imagination of mostly apathetic South Africans, even managing to surpass the efforts of his predecessors. Indeed, former African National Congress Youth League (ANCYL) president Fikile Mbalula's racist comments, made only a year ago, about the University of KwaZulu-Natal Durban–Westville campus resembling Bombay because of the number of Indians on it, seemed suddenly so playful in comparison.

We can all understand Malema's rationale, considering the elections are so close and he wants to stand out as an important and vocal arse-licker. But did he have to resort to such outlandishly dirty tactics? Yes, of course he did. He is young and spirited, and needs that tender before he's thirty.

Malema's agenda is mostly easy to understand. But understanding Zwelinzima Vavi's strident agreement with his outbursts is a touch more difficult. As an esteemed leader of the working class and not some firebrand rabble-rouser of the youth, what exactly does Vavi seek to achieve by supporting, even adding further artillery to, Malema's repulsive comments? On closer inspection, quite a lot.

Simply put, Vavi, Cosatu and the South African Communist Party have invested far too much of their energy, aspirations and hope in Zuma for some Mickey Mouse detail, like corruption charges or the rule of law, to come and spoil their party. There is no way in hell (a place very similar to Zimbabwe) that Cosatu would accept anyone linked to Thabo Mbeki, with his fervent pro-business and running-around-the-world agenda, as the president when South Africa goes to the polls next year.

But with Zuma having assumed party leadership at the memorable Polokwane ANC conference late last year, he could easily direct his puppets from Westville prison (or whichever jail Schabir Shaik is in) if necessary – meaning that Mbeki really is out of the picture. This signifies that, when the ANC wins next year (in 2009), Zuma will retain some sort of power, come what may. Why, then, would Vavi join all the illegitimate children of the left throwing their toys out of their cots, screaming about killing and shooting and talking about a revolution (read with a Tracy Chapman beat)?

Conspiracy theories abound, but what if Vavi's comments were not directed at the prosecutors, the judiciary, the HRC or the peanut gallery – but at Zuma himself?

Let me explain.

After the corruption and rape charges levelled at Zuma emerged in 2005, duly followed by Thabo Mbeki's upstanding (read convenient) decision to ask him to stand down as deputy president (with the world taking a bow in naïve appreciation), Zuma became an unemployed hero (like 40 per cent of all South Africans). Suddenly, his unemployed status, personal charisma and enviable SUV made him man of the hour and icon of the left. (How exactly this happened is anybody's guess, but do consult your local sociologist for a theory.) Viewing him as a new adversary to Mbeki's governance, South Africa's trade unions threw their bones behind Zuma and put all their money on him leading them out of bondage.

However, while Zuma was celebrated and touted as South Africa's possible answer to Hugo Chavez, he continued to pimp his ideals out to the highest bidder. Here he was showing a leg at a labour rally, there he was dropping his neckline at corporate meetings, and then again there he was joining the mile-high club with representatives of international monetary institutions – all the time making conflicting promises. While it was always clear that he was no *real* hero of the left, his victory at Polokwane gave his followers the audacity to believe.

But of late Zuma has been clearly drifting away from the workers, his words revealing signs of disinterest in real solidarity with the left. Just a few days ago Zuma admitted once more, this time to the *Financial Times*, that he had no intention of changing South Africa's economic policy. Not only did he publicly indicate his commitment to not interfering with Big Business's plans for world domination, he no longer considered it necessary to even counter this sentiment with some pro-labour byte-sized quote to keep the happy-clapping left believing. Before, he would ordinarily have been quick to throw them a couple of bones after a barbeque with business, but he's even stopped this pretence. So, having helped elevate him to glory, Cosatu, the trade union confederation, now sits like an expectant dog anxiously waiting to be fed and stroked, its ears erect, counting the days until its reciprocation – but none is forthcoming.

It took them a while, but Vavi and now Blade Nzimande have finally realized that Zuma has chosen sides: the *other* side. With a global recession looming (if not already here), Cosatu most definitely cannot afford Zuma jumping ship; not now. And so, through his latest support – quote: 'So yes, because Jacob Zuma is one of us, and he is one of our leaders, for him, we are prepared to lay our lives [sic] and to shoot and kill' – Vavi sends a message to Zuma: *don't you dare forget us*.

I'm not saying that Cosatu is threatening to kill Zuma. On the contrary, Vavi's message is really the scorn of that expectant dog desperately looking for attention from its master. By cheerfully offering to kill for someone, you're inadvertently claiming him.

Of course, Malema is too burdened by his oversized ego, too drawn to the gold-chain image of an embattled ghetto hip-hop star to catch the drift. But he'll get his black empowerment tender; he'll join the premier league next year and secure his financial future.

Malema's role is different. His words are less poetic. And thus, while Malema plays to the gallery of hungry ANC tadpoles, Vavi appears to have recognized an opportunity to send a nuanced message to his estranged lover (even if it meant that HRC hero Jody Kollapen would be on his tail). But again, the problem is that such comments undermine the South African judicial system and Constitution, and the ability of our sociopolitical institutions to function properly – which normally signals the beginning of the end, because the road to the banana republic is paved not long after Constitution-protecting institutions are peeled away.

The real tragedy is that Vavi's comments might be a hidden warning, with the latent message directed with as much force at Zuma as at his detractors. They also indicate, almost by perverted default, a willingness to kill and die – in other words, a willingness to fight for a cause, an arbitrary revolution, for someone they know is not really destined to lead them out of bondage.

No wonder Zuma is silent.

II

Fast-forward to April 2009, when millions of registered voters geared up to mark the X-spot on ballot sheets at 19,000 stations around South Africa. It was the fourth general elections since the death of Kurt Cobain. And apartheid.

Despite resounding victories at the poll in previous elections, the ANC stumbled into this election like an injured beast. Torn apart by internal ruptures including the formation of the Congress of the People (Cope), the 'kill for Zuma' debacle, internal bickering and the proposed disbanding of the elite crime-fighting unit, the Scorpions, the election was touted as the most significant one since 1994. At least Zuma could run for office without worrying about corruption charges hanging over his head; on 6 April the National Prosecuting Authority (NPA) announced that they had all been dropped.

As if the electorate could be any more bewildered by current goings-on in South African politics, the decision to drop all corruption charges against Jacob Zuma has turned ordinary South Africans into believers, converted sceptics into philosophers and undoubtedly got immigration turnstiles rolling. Just a week before the 'most important elections' and the electorate couldn't be more divided.

On the one hand, you have Zuma and his team of loyal supporters riding high after the decision by the NPA to drop all corruption charges against him. After years of screaming from the lungs, shooting from the hip and camping outside courtrooms, the decision is a vindication like no other. He is their Messiah; they are the Zumamaniacs.

On the other side, brimming with inconsolable rage and frustration marked by flared nostrils and shaking heads, are those who are maddened that secret tapes, legal technicalities and incompetent NPA administrators have probably botched the most important case in South African history. The case against Zuma was thrown out because political interference was reasonably proven, making the charges against him inadmissible. To this lot, the countless counts of corruption will never disappear until the day Zuma is tried in a court of law. To these sceptics, he is a disaster waiting to happen, a man representing Mugabe, Amin and every single post-colonial African leader who went wrong; they are the Zumaphobes.

South Africa's fourth elections since Nelson Mandela's release from prison has been touted as the electorate's opportunity to root out corruption, declare war on crime and deliver essential services to the economically disenfranchised. In reality, though, how South Africans decide to vote will be determined by where they stand in relation to Zuma. That's Jacob 'the black Jesus, working-class hero, chief borrower of taxpayers' money, husband of some, father of many, father of the nation' Zuma.

Forget about the complex political confrontations of the past; this is simply a battle between those for and those against Zuma. So let's take a closer look at the protagonists.

The classic Zumamaniac – hereafter Maniac, for short – is powered by ideology and guided by Julius Malema, Zwelinzima Vavi and Blade Nzimande, who argue that the work-in-progress revolution, led by the ANC, has finally reached working-class control. If the ANC has not delivered to the masses over the past fifteen years, that's because the revolution was hijacked by counter-revolutionaries, by the shiny suits and foreign educations of the Mbeki era. Now, with the conclusion of the ANC conference in Polokwane in late 2007, the ANC is finally the organ of the working class. Hence the leading positions of Vavi and Nzimande in Zuma's election campaign.

Sit down with a trade-unionist, card-carrying ANC member and ask him (yes, most are males) what is driving him to support Zuma in this election, considering how the ANC has let the larger union movement down in so many respects over the years, and he will reply, 'The ANC resolutions of Polokwane.'

Yes, the ANC might be suffering internal ruptures, but its resolutions *have* changed; they have shifted towards more working-class agendas, and all the concerns of Zuma's critics are meaningless, simply because these concerns are read as a direct attempt to undermine the working-class cause. The Maniacs' leader may still not be free from the cloud of corruption charges around his head (and he may yet be found guilty one day), but his supporters are nonplussed; they see these so-called democratic obligations as an unjust conspiracy to keep their leader from power and stifle the working-class cause. And they firmly believe that he has been put in this position by counter-revolutionaries who are probably guilty themselves of some or other wrongdoing. Most importantly, he is the man they have been waiting for (hence the 'black Jesus') to lead them out of bondage.

But the Maniacs aren't only working-class heroes hoping for a brighter future. Zuma is supported by a large band of champagne-toting elites, armed with the vision of a Zuma-led South Africa where government tenders and Black Economic Empowerment deals are plentiful. Theirs is an economic opening laced with greed and opportunism and the anticipation of their favours being returned. They know that economic policy is unlikely to change, regardless of what Zuma desires – and even if it does, they'll win the tenders to make it happen.

The average middle-class liberal South African is, on the other hand, the classic Zumaphobe – hereafter Phobe. This character is totally flabbergasted by the violent leanings of the ANCYL; the explicit and unashamed tolerance for corruption (recent highlights include the stirring revelations of Carl Niehaus, the Schabir Shaik fiasco and the hundreds of counts of corruption against Zuma); the end of the proven crime-fighting apparatus, the Scorpions; and the seemingly endless pit of poor governance as illustrated by the mismanagement of South African Airways, Eskom and other parastatals; the farcical street-name changes; and the great health, education and Zimbabwe failures. And he is, of course, appalled that Zuma has managed to sidestep his corruption trial – what he sees as a democratic necessity – just in time for the elections.

For the Phobe, the Polokwane process represents the absolute converse to what the Maniacs perceive it to have been: an event hijacked by the histrionics of the Zuma-mad. They may have tired of former President Mbeki, 'an authoritarian and power-hungry tosser' by the estimation of some, but Zuma's populism and his mass of blind followers are seen as an ever bigger threat to South Africa's democracy, a threat to the freedom of association, a threat to the liberties fought so hard for during the anti-apartheid struggle. Moreover, the rape trial and shower episode of 2006 has left a bitter taste for the Phobes, creating an unambiguous lack of respect for Zuma, the man. He is, to them, simply unfit for the job.

Zuma has not yet been voted in, let alone had sufficient time to prove himself a worthy or disastrous president; there is a long time before that particular verdict can be passed. But how will we end up measuring the Zuma presidency?

If he ends up delivering the *Animal Farm* allegory of rampant despotism, neglect and absolute disregard for human rights, renounces freedom of the press and hangs our beloved cartoonist Zapiro, all the while sipping whiskey and munching biltong while watching South Africa slip into Zimbabwe-like oblivion (meaning Zimbabweans would even leave) . . . would he then have failed?

You can bet there will be Maniacs backing him every step of the way. He can only succeed.

And what if he really does turn into an African Fidel or Chavez, and delivers the revolution by nationalizing everything from diamonds to gold to ostrich soup, and offers genuinely brilliant education and free health care, and sorts out Zimbabwe, and exports biltong-flavoured cigars to Sweden and knights Zapiro . . . would he then have succeeded?

The Phobes are convinced – better yet, 'know' – that the Polokwane resolutions are hardly bound to materialize. He can only fail.

For now, both sides speak different languages; both sides believe in a different victory; both sides want their way at all costs. In the struggle between the Zumaphobes and Zumamaniacs, there is no winner.

Now it's the vote – then the wait-and-see game begins.

POSTSCRIPT

In 2007, Cosatu told the ANC they were tired of being 'an election conveyor belt', used and abused by the ruling party in the lead up to elections. But they pretty much say that every year. To mitigate this inevitable reality, the confederation apparently designed a pact that would make its representatives working in government accountable to Cosatu, as opposed to the ANC.

But then Polokwane happened and Cosatu looked upon Zuma as the coming Messiah and identified the new ANC leadership as pro-poor heroes. The counter-revolutionaries had been usurped, we were told, and the ANC and the alliance were back on track to fixing our nation as they were meant to do. So the pact was abandoned.

The finicky bourgeoisie – that's you by the way, reading this book and thinking you're so clever, classless and free – are of course shaking their heads, wondering what the hell these union bozos were thinking by backing Zuma. Everyone knew that Zuma could never jive with the working class, other than during concerts.

But I don't think anyone realizes how seriously Cosatu took the possibility, or at least pretended to believe in deliverance by the Zuma presidency.

It's sort of sad, but also sort of funny – in a sad way.

At the tenth Cosatu national congress held shortly after Zuma was elected president in 2009, the confederation celebrated that the movement – that is, the National Democratic Revolution – was firmly in their hands. The congress recalled the number of job losses under the Mbeki administration and the flawed approach to HIV that had cost so many lives, and called on the movement to celebrate the election of Zuma as a complete break from the ANC that had been hijacked by those uninterested in the plight of the poor. More than anything else, Cosatu pinpointed with glee all their big shots now in influential positions in government or within the alliance. The country's deputy president, Kgalema Motlanthe, and the ANC secretary general Gwede Mantashe were both former general secretaries of the National Union of Mineworkers; Ebrahim Patel, hero of the South African clothing and textiles workers, was now minister of economic development; Blade Nzimande, general secretary of the South African Communist Party, was now minister of higher education. This was some serious clout. The farm animals had finally replaced the farmers; revolution was on the cards and there would be no excuses this time.

This is what Cosatu concluded at the congress: 'If we cannot make the relationship with our alliance work under these conditions, then we simply have no capacity to make a relationship work with anyone else. If we can't make our relationship with government work, then there will be something wrong with all of us in the alliance. Equally, there will be something wrong with all these comrades in government if they allow the relationship to collapse.'

One year later, mid-2010 to be precise, Cosatu realized that the firm working-class fists they thought would be directing government policy, leading the revolution to the next stage as they painted the town red, were firmly up their own bums. Zuma shrugged his shoulders and danced on to the next flight to China as Cosatu failed to make any headway in the direction touted as the path to salvation. And Cosatu seems to have looped back to square one.

Ultimately, Vavi and the Cosatu leadership are responsible for releasing opium to the workers and ordinary card-carrying members on the ground who were desperately searching for something to believe in – the same people who stood outside the courts and bayed for the blood of those who would obstruct Zuma from becoming the president this country needed – and for ultimately failing them.

Well, this is politics.

And now Cosatu resumes its daily role as the ANC's little big bitch with heavy balls and no bite. Suddenly 'kill for Zuma' seems like a lifetime ago.

And what of the Maniacs and the Phobes?

To be fair, many of his detractors decided to give Zuma a chance following his election into office. Zuma selected a cabinet that was widely judged as brilliant. (I don't know why; most of them have done bugger-all since.) And almost three years later the Phobes are reasonably relieved by Zuma's inaction to this point. In fact, it is precisely because Zuma hasn't done anything dramatic that he has kept the Phobes at bay. But we all know that they're just waiting for him to screw up.

For instance, the surge of anti-Zuma sentiment following the birth of his twenty-somethingth child in late 2009 told a tale of a readymade criticism just waiting to make out the president as a bigger tool than we suspected him to be. Columnists, bloggers and newspaper editors – from independent newspapers to the *Times* and even the *Daily Sun* – came alive with the sound of condom-nation for Zuma and his (latest) bastard. Some writers predicted that the latest exposé on his shenanigans would prove to be the final nail in his PR coffin. Others suggested that the negligence would reduce his influence in the ANC and this would in turn create setbacks for the businessmen waiting for their promised lucrative deals and the criminals who were guaranteed amnesty for their misdemeanours. The criticism was fierce for a while, but it eventually died down. Once again Zuma survived. And not unpredictably.

The successful hosting of the World Cup softened the Zumaphobes for a while, perhaps even endeared them towards the Zuma presidency, but the damaging public-sector strikes and their tragic consequences on education and the health sector, the draconian nature of the government's proposed Protection of Information Bill and the re-emergence of Julius Malema's random rants about nationalizing the mines have always kept the Phobes feeling vulnerable. But Malema's suspension from the ANC has brought a new dynamic to the manner in which Zuma will be viewed. At the time of going to press, Malema had vowed to appeal his expulsion from the ANC, but the move to sideline the firebrand leader would have opened a hornet's nest in the ANC and confused the Phobes – who would be left wondering if this was yet another charade designed to distract from the real tears in the party.

I get the feeling that it's going to be difficult to judge Zuma's presidency for some time yet. Each side is still waiting for Zuma to deliver their version of the prophecy, be it success or failure. And there seems to be a growing impatience for decisions – big, immediate decisions.

The Zuma roller-coaster ride shows no sign of stopping . . .

A pub crawl for the president

As a lifelong non-drinker, I know almost nothing about pubs and bars save for what I've picked up from a few amateur rounds out with friends – and of course what Hollywood has taught me. This means my visions of a typical bar are predictably clichéd: the all-knowing barman, the college-dropout barmaid serving cheap shots, depressed henpecked sods drowning their sorrows with a pint before going home to deal with 'Government'. But when I was tasked by my editor to see if scores of muscled workers in blue overalls and gumboots would be gathered around a TV at the local bar, cursing, chanting and clunking over-filled glasses of Castle as president Zuma delivered his first State of the Nation speech, I somehow doubted it was going to be like a scene from the movies.

The delivery of this particular State of the Nation address, in February 2010, had been rescheduled from its traditional weekday morning slot to a live 7 p.m. broadcast, presumably so that the awestruck South African public could watch its governmental goons hit the red carpet. And – who knows? – perhaps the powers that be expected the people of the land to stop their pub brawls, take a breather in the brothels, and step off their treadmills to listen to our prez remind us of the state of things.

Let's see.

I walk confidently into my first bar in Overport in the whimsical hope that once I've taken my seat a lonely one-time stripper called Shelley might lean over under dimmed lights and whisper, 'What can I get you, stranger?', after which I'd seduce her with sweet nothings and explain how real men don't need a hard drink to get going . . . But the bar I walk into has no electricity.

'The barman is over there somewhere,' a lean silhouette sitting on a plastic chair chuckles as he points ahead. 'He is so fucking black you won't see him.'

In the dark I discern the whites of roaming eyes checking me out and the shimmer of the usual suspects in glass fridges behind the counter, their glamorous green-and-gold wrappings reflecting the last moments of sunshine filtering through the empty room.

'Howzit,' I say to the bulky shadow across the bar.

It grunts back at me.

'Do you have a television here? Tonight is the State of the Nation addr—'

'I know what he's going to tell us,' croaks a voice in the dark behind me. 'He's going to tell us how he's going to use our money to support his fifty-two children and his ten wives. Fuck the State of the Nation speech!'

I look around expectantly, but no one crashes through the windows to take out this contemptuous disbeliever. Ah, freedom of expression, democracy, liberty and all that – invented to prevent fascism, avert incestuous dynasties and rid the world of communist Russians. Can it be so?

Our president and his ministers may have been voted in by the electorate, but surely this process was the practical assimilation of royalty – just without the bloodline, creed or caste designate, or the obligatory majesty of propriety that was adhered to in most kingdoms some centuries back (and, of course, in present-day Saudi Arabia, Zimbabwe and rural KwaZulu-Natal)? Zuma may not be our blue-blooded king, but ordinary citizens' taxes still feed, clothe and transport our First Citizen and his entourage, suggesting that some things haven't changed since the times of Julius Caesar. Have any doubts? Yesterday's bullish chariots are today's blue-light SUVs; the archaic French *parlement* is today's Parliament; and gladiator fights in an ancient colosseum could easily be today's Victor Matfield tearing up the Brumbies at Loftus.

Still, it appears a man can curse the president of South Africa and get away with it – well, for now at least.

Back in the bar I order a Coke. The barman gives me a Sprite. I lift myself onto a bar stool and spin around to face the voice. Like they do in the movies.

'This Zuma guy won't last long,' says the mystery man from a table in the gloom. 'If he carries on like this, the ANC will pull an Mbeki on him. They'll get rid of him.' He takes a swig from his bottle.

'You know, Deevi,' he continues, 'this country isn't getting any better. Everything's in a state of corruption. In some years' time, Deevi, if this country doesn't turn into Zimbabwe, it will be taken back by the white man. I think I better move to Botswana or Uganda.'

The guy sitting opposite him, presumably Deevi, nods his head. But the mystery man isn't finished yet.

'Every year they have the State of the Nation speech at 10 a.m.,' he declares to his tiny audience. 'You know why they suddenly changed it? You know why?' His croak is now a drunken slur.

'How do you know?' Deevi asks.

'I read the paper, watch the news,' he replies. But he doesn't tell us why.

My new friends are entertaining in their way, but sitting in the dark isn't going to help me much. A fault at a substation has apparently killed the electricity in the entire area and the barman has no idea when the power will return. So I bid them goodbye, jump into my car and race off towards the city in the hope that I'll find a suitable bar along the way. Switching on the radio to listen to the live broadcast, I am greeted with, 'We seem to have lost the signal from inside Parliament . . .'

I chuckle at the peculiar start to my evening. As the feed improves, I drive past an upmarket café in Musgrave and notice three huge flat screens showing a bunch of Italian men sprinting after a football. I decide to pull over and ask the manager if he wouldn't mind switching from the sports channel to the speech. He complies and adjusts the volume slightly – but not above the middle-class din presiding over exorbitantly priced suppers.

Zuma's mouth moves slowly; I lip-read 'job creation' and 'poverty'. I look around and not a soul has even noticed the president's presence. Is this what the speech means to us? Lip service?

'Do you want to keep watching?' the manager asks me.

I smile and decline. What's the point in a place like this? I race back to my car. One more place, I think to myself.

Back in my vehicle, Zuma reminds us how far the nation has come; how Mandela and Co. sacrificed their lives for justice; that 480,000 jobs have been created through the expanded public-works programme despite the fact that 900,000 jobs have been lost in the recession – 900,000 jobs that probably weren't there in the first place, I cynically think to myself.

I scan the streets for my last-chance saloon. The time is 7.30 p.m. It's not yet completely dark and the street, scattered with workers and vagabonds, mirrors the murkiness of an awkward twilight. A couple of junkies sit on the pavement at a street corner, their demeanours unflattering. Nearby, a coffee shop with a restaurant above also broadcasts soccer – from a different league – on its television screens.

I pass a string of busy gourmet burger and pizza joints, then a bar with an enormous flat screen facing the street, flashing a fashion catwalk or music video (what's the difference?). On the radio, Zuma tentatively advocates a five-year plan to improve housing and health and decrease crime; it's as if the same worlds are ceremoniously spinning in opposite directions.

Eventually I find my next stop. I walk into the bar and, radiating charm not seen since the times of a young John Travolta, I order a ginger ale. Three men sit beside me with huge glasses of golden liquid on the tabletop before them. I acknowledge their company by simultaneously raising my eyebrow, slightly nodding my head and lifting my ginger ale in their general direction. They nod back.

'Heard they're showing the State of the Nation speech tonight,' I say to all three of them.

'Tonight?' one of them asks.

'Yeah, tonight. I think it's now,' another says.

The third guy just stares at me, dryly, sipping his beer.

I ask the barmaid to change the channel. She declines. 'I think we'd rather stick to the sports, hey.'

'I suppose we can do that,' I say to the man beside me. 'Zuma's only talking about our future.'

The barmaid laughs. The two men also laugh. The third man keeps staring at me.

With less than ten minutes left before the historic speech ends, I decide it's time to throw in the towel. I check my email on my phone. Excerpts of the address are already appearing in my inbox. In a couple of hours there will be a plethora of write-ups, commentaries, analyses and the usual dramatics surrounding a speech of this nature.

I watch Mancini score some goals as part of a promo for AC Milan. I pick up my ale and join the others in drowning their sorrows.

Betting on jobs at the casino

It was August 2009. We were in the midst of recession. With hundreds of thousands of jobs being shed across the country, the powers that be at KwaZulu-Natal's Department of Economic Development came up with a master plan to reinvigorate the economy. This is their story . . .

KwaZulu-Natal always leads the pack. During the ongoing economic recession that began in 2008, the province held the dubious distinction of playing host to not only the most job losses, non-functioning traffic lights and street-name changes in the country, but also the most cases of swine flu . . . So it was hardly a surprise when the KZN Department of Economic Development (DED) decided to host the first Economic Recovery and Job Summit, a very important-sounding event.

In the first three months of 2009, about 119,000 jobs were lost in KwaZulu-Natal, a truly shocking statistic. (I didn't even know that many people in the province had jobs in the first place.) And so high-flying businessmen, bureaucrats and labour representatives were summoned to the Sibaya Casino outside Durban in an attempt to create a road map for a sustainable economic turnaround; that is, keeping the poor people occupied by creating work, halting our Gini coefficient's blastoff into orbit and creating more Internet bandwidth.

Keep in mind that KZN is really a backwater province, where the somewhat slower locals remain to live a more relaxed existence rather than taking on the rat race of Jozi or considering the marathon trek to distant Cape Town (where the locals don't speak much Zulu). For us rural Durban people, such a road-show-type conference seemed a once-in-a-lifetime experience and the fact that KZN was leading the response to the economic crisis really was something for us to celebrate. Not much ever gets done here, what with all our sunshine and seaside to distract us, and Schabir Shaik still taking up most of the province's attention.

Naturally, the DED selected a fabulous venue for the summit. Away from the manic city centre, away from the cluttered informal traders and dirty pavements, away from street children, drug pedlars and other undesirable vagabonds, Sun International's Sibaya Casino and Entertainment Kingdom, thirty kilometres north of Durban, was deemed perfectly suitable.

In fairness, the organizers' choice was really limited, since the International Convention Centre in the Durban CBD had been booked out already and every other conference venue was too sterile for a meeting of this nature. Where else could the province have possibly held it? At the early morning market at Warwick Junction, where poor veggie sellers struggle for survival while dodging rubber bullets, signing court papers and escaping Michael Sutcliffe's Marxist tear gas? Not likely . . . Would it have made sense to hold it in one of those not-so-secret sweatshops downtown (suggesting intentions to revive the clothing sector)? Not convenient . . . Or would it have tickled the fancy of the elite to have hosted it on the top floor of the King Edward VIII Hospital – where the effects of the recession are visible on the faces of the poor who have been queuing up since 2008 to see a specialist? Not healthy . . .

So the Sibaya Casino was selected, a tidy little drive up the north coast. Propped up elegantly on a hill, surrounded by beautiful sugarcane plantations and facing the vast Indian Ocean, the casino is a holiday-maker's dream. Sure, certain visitors may think the castle-façade walls give it something of a lost-cardboard-palace-of-the-Zulu-Empire feel, but others would say it's 'the ideal getaway for those seeking all the thrills and spills, laughs and luxury KwaZulu-

Natal has to offer. With every convenience from state-of-the-art conference facilities to placid ocean views, Sibaya is nothing short of being home away from home.' Either way, the organizers of the summit clearly bought into the branding.

Dignitaries arrived in fancy cars sporting expensive suits, and the journalists in wait lapped them up, running around and doing Jim Carrey-type renditions with the premier, the new economic development minister and various other famous personalities, I think. (I can't be sure. I am not very good with faces.) SAfm is obviously quite a serious news station – well, that's what my mother says – and even they came to camp outside the casino, so it was all very important. And when it finally got underway, the not-so-important people were more than thrilled to stand up in awe when the various ministers took their seats on stage. I guess that's what church would feel like should I decide to convert.

The focus of the delegates was really impressive. They walked straight past the slot machines, poker tables and early-morning gamblers (people gamble, have breakfast and go to work) and, to the surprise of many, headed straight to the conference centre. Good to see politicians drawing the line between gambling with our lives and with their money.

Despite starting late, the summit was well organized. Arrangements were so thorough they even brought in pretty girls to escort delegates from the entrance of the ballroom foyer to the registration tables (a good five metres), making all the important people feel more than comfortable as they prepared to robustly discuss what needed to be done to save the newly unemployed masses from rioting and making a nuisance of themselves. I particularly enjoyed the eye candy – after all, I'm a guy and August is national women's month in South Africa and all that – and was glad to see the organizers had got this vital aspect of the event right.

Economic Development Minister Ebrahim Patel spoke eloquently about his 'six-pack plan' (I'm dead serious) in the casino's ballroom – quite a clever response to the crisis. I battled to take him seriously, though, as the affluent ambience frequently forced Patel to break into a waltz with the economic development and tourism MEC Michael Mabuyakhulu. This was a ballroom after all and I do have ADHD . . . Thankfully, Patel maintained his composure and the singing and dancing remained strictly in my own head.

Likewise, over the next day and a half, stakeholders from the many sectors maintained their composure when they met separately in various locations inside the casino. The tourism sector met under a crystal disco ball inside the Krakatoa nightclub. I understand that they somehow managed to sit still.

Some of the discussions and points raised were poignant. The tourism sector resolved, among other resolutions, to support local craft-makers; the old women on the Durban beachfront – beading away, crafting away, tearing their hair away – often make their first sale of the week at 3 p.m. on a Friday afternoon and would be very excited since they have only heard this commitment for the past ten years. The clothing-and-textile industry reportedly had some fierce discussions; apparently labour representatives actually pitched up to that session with a real agenda.

The IT professionals at the nerd end of the summit drummed home the need for increasing Internet bandwidth and investing in Business Process Outsourcing, BPOs or call centres as we know them. I think this was a fruitful exercise because the sector's insistence on developing call centres is really a positive one; we definitely need a generation of educated, smart, middle-class youngsters living underground and talking in foreign accents to irate customers in New York and Melbourne. Research suggests that Durban's weather will keep call-centre consultants relaxed, stress-free and in a good mood, which they'll need to be since they will get paid 10 to 18 per cent less than their counterparts in Johannesburg or Cape Town. This way about 25,000 zombies could be created without breaking a sweat . . . But at the agricultural meeting, the farmers were upset once again that no one cared about their cows unless there was no milk on the shelves. I'd never thought about it like that before.

The superficiality was impressive. Cocktail parties, lavish suppers and free dancing girls were the order of the day. Delegates fluttered out of the conference room in the evening, meandering among tourists, Zulu dancers and some Fong Kong Dolly Parton wannabe dancing and singing around the casino and the lobby area. This was, I realized, just reward for a hard day's serious work.

As I watched our extraordinary leaders disappear into the night, I smiled to myself. We're definitely on the right path, I thought. These extravagant summits and conferences made absolute sense, especially when rich, established politicians took time off from their busy schedules to discuss the path forward, how they might 'create some jobs' and the type of tenders they could be lining up. How noble, nay gracious of them. Somewhere in there they might even give the poor reason to feel good about themselves.

Later, I decided to ask a friend what she thought of my conclusions.

'Am I being unfair?' I asked her.

'Yes, you are!' she replied. 'Don't you realize that they really think they are doing something great?'

But this is what I am saying . . . Am I not?

POSTSCRIPT

I never heard about Minister Patel's six-pack plan again. Evidently, neither did Benni McCarthy.

BEYOND THE BOUNDARY

When we snubbed His Holiness

I

While studying at university in Delhi back in the days when I was young and happy – in 2004 to be precise – the sociology department organized a 'study trip' for our class to the north Indian hill station of Dharamsala. Situated in the upper reaches of the Kangra Valley in a branch of the Himalayan mountains known as the Dhauladhar Range, Dharamsala is famous as the town where His Holiness the Dalai Lama has lived in exile for the last five decades, along with thousands of Tibetan refugees.

Like most 'study trips', there was no real studying on this little adventure, and we spent most of our time just chilling. I remember the experience for the oddest reasons: the long trip on a rickety bus that threatened to off-load us at every hairpin on the cliffhanger route, and a bunch of kids trying to lynch me for teasing them in some made-up Tibetan–Turkish–Hindi–Russian dialect, come to mind. Freshest in my memory, though, is my European classmates' fascination with the holy (read sexy) Buddhist monks – their admirably shiny scalps and flowing robes, their tight calves and supposedly high resistance to getting laid . . . I remember this particularly because my Polish friend insisted I check them out with her.

It was a memorable trip precisely because it was so relaxed. Instead of hopping around the town with silly questionnaires, we were allowed to simply soak in the ambience. We learnt more this way, as we immersed ourselves in every last morsel of experience with our limited funds. We were the poor tourists, the vagabonds, but it helped our cause that our professor was well hooked up, and he used his magic charm to facilitate a couple of valuable trips for us.

We trekked up to the impressive Tsuglagkhang Temple complex, commonly known as the Dalai Lama Temple, where we were able to swoon at the sight of His Holiness leading a prayer. We hadn't known he would be there until someone started the whispers: 'Look, the Dalai Lama, the Dalai Lama!'

Tibetans aren't the tallest of folk, but we all found ourselves, between the conspicuous murals and the antique statues, on the tips of our toes trying to capture the perfect view of the icon before us, the fourteenth Dalai Lama. Sure, he may look like a regular Asian fellow, but his deep verses and intermittent deeper breaths reverberated through our insides like the thunderous, compulsive bass in a Buddha Bar. In contrast to our ogling of the monks and indulgent amusement at the Indo-Tibetan bazaar, this was whack intense. He was truly impressive – but despite being in awe, I still could not stop an electric cynicism from sparking along my nerves.

Here was a holy man, I thought to myself, who spent far too much time touring, lobbying and smiling, with his palms pressed in a charming namaste pose, for the benefit of Westerners looking to detoxify their ordinary city lives. Surely this luxurious passive-resistance thing died with Gandhi, Luthuli and Lennon, I figured – but it was this holy bloke who gave the world's hippies a second coming: an excuse to draw flowers, play the guitar and have sex without condoms as they searched for a worthy anti-something-exotic-something-else rallying point to give purpose to their lives. Tibetans needed action and here was their leader dining with the world's elite, who were happy to bask in his presence while merrily gobbling up the profits generated by rapidly proliferating trade with China. After all, and let's be frank, the Tibetan peaceful resistance was now a way of life, the talk and inaction a deal wedged ajar.

I couldn't help asking myself a question: having received the Nobel Peace Prize a decade and a half before, in 1989, when was he ever going to get his hands dirty to get a hold on the main prize? At the same time, and despite my cynicism, it was really quite something to be in the presence of this esteemed individual. Even one of my Chinese classmates attested to being star-struck, as His Holiness stood right before us, leading a congregation of monks.

Effective or not, in a world so quick to resort to violence, we were all inimitably drawn to the indomitable values of non-violence and the reconciliatory politics that resonated from this holy man hollering his incomprehensible syllables. My friend looked on, his arms folded and his feet still, as he carefully observed the Dalai Lama and his devout followers searching for the Divine.

II

Dharamsala, high up in the mountains, is an extraordinary sight. The Himalayas sprawl out to the north-east and the magnificent summer colonial escapes of Simla and Kasauli lie to the south. The province of Himachal Pradesh, which encompasses all these towns, is a far cry from the hustle and bustle, shit and grime of ordinary Indian life. It's almost another world.

The upper town of Dharamsala, known as McLeod Ganj, lies at around 2,000 metres and survives on Tibetan-refugee tourism. FREE TIBET t-shirts, tattoos, snow-lion flags, getting high, meditating, seducing sex-starved monks . . . This is the end destination for hippies looking for a trip back in time to another era. The town is literally caught in a time warp, incorporating certain trappings of modernity with the ideals and ambience of 1960s' flower power. It is a particular disposition that the local community effortlessly pulls off – so there are Internet cafés dotted around the place and even Coca-Cola vendors on the highest peaks, but as you walk around you could be forgiven for thinking that when the Cold War ends they'll all just pack up and go back home . . .

How can you blame them? They've been dreaming of home since 1959.

But their dislocation is seemingly complete, and the Tibetan museum in Dharamsala tells of a powerful discord: they are at once rebelling, documenting and living against the occupation of their homeland, and yet they seem strangely content for now. The museum itself is a collection of original texts, images and installations documenting the community's flight from China to India. It showcases in painstaking detail the Chinese occupation of Tibet, and documents the great escape of a young Dalai Lama with his entourage of twenty men and six ministers to India in 1959. Of course, China still sees its invasion of Tibet as a mere reunification of the provinces.

The Dalai Lama's epic getaway and relocation to India is well documented, with a number of emotive 'before the border' and 'after the border' photographs. It is noted that he had to travel at night, tolerate harsh weather conditions and cross the 450 metre-wide Brahmaputra River (which incidentally gave its name to my student hostel back in Delhi). More than 80,000 Tibetans soon followed suit and settled in what is now known as 'little Lhasa', after the name of the Tibetan capital. There are also snaps of Tibetan rebels or freedom fighters with rifles ready to defend themselves in the event of an attack from the Chinese.

Needless to say, my Chinese mate was bemused by the museum. 'Wasn't it strange,' he asked me, 'to have documented an escape so purposely and thoroughly?'

My friend argued that considering all the posing going on in this 'photographed middle-of-the-night-type getaway', was it not obvious that the Chinese let the holy man escape, and if they wanted they could have put a bullet in him on that very night or any time later? 'And,' he continued, 'while the Tibetan struggle has always been presented as vehemently non-violent, what were all these Tibetan freedom fighters doing with guns in their hands?'

'I don't know', I replied, grinning at my friend's battle to debunk the Chinese propaganda fed to him as a child.

Just then, as if he hadn't enough on his mind already, one of our classmates, a North American girl, obviously scarred by the dismal imagery of persecuted monks harassed by deadly Chinamen, walked over to him, tapped him on the shoulder and looked him right in the eye. 'I want to know,' she asked solemnly, 'when you see this . . . do you feel guilty?'

North Americans, whether they're Yanks or their cousins with the inferiority complex, the Canadians, often seem to possess an uncanny lack of tact. That it comes with a discernible McDonald's twang makes the candour even more resentful.

This, I thought to myself, was probably the same question white South Africans always faced from overzealous tourists. 'Did you know about the black people dying in the townships?' Or, 'Did your family ever discuss Nelson Mandela's imprisonment?' Or, most likely, 'Hey, is Sandton safe or are there many blacks there?'

But I wondered if it was a fair question to ask my Chinese friend, an individual, who like most Chinese, never benefited in any way from his country's continued conquest of Tibet. It wasn't as if Tibetan children made cheaper slaves in local Beijing sweatshops or the Tibetan mountains bore a secret potion that gave the Chinese a longer you-know-what.

At the same time, there were real abuses in Tibet. Did this mean that as a thinking citizen he ought to feel guilty, even if he was merely a bystander to his country's policy? Is it his fault that the Chinese government had an insatiable phallic urge to pin down Tibet as a pet project of oppression?

The Germans were (and sometimes still are) picked on for obvious power-hungry reasons, and today Americans are frequently tormented for being stupid and politically meddlesome, but was it really reasonable to chastise a Chinaman for his country taking over Tibet some five decades earlier?

III

In March 2009 the Dalai Lama was denied entry into South Africa. The government explanation was that his presence in South Africa at a conference about peace a year before the soccer World Cup could shift the focus from our staging of the biggest show on earth to the ongoing quest for the liberation of Tibet. Though our presidential spokesperson denied any suggestion, whatsoever, that the ban was a result of Chinese pressure, a Chinese embassy official confirmed that Beijing had indeed urged South Africa to take this action, warning that a visit would harm bilateral ties between the two countries and could lead to the reversal of billions of dollars' worth of trade agreements.

I am pretty sure no one ever saw that official again.

South Africa's refusal to admit His Holiness into the country achieved two notable things: first, it focused the spotlight squarely on China's shenanigans in Tibet; and, second, it reaffirmed South Africa's status as a ruthless, amoral player in international politics.

From a South African's point of view, what our government effectively did to the Tibetan movement was even more painful than the debauchery of plastic smiles and stained handshakes that is the resort of the rest of the civilized world's reaction to the Tibetan cause. Case in point: in 2007 the Dalai Lama received a Congressional Gold Medal from the then American president, George W. Bush. A year earlier he was given honorary Canadian citizenship. Never mind that the Dalai Lama would have done a whole lot better if he had managed to get an item number in that awful comedy, *From Chandni Chowk to China*, but consider that His Holiness is a recipient of more than a hundred prizes and gestures from around the world – all of which do little but humour the Tibetan struggle.

In fact, the decision to ban His Holiness from entering South Africa did little to hinder the Tibetan movement; it hardly trimmed the wings of a movement that hasn't flapped in years. But it reeked of a new self-interest that is just too willing to bend over to the highest bidder. Yes, there is hypocrisy in the half-hearted gestures of the United States, Canada, even *Masterchef Australia*, and everyone else who might have patted the Dalai Lama on the back over the years, but at least there has mostly been an acknowledgement of an ethical awareness, of what is right. Call me naïve, but the South African decision to refuse him access into the country only serves to further taint South Africa as a country that considers flaky trade to be more important than giving a voice to the oppressed. This, surely, is the most profound hypocrisy imaginable, given our government's own political history, which relied on the moral support of foreign leaders for its very survival not too long ago. And it is not the first instance.

First it was South Africa's despicable decision to vote against a UN Security Council resolution aimed at sanctioning the military junta running Myanmar in 2007. Then it was Thabo Mbeki's 'no crisis in Zimbabwe' comment following the flawed 2008 elections, as well as his diplomatic strategy of simply appeasing Mugabe that killed our integrity as a worthy broker in that (or any other) peace process. The Zimbabwean example is particularly painful when we consider that Zimbabwe is our immediate neighbour and its well-being directly affects us; the consequences of our 'silent diplomacy' reveals itself in the faces of the millions who have had to cut through our fences and make a life in South Africa. South Africa is understandably against foreign intervention in African affairs as demonstrated in their opposition to outside interference in the 2011 election standoff in Cote d'Ivoire and in their anxiety over NATO intervention in Libya (though they voted for a no-fly zone over Libya). But their protests appear more symbolic than rational arguments. The priority ought to be immediately ending a conflict and protecting the lives of ordinary people directly affected by a standoff, and not patronizing leadership that won't go. Instead, they have continuously insisted on political road maps when the game has already changed and 'power sharing' when the people have already spoken, suggesting purely self-serving intent.

As with the Dalai Lama example, there are certain political reasons for the stances our government has taken, but they pale in comparison with the moral obligations that have been abandoned in the process. With Myanmar and Zimbabwe, South Africa had a unique opportunity to claim the moral high ground in partitioning the rights of the marginalized in both countries. Instead, we cast off our humanity so we wouldn't offend a repressive junta and our uncle Bob.

The issue now is that our current government – that is, the post-counter-revolutionary-Mbeki-era government, also known as the Zuma government – has simply assumed Mbeki's foreign policy, which abandons the politics of the liberation struggle and neglects the concept of solidarity with oppressed communities. While the Cosatu, with all its faults, managed to stop a Chinese shipment of arms from travelling through South Africa to Zimbabwe in April 2008, and achieved a similar triumph when refusing to off-load an Israeli ship in protest of that country's ugly invasion of Gaza in December that year, the South African government has consciously kept its distance from any controversial activity that might hurt its short-term self-interest. We may have successfully staged the World Cup, with hundreds of millions glued to their screens during the tournament, but we are rapidly losing credibility as the vanguard of human rights, free speech and equality on the continent.

Ultimately, the Dalai Lama is not so important, and denying a visa to a jet-setting freedom fighter who won't fight isn't quite the same as, say, colonizing Swaziland (though that would be cool because King Mswati III needs to go). Besides, the Tibetan cause is probably a lost one. Whereas there was once a drive for an independent Tibet, it was announced in 2008 that the Tibetan people would settle for autonomy. Tomorrow, they might just settle for an electric toaster. Not for ordinary monks it would seem; acts of defiance, including horrific cases of self-immolation, continue as some refuse to give up the cause. This only makes South Africa's stance towards the Holy Man and the Tibetan movement only more unconscionable.

I remember how my Chinese friend replied to the question posed to him by his North American accuser.

'I don't think I feel guilty,' he shrugged.

I think he just felt sick.

POSTSCRIPT

In October 2011, the Dalai Lama cancelled a scheduled trip to South Africa after the South African government dilly-dallied with his visa application once more. His Holiness was meant to attend Archbishop Desmond Tutu's eightieth birthday celebrations on 8 October – but with less than three days before his scheduled departure and with no confirmation of a visa forthcoming, he pulled the plug on joining the soiree. The decision to cancel his trip prompted Tutu to lay into the ruling ANC, comparing the South African government with the apartheid regime and warned that the day will come when 'we will pray for the defeat of the ANC government . . .'

'Many, many people are appalled in many parts of the world, especially people who supported us during the struggle. They are weeping and saying, "South Africa? It can't be",' he added. With all due respect to Tutu (one of the few celebrated crazies left on this planet brave enough to speak his mind) the Dalai Lama might still be revered by millions of monk lovers across the globe, but the Tibetan leader is finding it increasingly difficult to gain an audience with international statesmen fearful of the wrath of the Chinese. In 2009, Barack Obama refused to meet him but went ahead with a low-key meeting at the White House in July 2011, much to the dismay of the Chinese. Likewise, Julia Gillard, the Australian PM, snubbed His Holiness in June 2011 in an apparent attempt to appease the Chinese. But Mexico's president Felipe Calderon decided to met His Holiness in his presidential palace in Mexico City in September 2011, a move that prompted China to release a statement saying that the meeting had 'grossly interfered with China's internal affairs, hurt the feelings of the Chinese people and harmed Chinese–Mexican relations'. As a result, Brazilian government officials carefully ignored His Holiness on his trip to Brazil a week later. And of course, the list of diplomatic games goes on.

Fact remains that with China's soft power reaching a crescendo, Tibet's window of opportunity to gain tangible support for its cause continues to shrink with every stitch. Such is the disconnect, that it does not even matter that the Dalai Lama has withdrawn from public office and no longer demands independence from China. He is public enemy number one for China and authorities are determined to pull out all the stops in isolating him from the rest of the world.

Meanwhile, as the official line goes, the South African government did not deny him a visa this time around; they managed to do just enough to let him know that he was no longer welcome to the country.

How times change.

Nobel Obama trumps Superman

During my European adventure of 2009 (while taking time out from being harassed at airports and train stations by terror-obsessed European officials), I received an invitation from a friend in Oslo offering me a free guided tour of the city, provided I could get my ass there. A UN classmate and quite the jet-setter, she had freshly returned home to Norway after a stint in Sarajevo or Belgrade or somewhere, and she suggested I visit Oslo while she was still around. 'When else will you ever come to Norway anyway?' she motivated. Unfortunately, I am no Nobel Prize laureate in the making, so she had a point. When I got to know that another close friend of mine, a South African, was also in Oslo, I knew I had found my purpose. I promptly found a cheap flight and headed off to check out the kingdom of the Vikings. I found fjords, a lovely city and respectable Pakistanis, and even managed to scheme a free journo tour of the Nobel Peace Centre, providing inimitable insight into Norway's quest to be the world's greatest promoter of peace.

Several months later, on 9 October 2009, Barack Obama was awarded the Nobel Peace Prize. Clearly I'd been destined to write about it.

The Nobel Peace Centre in Oslo is something of a religious site. Sitting adjacent to the harbour at the centre of the city, a spot that could easily double for Cape Town's waterfront, the Peace Centre is a temple for serious diplomats, earnest hippies and wide-eyed, encyclopaedia-stuffed kids.

Walking through the Peace Centre is like making your way through a handmade, leather-bound history book. It pulls out all the stops to showcase the most positive influential leaders, thinkers and do-gooders of the past century: magic history tomes tell Alfred Nobel's story, electronic stems hosting mini-interactive screens summarize each laureate's distinction, looping documentaries advance the various legends, and trees bearing international messages of peace yield fruits of hope – every part of which makes the experience as gratifyingly ethereal as possible.

The impressive gizmos were all very, well, impressive – but pardon my heresy if I say it all rather bored me. Even though I felt right at home with the four South African Peace laureates looking at me through interactive screens, I couldn't help but think that something was amiss. I got the impression that the plush building is to idealistic peace-mongers what the Neverland ranch was to Michael Jackson fans: a theatre of make-believe designed to make you feel all fuzzy inside while you try to exorcize the monsters in your head (or bed).

At this point, a quick Nobel overview. Story goes that in 1895 the Swedish inventor and arms dealer Alfred Nobel bequeathed his fortune to the creation of a series of prizes that would celebrate human spirit and ingenuity. They came to be known as the Nobel Prizes, and are generally acknowledged as the most prestigious awards in their respective fields, with categories including literature, physics, medicine, chemistry and, the most famous of the lot, peace. (It was also the most poignant, given that Nobel's most noteworthy invention was dynamite.) In 1968 an economics prize was added to the list by the central bank of Sweden, though it is not technically a Nobel.

Interestingly, the Peace Prize is the only one of the six to be judged and awarded in Norway; the others are Swedish. Given that I was at the Peace Centre in Norway, that, unsurprisingly, was the prize I was focusing on – and the one leaving me somewhat nonplussed.

The first Nobel Peace Prize was dished out in 1901. Associated with a hefty booty, and quickly linked with enough statesmen and international organizations to outshine the northern lights, the prize soon became the Holy Grail for modern civilizations to aspire to. One sip from its chalice and the winner would have bestowed on himself the neo-pagan version of prophethood, reserved only for those who strive with honour to make the world a more harmonious place.

The irony of course is that the award has, from its earliest days, been a caricature of the world's imperialist power basins. When Albert Luthuli received the prize in 1960, it was only the second time it had been bestowed on someone outside of North America or Europe. Martin Luther King, the youngest recipient of the prize, received it in 1964 for leading the civil rights movement in the United States, but it was only really in the 1970s, when flared jeans, short skirts and flower power won over the Nobel committee, that they began acknowledging heroes in less fashionable realms. Until then, it seemed nothing more than an elaborate pat on the back of Western statesmen for putting out fires they had mostly started in the first place.

Mahatma Gandhi, for example, was nominated five times for the award but never won. Certain critics say it was because he was obsessed with the human rights of Indians only and thus lacked universality. (Others now argue that the Indian population explosion of the last half-century is India's way of taking his values global.) But the real story has probably more to do with Norway's close relationship with Britain at the time and the fact that Gandhi was, after all, just a coolie. In the Western world, no underwear meant no prize.

Gandhi was assassinated in 1948, having become the pioneer of non-violent resistance. Along with Mandela, he was the very icon of peace in the twentieth century – and the fact that he was never awarded a Nobel is a huge indictment of dubious standards. Indeed, it was embarrassing enough for the committee to realize that their insistence on courting the most fashionable statesmen and the choicest causes was inherently flawed. The reality is that prizes may be intended to recognize great deeds, but people don't revere individuals because of their prizes; they revere them for their noted deeds. Take a few South African winners, for example. The fact that Luthuli and later Desmond Tutu received the Peace Prize for their insistence on a non-violent struggle against apartheid is rather arbitrary compared with their tangible world-changing achievements over their respective lifetimes. Likewise, Nelson Mandela's charismatic move towards reconciliation and his twenty-seven years of sacrifice in prison come to mind long before we talk about a CV lined with loads of awards, one of which is the Nobel Peace Prize.

Western prejudices aside, the Nobel Peace Prize has always been a well-intentioned attempt to highlight, inspire and motivate long-lasting efforts for peace and prosperity. At the same time, in the real world it was also always Norway's ticket into the big league of international diplomacy, an annual event for that country to set the agenda regarding human rights, democracy and disarmament – ideas close to Norwegian hearts. As a result, it has always been influenced by a certain worldview, a political approach suiting a country with particular needs and allies.

Consider the awarding of the prize to American president Theodore Roosevelt, the first statesman to receive it, in 1906. Supposedly he got it for mediating in the Russo-Japanese war, but it has been plausibly argued that his name was called as a way of manufacturing goodwill and allegiance between the United States and the newly independent Norway. Back then, the Norwegian foreign minister chaired the prize committee and so this conclusion is hardly unfair. But this set a trend whereby so many winners turned out, less than coincidentally, to be the world's most powerful personalities – 'they that have the power to hurt', as Shakespeare wrote. Whereas the prize may have been designed for philosophers, writers, activists and those challenging the structures of power – I like to think modern journalists like John Pilger, Robert Fisk or even a Rian Malan (!) should warrant nomination – the committee focused its attention on those with direct access to the machinations of power.

In so doing, Norway twists noble acts that deserve divine

reparation into their annual attempt to remain in the spotlight of modern human history. How else would such a small and unimportant nation posit itself as a world leader in humanitarian assistance, developmental policy and mediation? We like to imagine the Nobel Peace Prize and its recipients as the ultimate endorsement of humanity, when the thing is hardly more convincing than an Oscar. At least everyone admits the Oscars are just a performance.

Which leads me on to Barack Obama, who has now become the third American president to win the Nobel Peace Prize (the other one was awarded to Woodrow Wilson in 1919, while Jimmy Carter won it in 2002 after leaving office). Officially, it was for 'capturing the world's attention and giving its people hope for a better future' and 'for his extraordinary efforts to strengthen international diplomacy and cooperation between peoples'. But I'm not buying it. Is anyone?

With this endowment of the award, the noble gimmick has surely only shrunk further into a feverishly farcical limerick of an accolade. They might as well have given it to Superman.

Don't get me wrong. I like Barack Obama. I like how he delivers a speech. I like his chiselled face. I even agree he is the sexiest politician since Clint Eastwood became mayor of Carmel-by-the-Sea. But then, they should have just given him that Oscar.

Sure, Obama did make some noble promises and, well, he isn't George W. Bush, but what, in all objective honesty, has he achieved in terms of tangible positive and meaningful change in a world so incessantly divided? And by contrast, what does the Nobel Prize committee, and by association Norway, have to gain from validating the agenda of the most powerful man in the world? The answers are: not much, and quite a lot.

The fact that the nominations for the award closed less than two weeks after Obama was inaugurated as US president – that is, two weeks after he assumed the position of power in which he is able to actually *do* something tangible about peace rather than just talk about it – suggests, to me at least, that the prize has become nothing more than a charade.

If only Obama had responded something along these lines to news of his award:

'I am shocked, surprised and moved by the committee's choice of me for an award that is the pinnacle of honour for human rights, equality and justice. With it, I have been invited to join the ranks of all those men and women before me who have sacrificed their lives in fighting for a better, more peaceful world. I would like to honour the Luthulis, the Mandelas, the Suu Kyis who have been awarded it in the past – individuals who have inspired millions through personal sacrifice. But I am only a few months into my new job, and while I appreciate the honour of this award, I humbly request that I be judged by what I accomplish in the coming years and not by the promises I have made in the past few months. Therefore, I cannot accept the Nobel Peace Prize just yet. God bless America.'

It is obviously difficult to turn down such an award. It could be construed as an arrogant and unnecessary slap in the face; it could even be regarded as anti-peace. But had he done so, Obama would have exchanged a farcical award for immortality, and the Nobel Peace Centre might have stopped looking like Never, Neverland.

POSTSCRIPT

In October 2011, three women were awarded the Nobel Peace Prize for their non-violent struggle for the rights of women in their respective countries. While Leymah Gbowee and Tawakkul Karman received their plaudits with some international conviction, the awarding of the prize to Ellen Johnson Sirleaf, the Liberian president, brought donkey-carts to a standstill in Monrovia. The timing of the award could not have been more telling of the dubious agenda of the Nobel committee who chose to honour her just days before a contentious presidential elections in Liberia. The move was seen as an endorsement of Sirleaf by 'Western' powers. In Sirleaf's case, the award felt purposefully planned, and rubbed the shine off the achievements of the other two deserving recipients. There could be no other reason for awarding Sirleaf the coveted prize in 2011, unless of course the Nobel committee had earmarked the year to honour women and found three for the prize of one. A year earlier, Liu Xiaobo, the Chinese pro-democracy activist, was announced as the 2010 recipient of the Nobel Peace Prize. He would have heard about his honour while sitting in jail in some random town in China, where he is due to remain until 2020. Of course, the move to recognize him and his cause is a 'good' one, though it is unlikely to inspire much change in China's approach to governance, human rights or jailed political activists. And, of course, it proves to be yet another impotent white liberal political statement by the Nobel committee.

Meanwhile, Obama's prize appears ever more ridiculous as the drones go by. Obama should have taken inspiration from Jean-Paul Sartre. In 1964, the French writer, philosopher and philanderer was named the Nobel Prize laureate for literature. But he snubbed the award, becoming the first person ever to do so for 'moral reasons'. (In 1958 Boris Pasternak, author of *Doctor Zhivago*, was forced to refuse the award after coming under pressure from Soviet authorities.) Sartre argued that he did not want to be 'transformed' by such a prize; neither did he want to partake in the mass glorification of literature, something he objected to as a bourgeois privilege. Of course, if you didn't study sociology, philosophy or literature, you probably never knew this life-changing fact. Now you do. Deep down you knew there was a reason for buying this book . . .

Let's all jerk off to climate change

If you haven't blogged, climbed a crane, bolstered a sand castle or run naked through the streets screaming 'the climate changers are coming', then you must really be a tough cookie. You must at least have switched off the lights and sat in the dark, sacrificed the luxuries of 3-ply for the austerity of organic toilet paper, or experimented with recycled bath water in your kettle to reconnect with your inner greenie.

Else you're really just a selfish, urbanized bourgeois prat. I mean, everyone else is going green!

Climate change has been the most widely discussed subject across the globe since Priyanka Chopra's nose job. And if you still think it's an overblown hoax, designed and marketed by the scorn of a betrayed woman sitting on an island called Al Gore, bite your tongue. Such a public declaration will lead to an even more public lynching.

Even if you are remotely correct to believe that our current environmental concerns are a tad exaggerated, it would be retarded to defend humankind's existing levels of industrialization and rapacious appetite for the earth's resources as anything but harmful to the mother ship.

Exaggerated or not, the consequences of our actions are more than quivering numbers on a chart.

The United Nations said there were about twenty million people displaced in 2008 as a result of climate change – which is more than war-induced displacement. Among other dire predictions, it is reported that some of the world's greatest river basins in southern Asia are now intensely threatened by human activity. If these vital rivers – the Indus, the Ganges, the Mekong – decide to stop flowing, or morph into shopping malls, some 750 million livelihoods will dry up.

Indian farmers have already been resorting to suicide or selling their daughters for anything from $40 to $100 (depending on their Indian accent) in a bid to survive. Sure, the inhabitants of these parts have heavily burdened their ecosystems by procreating like bunnies, and you could argue that they actually deserve to drink their own sewerage if fresh water dries up as just penance. But we shouldn't judge them. This is not a Libyan revolution. Even Robert Mugabe deserves a trial before we hang him.

Speaking of uncle Bob, we needn't look further than north of the Limpopo for the first signs of trouble. In parts of southern and East Africa, shifts in the climate have wreaked disastrous consequences on farmers and their communities.

With a dearth of man-made irrigation in certain parts (allied with a bit of political maladministration here and there), the advent of drought effectively means you die – or at the very least you watch your cows die.

Mozambique, Malawi, Zimbabwe and even parts of northern KwaZulu-Natal and the eastern Cape have been experiencing intermittent bouts of severe drought in recent years. As custom dictates, it's always worse in the Godforsaken Horn of Africa. In 2009, Oxfam issued a warning that if $115 million in food aid didn't fall from the sky, some six million Ethiopians were going to starve. Of course, if we had known in advance, we could have transferred the $450 million used for the Moses Mabhida Stadium in Durban to feed them all three-course meals until the rains returned. And then again in 2011, the UN said they needed a modest $1 billion more to save twelve million Somalis from drought and famine.

Of course, famine is often a consequence of poor governance and war and Somalia is not exactly run like the West Wing, but we have continued to deny how our moronic behaviour has contributed to the problem. Shifts in the climate have led to shifts in the way people have lived for hundreds of years on the ground. Of course Somalis, like Ethiopians, like so many other poor and 'luckless Africans', are as used to starving as the Bangladeshis are probably used to drowning and, well, they'll just have to get over it.

We are so inundated with climate-change talk you could swear we are actually shedding our egos, altering our collective behaviour and looking nature's appointed bush-whacking locusts in the eye as they prepare to teach us a good lesson for banging up the Earth. You'd think by now that everyone would have realized that our methods of industrialization need an immediate rethink if we ever want our great-grandchildren to visit the glorious Kruger National Park and not find an island surrounded by shoals of great white sharks. But our actions remain nothing more than paint on a glazed brick wall.

In 1997, more than 160 countries signed an agreement to reduce carbon emissions. This became known as the Kyoto Protocol, because it was held in Kyoto, Japan (not because the UN wanted to brand climate change as a sci-fi flick starring Bruce Willis).

The fact that China did not bother to attend the meeting and that the United States chose not to sign the agreement, took the piss out of all those good intentions to slow climate change, contain the earth's temperature and save the world.

Twelve years later, in December 2009, we got the Copenhagen Accord, the farcical sequel to the Kyoto Protocol. Despite its billing, no one expected anything spectacular from the final sets of climate talks in Denmark, and the Accord was predictably lame: it was drafted by only five countries (including South Africa, interestingly enough), it set no real targets for emission reductions and it was not even legally binding.

And even before the 2011 Conference of the Parties (otherwise known as COP17) was to take place in my hometown Durban in late November, there was talk that there would be no legal binding agreement (again) aka a second generation Kyoto Protocol that would oblige developed countries to cut emissions. But word on the web was that the conference would improve chances of 'an agreement in the future', 'perhaps by 2015' or 'more likely by 2020'.

Say what?

Apparently the economic crisis would be the excuse this time. As if the economy ran on a tablet created by God and not the late Steve Jobs.

But what I would really like to know – why can't they communicate over email in the interim?

And so here we are, heading towards the 20-teens, with polar bears almost already roaming our gardens, and seals almost already swimming in the neighbour's pool (note to neighbour: dude, please clean your pool), but the developed, industrialized governments – which is to say, the biggest violators – still want to negotiate humankind's future on their own terms.

Indeed, China may well have replaced the US as the biggest violator, reportedly producing 23 per cent of the world's greenhouse gases, but the G8 together produces half the world's output of greenhouse gases, which kind of puts our world into perspective. The biggest violators run the roost. It's akin to the permanent members of the UN Security Council being the biggest arms dealers (which they are). And the fact is, despite being brave, the Yanks simply didn't pass the necessary legislation in the Congress by the time Copenhagen came around, meaning they weren't 'in a position to pledge sizeable reductions'. In other words, the United States performed nothing more than a perfunctory visit to Denmark. Meanwhile, China and India – now at the crest of their industrialization and having initially indicated willingness to make 'notable' reductions to greenhouse emissions – predictably refused to make any worthwhile concessions at Copenhagen without full participation from the developed world, especially the United States. And why should they? It's 'their turn' now.

But some of this developed–developing world dynamic changed in Durban. Albeit, ever so slightly.

Known as the Durban Platform for Enhanced Action, COP17

managed to commit all nations (for the first time) into reducing greenhouse gas emissions from 2020. But critics say they have heard it all before. It had been agreed back in 2007 that a deal would be reached by 2009 (Copenhagen), but we all know what happened there. So even though China, India and the US are now committed to the formulation of a legally binding agreement, there is no guarantee that it will *actually* happen come 2020. Moreover, by pushing the agreement to 2020, the Durban platform falls short of previous pledges to regulate global warming to below two degrees celsius. I don't know what this will mean for pig farming in Osnabrück, but experts say if this continues, by 2020 it will be too late to reverse for hog, or human.

Durban managed to renew the Kyoto Protocol but the extension will exclude the United States, Russia, Japan and Canada, turning up the volume on the good old days when poorer countries were expected to fuck themselves while industrialized countries, the United States in particular, continued on their merry way (and shirked their responsibilities).

And so once again, the average man in the street must bear the brunt of yet another buzz kill. Expectations of a timely resolution have been dashed once more. Yet, the farmer in the field will be advised to stop herding methane-producing cows to reduce greenhouse gases; consumers in the supermarket will be told to buy exorbitantly priced eco-friendly foods; porn addicts at home must forget about those magazines and indulge in digital viewing to save the trees . . .

As it stands, climate change is no different from South Africa's policy of appeasement with Robert Mugabe, the impotent Middle East peace process, or the lack of effective action in Tibet, Myanmar, Kashmir, Somalia and on and on. In other words, an effective response to climate change has yet to take its place in the collective human conscience. Meanwhile, ordinary sods must pay the price for it.

Where there is no political will, causes remain feeble – no more than whimsical blog posts and idle dinner talk. But this farce is becoming rather jaded now. Isn't it time we shifted gears?

Unfortunately, climate change remains just another debate spawned for political and economic gain in the chess game of international relations. It is not yet a separate dilemma. And as such, without a binding international treaty *today* which includes the (wholehearted) participation of the United States and China, and without consequences for non-participation, the millions and millions of dollars spent on publicity, travel, rigorous debate and dancing girls amounts to nothing more than, well, just jerking off your hose.

POSTSCRIPT

Please think about the environment before you photocopy this article and send it to your friends.

In search of an African revolution

First Tunisia and Egypt, then Libya, Bahrain, Syria and Yemen: 2011 was quite a year for north Africa and the Arab world, or 'for dictators' as a friend put it. Hundreds of thousands flocked to the streets to oust their authoritarian regimes – the biggest turnout of folk since Woodstock (without the sex, I presume).

But with rising food prices, unemployment and rampant corruption, countries in sub-Saharan Africa are ripe for revolution themselves. Besides, the region is no stranger to authoritarian regimes or leaders who simply refuse to leave: up to ten countries in sub-Saharan Africa have had the same head of state for the past two decades and young, frustrated, educated youth are baying for their blood and well, change. Inspired by the people in north Africa and the Middle East who stood up to their authoritarian regimes, ordinary people in countries south of the Sahara started twitching, rolling up their sleeves and gearing up for some action themselves.

But no one noticed.

Demonstrations are continuing across the Middle East, interrupted only by the call for prayer when protesters fall to their knees on cheap carpets and straw mats and the riot police take a tea break. Egypt, in particular, with its scenes of unrelenting protesters staying put in Tahrir Square, playing guitars, singing, treating the injured and generally making Gandhi's famous salt march of the 1940s look like an act of terror, captured the imagination of an international media and audience more familiar with the stereotype of Muslim youth blowing themselves and others up.

A non-violent revolution was turning the nation full circle, much to the admiration of the rest of the world.

'I think Egypt's cultural significance and massive population were very important factors in ensuring media coverage,' says Ethan Zuckerman, the co-founder of Global Voices, an international community of online activists.

'International audiences know at least a few facts about Egypt, which makes it easier for them to connect to news there,' he continues, drawing a comparison with Bahrain, a country Zuckerman says few Americans would be able to locate on a map.

Zuckerman also believes that media organizations were in part motivated by a 'sense of guilt' over their failure to effectively cover the Tunisian revolution and were, therefore, playing 'catch up' in Egypt, culminating in the extraordinary coverage of its revolution.

'Popular revolutions make for great TV,' he adds. 'The imagery from Tahrir Square in particular was very powerful and led to a story that was easy for global media to cover closely.'

The African Egypt versus the Arab Egypt

Egypt swiftly became a sexy topic. But, despite the fact that the rich banks of the Nile are sourced from central Africa, the world looked upon the uprising in Egypt solely as a Middle Eastern issue and commentators scrambled to predict what it would mean for the rest of the Arab world and, of course, Israel.

Few seemed to care that Egypt was also part of Africa, a continent with a billion people, most living under despotic regimes and suffering economic strife and political suppression just like their Egyptian neighbours.

'Egypt is in Africa. We should not fool about with the attempts of the north to segregate the countries of north Africa from the rest of the continent,' says Firoze Manji, editor of Pambazuka Online, an advocacy website for social justice in Africa.

'Their histories have been intertwined for millennia. Some Egyptians may not feel they are Africans, but that is neither here nor there. They are part of the heritage of the continent.'

And, just like much of the rest of the world, Africans watched events unfold in Cairo with great interest.

'There is little doubt that people in Africa are watching with enthusiasm what is going on in the Middle East, and drawing inspiration from that for their own struggles,' says Manji.

He argues that globalization and the accompanying economic liberalization has created circumstances in which the people of the global south share very similar experiences: 'Increasing pauperization, growing unemployment, declining power to hold their governments to account, declining income from agricultural production, increasing accumulation by dispossession – something that is growing on a vast scale – and increasing willingness of governments to comply with the political and economic wishes of the north.'

'In that sense, people in Africa recognize the experiences of citizens in the Middle East. There is enormous potential for solidarity to grow out from that. In any case, where does Africa end and the Middle East begin?'

Rallying cry

The 'trouble' started in Tunisia (another African country) on 17 December 2010, when street vendor Mohamed Bouazizi set himself alight in protest after being humiliated at the hands of a policewoman. His self-immolation articulated the frustrations of a nation, spread briefly to Algeria (yes, another African country), and then Yemen, Bahrain and Syria just as Hosni Mubarak made himself comfortable in a Sharm el Sheik spa.

Meanwhile, in 'darkest Africa', far away from the media cameras, reports surfaced of political unrest in a west African country called Gabon.

With little geo-political importance, news organizations seemed largely oblivious to the drama that began unfolding on 29 January, when the Opposition protested against Ali Bongo Ondimba's government, whom they accused of hijacking the recent elections.

Demonstrators demanded free elections and security forces duly stepped in to lay those ambitions to rest. The clashes between protesters and police that followed showed few signs of relenting.

'In Tunisia, Ben Ali left. In Gabon, Ali Ben out' – read a banner held at a protest rally in northern Gabon on 2 February 2011.

'The events in Tunisia and Egypt have become, within Africa, a rallying cry for any number of Opposition leaders; every day people are harbouring grievances and political opportunists are looking to liken their country's regimes to those of Ben Ali or Hosni Mubarak,' says Drew Hinshaw, an American journalist based in west Africa.

In some cases that comparison is outrageous, but in all too many it is more than fair.

'Look at Gabon, a tragically under-developed oil exporter whose GDP per capita is more than twice that of Egypt's but whose people are living on wages that make Egypt look like the land of full employment.

'The Bongo family has run that country for four decades, since before Mubarak ran nothing larger than an air force base, and yet they're still there. You can understand why the country's Opposition is calling for new rounds of Egypt-like protests after seeing what Egypt and Tunisia were able to achieve.'

Elsewhere on the continent protests have broken out in Khartoum, Sudan, where students held Egypt-inspired demonstrations against proposed cuts to subsidies on petroleum products and sugar. Following the protests there on 30 January, the Committee to Protect Journalists (CPJ) reported that staff from the weekly *Al-Midan* were arrested for covering the event.

Ethiopian media have also reported that police there detained prominent journalist Eskinder Nega for 'attempts to incite' Egypt-style protests. In Cameroon, the Social Democratic Front Party said that the country might experience uprisings similar to those in north Africa if the government did not slash food prices.

'There are lots of Africans too who are young, unemployed, who see very few prospects for their future in countries ruled by the same old political elite that have ruled for twenty-five or thirty or thirty-five years,' says the Christian Science Monitor (CSM) Africa bureau chief, Scott Baldauf.

'I think all the same issues in Egypt are also present in other countries. You have leaders who have hung onto power for decades and who think the country can function only if they are in charge. A young Zimbabwean would understand the frustration of a young Egyptian.'

Divide and rule

Sure, the continent is vast and acts of dissent and their subsequent suppression are the bread and butter of some oppressive African states. But just as self-immolation was not new in Tunisia, discontentment and rising restlessness is not alien to Africans.

In the past three years, there have been protests against poor service delivery in South Africa and food riots in Cameroon, Madagascar, Mozambique and Senegal. But whether the simmering discontent in Africa will result in protests on the scale of those in Egypt remains to be seen.

'All the same, dry wood of bad governance is stacked in many African countries, waiting for a match to set it alight,' says Baldauf.

'But it takes leadership. It takes civil society organization,' something the CSM Africa bureau chief fears countries south of the Sahara do not have at the same levels as their north African neighbours.

Emmanuel Kisiangani, a senior researcher at the African Conflict Prevention Programme (ACCP) at the Institute of Security Studies (ISS) in South Africa, believes the difference in the success levels of protests in north and sub-Saharan Africa can be attributed in part to the ethnic make-up of the respective regions.

'In most of the countries that have had fairly "successful riots", the societies are fairly homogeneous compared to sub-Saharan Africa where there is a multiplicity of ethnic groups that are themselves very polarized. In sub-Saharan Africa, where governments have been able to divide people along ethnic–political lines, it becomes easier to hijack an uprising because of ethnic differences, unlike in north Africa.'

'Where is Anderson Cooper?'

Egypt and Tunisia may have been the catalysts for demonstrations across the Arab world, but will those ripples spread to the rest of Africa as well and, if they do, will the international media and its audience even notice?

'What the continent lacks is media coverage,' says Hinshaw.

'There's no powerhouse media for the region like *Al Jazeera*, while European and American media routinely reduce a conflict like that in Ivory Coast or eastern Congo to a one-sentence news blurb at the bottom of the screen.'

Hinshaw is particularly troubled by the failure of the international media to pay due attention to events in Ivory Coast, where the UN estimates that at least 300 people have died, with the country's Opposition claiming the figure to be closer to 500.

'With due deference to the bravery of the Egyptian demonstrators, protesters who gathered this weekend in Abidjan [in Ivory Coast] aren't up against a military that safeguards them – it shoots at them.

'The country's economy has been coughing up blood since November, with banks shutting by the day, businesses closing by the hour and thousands of families fleeing their homes,' he continues.

'And in all of this, where is Anderson Cooper? Where is Nicolas Kristof? Why is Bahrain a front-page news story while Ivory Coast is something buried at the bottom of the news stack?'

The journalist is equally disappointed in world leaders.

'This Friday, Barack Obama publicly condemned the use of violence in Bahrain, Yemen and Libya. When was the last time you saw Obama come out and make a statement on Ivory Coast? Or eastern Congo? Or Djibouti, where 20,000 people protested this weekend according to Opposition parties?

'The problem is that most American media compulsively ignore everything south of the Sahara and north of Johannesburg. A demonstration has to be filmed, photographed, streamed live into the offices of foreign leaders to achieve everything Egypt's achieved.'

Nanjala Nyabola, a political analyst at the University of Oxford, suggests this journalistic shortcoming stems from journalists' tendency 'to favour explanations that fit the whole "failing Africa" narrative'.

Filling the void

So with traditional media seemingly failing Africa, will social media fill the void?

Already, so much has been written about the plethora of social media networks that both helped engineer protests and, crucially, amplified them across cyberspace.

Online activists, sitting behind fibre-optic cables and flat screens, collated and disseminated updates, photographs and videos and played the role of subversive heroes from the comfort of their homes.

Of course, not all tweets or Facebook uploads came from pyjama-clad revolutionaries far from the scene of action – an Internet-savvy generation of Egyptians was also able to keep the world updated with information from the ground.

'It's not clear to me that social media played a massive role in organizing protests,' says Zuckerman. 'But I do think it played a critical role in helping expose those protests to a global audience, particularly in Tunisia, where the media environment was so constrained.'

So, could the same thing happen in Africa? 'I think it's important to keep in mind that African youth are far more plugged in than most people realize. The spread of mobile phones has made it possible for people to connect to applications like Facebook and Twitter on their telephones,' says Nyabola, adding: 'At the same time, I think most analysts are overstating the influence of social media on the protests.

'The most significant political movements in Africa and in other places have occurred independently of social media – the struggles for independence, the struggles against apartheid and racism in southern Africa. Where people need or desire to be organized they will do so independently of the technology around them.'

Baldauf concurs: 'In every country you see greater and greater access to the Internet and greater access to cellphone networks. I remember getting stuck in a muddy road in eastern Congo, out where the FDLR [Democratic Forces for the Liberation of Rwanda] controls the mining industry. We had to stay the night in a village, the guests of a lovely old man in his mud hut. It was at the end of the world, but to get phone calls off to my wife and to my editor, I just had to walk out of the hut and use my cellphone.'

The ballot box

The next twenty-four months are important for Africa.

Elections are scheduled in more than twenty countries across the continent, including Zimbabwe, Nigeria, the Democratic Republic of Congo and Kenya.

But as food prices continue to rise and economic hardship tightens its grip on the region, it is plausible to imagine Africans revolting and using means other than the often meaningless ballot box to remove their leaders.

'What people want is the democratization of society, of production, of the economy and, indeed, all aspects of life,' says Manji. 'What they are being offered instead is the ballot box.'

He adds: 'Elections don't address the fundamental problems that people face. Elections on their own do nothing to enable ordinary people to be able to determine their own destiny.'

This, according to Kisiangani, is because 'the process of democratization in many African countries seems more illusory than fundamental'.

Gabon, Zimbabwe, even Ethiopia may never have the online reach enjoyed by Egyptians, and the scale of solidarity through linguistic and cultural symmetry may not allow their calls to reach the same number of Internet users. But this does not mean that a similar desire for change is not brewing, nor that the traditional media and online community are justified in ignoring it.

Screens were put up in Tahrir Square broadcasting *Al Jazeera*'s coverage of the protests back to the protesters. And while it might be difficult to qualify the role of social media in the popular uprisings gaining momentum across the Arab world, it would be even harder to quantify the impact of being ignored, of not being watched or discussed and, well, re-tweeted to the throngs of others needed to pass on the message.

Ignoring developments in Africa is to miss half the story.

'The protests have created the "hope" that ordinary people can define their political destiny,' says Kisiangani. 'The uprisings . . . are making people on the continent conscious about their abilities to define their political destinies.'

POSTSCRIPT

Keep a watch out over sub-Saharan Africa over the next five years . . . blink and you will miss an opportunity to invest (because that is all that matters, right?).

Tweeting the Arab revolutions

Bravo, bravo! Social media outdid itself in 2011.

A memorable year for journalists it was, as they reinvented the profession, chasing 140 characters instead of roaming the streets . . . but it was an even bigger year for ordinary folk who donned capes, copied, pasted and tweeted the hell out of the events taking place on the ground.

Such was the enthusiasm for the online, ordinary tweeters gave up their office jobs and stayed home to tweet about a revolution taking place some 5,000 kilometres away, new media consultants morphed into centrestage activists, collating, disseminating, directing web traffic as their sentiments dictated . . . and well, just about everyone and their cocker spaniel with access to a smart phone or the Internet clamoured on board the social media thinking that democracy in the Middle East relied on their tweets.

While online conversations spoke truth to power, it was easy to forget that online conversations were often still the respite of those with power . . . those outside were still living regular voiceless lives in the bogs of their meagre existence.

Poetic, dramatic and self-indulgent.

Quite like the alchemy of social media: the deception of self-importance.

Or so they thought.

So we've all been talking about the 'Arab Spring'. Mubarak and Ben Ali, Libya and Syria, Shias and Sunnis, dictators and democracy, Twitter and Facebook . . . at the heart of the discussion, we've pulverized the use of social media in galvanizing, organizing and disseminating news of a new order. The use of language, the dependence on technology and the curiosities of media coverage have dominated discussion but much of the self-congratulatory conjecture has lacked critical introspection.

In other words, so much of the discussion has been a load of blistering bullshit.

First and foremost, the very term 'Arab Spring' does little but insinuate that an entire region slept unobtrusively over a long winter under siege by externalities that rendered them to the mercy of their surroundings.

As if the Arab world sat like harebrained turtle doves patiently waiting for flowers to bloom.

If anything, the Arab world has endured multiple convulsions over their postcolonial history – as all people under repression might.

Another myth, linked to the other misnomer of 'an awakening', is the overestimated talk of causality linked with the invention of social media. It is as though the region's struggle for democracy started with a tweet, an indulgent poke on Facebook. Nothing can be further from the truth, except of course thousands of virtual characters and make-believe bloggers in Edinburgh pretending to be gay girls in Damascus. The ongoing struggle for democratic change in the region is a grassroots' people-driven movement that has only enjoyed acceleration through new technology. The technology did not invent the cause.

Across North Africa and the Middle East, streets see protesters face off against state security in a daily battle for liberty, life and bread. Technology, wonderful as it has been to these protesters, is blunted against the harshness of bullets, tear gas and incarceration. The enduring fight, continual loss of life and daily sacrifice started on the ground remains primarily a street fight.

It is, however, still difficult to debunk the emphatic role that new media gadgetry continues to play in coaxing a readymade online audience lusting to direct, participate and shape history.

For instance, news that Tunisia's Zine al-Abidine Ben Ali had skipped the country to seek refuge in Saudi Arabia following weeks of protests broke on Twitter on the evening of 16 January 2011. While traditional wire services tripped over one another to cover the ongoing protests in the country, twitterati spread the word that the army had surrounded the Tunisian airport and further speculated that Ben Ali had fled.

Granted that allegations, developments and mere fabrications have yet to be filtered, separated before becoming confident news lines, Ben Ali's documented flight over Twitter, as confusing as it might have been at the time, became one more reason to shift the emphasis of news gathering from the relative order of traditional news gathering to the chaos of citizen media sources. Between Lady Gaga and the vagaries of trending topics, the tool could break news, tell a story and with enough muscle, force 'the mainstream media' to take the story to the next level.

Social media acolytes claim new media is the ultimate step towards the democratization of information; ordinary people are now able to tell their stories, even set the news agenda.

Technological inequities, politically unimportant regions and unfriendly media terrain notwithstanding, grounds for such pompous assertions have definite anecdotal backing.

iPhones for wands

Social media's love for immediacy, shocking content and latent anarchic zeal provided protesters with the confidence that they were not alone – there was an inimitable sense of being watched, of being followed by millions across the globe. It is a fact that new media gave activists a virtual meeting ground to meet, discuss, flesh out ideas without having to get out of their pyjamas. It is also true that the collective rage evidenced on social media platforms turned shy geeks into heroes, defying draconian censorship measures in an effort to keep up the flow of information.

Importantly, the pervasiveness of these new platforms allowed everyone with access to the technology the opportunity to speak out. The days of stagnant, co-opted activists monopolizing the airwaves and mobilizing non-events were over. This was organized anarchy; eccentric young voices raising iphones like magic wands

And 'confidence' might just be the difference between the protests of the post-colonial past and those that fashioned changes in the revolts of 2011.

Mohamed Bouazizi's act of self-immolation in the remote town of Sidi Bouzid might be credited for sparking the revolution in Tunisia and creating a domino effect of popular protests across Egypt, Libya, Yemen, Bahrain and Syria, but Facebook gave his cause a loud, international voice.

Bouazizi's act wasn't unique in Tunisia, but a video of the incident posted on Facebook and the resultant protest turned viral within days.

It forced a reluctant mainstream media to cover the story, and therefore fuelled this newly found 'confidence' in protesters so used to being ignored. Subsequently, the events firmly located social media as a platform to organize, disseminate information and rally mainstream media to tell a story.

The same could be said of the events of '#Jan25', where the hashtag created a rallying point for the Egyptian protests. It translated into an estimated 10,000 people initially turning to the streets, and then transcended into millions descending onto Tahrir Square three days later in an iconic 'Day of Rage'.

Even blocking of the Internet and mobile phones managed to achieve precious little as activists found a way around the censorship and the popular revolt had enough momentum to survive on the ground.

Sentiments of the twitterati

Twitter was certainly not the reason thousands of people came out on the streets of Sanaa in Yemen or Homs in Syria.

But the immediate ability of social media to transmit images, scenes from the ground did help persuade migrant professionals to leave the safety of their homes in the UK and join the armed rebel movement in Libya.

It also did tangibly affect the manner in which journalists collected information.

In February 2011, while Gaddafi's forces were cleaning up Tripoli, ridding the city of dissidents, I sat up repeatedly until the wee of hours of the morning chatting on instant messenger with a grief-stricken Libyan doctor who passed on valuable information on the acts of violence in the streets, the state of the hospitals and the movements of marauding mercenaries. He would lie in the back seat of a car, and chat with me as he peered out of the window. Our chats were punctuated by constant interruptions; the line would get cut, or he would just disappear and come back in a rage, hoping to speak to someone. I was his lifeline. He was our window into the streets of Tripoli. No wire carried his story.

And then there were the images and videos that came in droves – more brutal, more devastating than the most convoluted horror movie scripts. Heads blown off bodies by shotguns at point-blank range, security vehicles running over protesters, severed limbs strewn across the street. The jagged cut of the images, the screams and shrieks, almost implausibly real.

The Libyan doctor would send words over instant messenger – typed scribbles that didn't make any sense. Such was his nervousness he would just type and send.

On more than one occasion he told me not to ask him to calm down. On more than one occasion I came home and cried myself to sleep.

The liberal agenda

Libya's revolution might be over, or at least Muammar Gaddafi might be gone, but it took some time to track down the charming doctor I repeatedly spoke to, and occasionally laughed with, in a town in Romania, apparently working on a medical project related to the recovery of injured revolutionaries.

I spent months wondering if he had made it. Such is the nature of social media that reality is often reduced to a phantom.

And for every bizarre tale during these people's revolutions, relayed through social media, there are thousands of others left outside the realm – outside the club and camaraderie of 'the network'.

With social media, one gets the sense that a topic turning viral is directly proportional to the sentiments of the twitterati which are 'usually middle class, upwardly mobile youth with mostly liberal sensibilities' – or at least this is how the adage goes.

In fact, effective social media requires a range of conditions to make it useful as a political tool or as a journalistic add-on. It first requires a specific historical moment, developed and nurtured over time, linked to the collective aspirations of the people. Like most things in life, timing is everything. Second, it requires a readymade audience already pre-vetted to live out, act out, effectively 'retweet' these aspirations. If anything, social media has shown itself incapable of looking further than the immediate because it was always built to be an introductory tool: a means to an end.

This is not to undermine the intent, ambition or even intellect of social media users, but the mass appeal of social media relies far too much on the immediacy of 'a shock' to propagate a sizeable discussion that details the edges, airbrushes the details and neglects the mechanics. Complex problems need immediate solution and according to the legion of new experts, they are readily available. It took eighteen days to oust Mubarak and social media users felt they were out to change the world.

This perceived invincibility is often a problematic hyper-reality of the scope, reach, even universality of the values propagated over social media. The online world might be filled with conflicting opinion, but building legitimacy still requires a euro-centric zeal.

The liberal agenda often needs you to prove your liberal credentials, be it caring for the environment, or Palestine, promoting democratic values – this club can often be an exclusive, self-congratulatory pit.

No one is going to take you seriously if they catch you tweeting about Kim Kardashian's butt.

Meanwhile, Mubarak can leave and the twitterati struggle to handle the junta that takes over. Gaddafi will trend when flayed but silence accompanies the rebuilding of Libya. Homs burns but remains off the keg if power is turned off in Syria.

Of course, no one really tweeted or posted a photo about their hunger from famine-stricken Somalia during the horrific drought of 2011.

To offer a revision to an oft-quoted famous tweet: one world tweets while the other half doesn't eat.

POSTSCRIPT

Just when you thought social media could not possibly become any bigger, any more frivolous, any more self-indulgent, simplistic and downright spectacular, along came the bold #Kony 2012 campaign and pissed over all of us. But the #Kony 2012 campaign is another fight, for another day. I have earmarked it for the sequel . . .

'I DRINK POISON AND VOMIT DIAMONDS'

The road to Dadaab

In July 2011, I joined Al Jazeera's *East Africa team in Nairobi and headed to Dadaab, the largest refugee camp in the world, situated close to the border with Somalia. The UN reported at the time that the refugee complex was dealing with an unprecedented number of new arrivals fleeing famine and war in Somalia. Some thirteen million people in the Horn of Africa, including Somalia, Ethiopia and northern Kenya as well as pockets of Uganda, Dijbouti and Sudan, were affected by a drought said to be the worst in sixty years.*

It takes a while to weave our way through the dusty streets of Nairobi and surface from the coagulated gunk that is the city's air. The city confuses me. In one moment it takes me home, further south of the African coast, to Durban. And in the next, it startles me with an air of Delhi.

The orchestrated chaos of informal traders unwrapping their bright, fresh vegetables onto wooden tray tables beside oversized football shirts and mobile phone accessories would pass easily for a scene from Durban's CBD, where messy informality and sneaky formality contest with each other for the remaining vestiges of crucial business space.

Yet, at the same time, the area around Nairobi's Jomo Kenyatta monument, opulently wide, with an affectation of stateliness, together with the perennial haze that hangs over the city's skyline like a soiled sheet, takes me back to Connaught Place in the Indian capital.

It's funny what malaria tablets can do to you, or the British for that matter.

African skies

When you do eventually make your way out of Nairobi, the road furrows indolently, but the skies open with dramatic generosity. Stereotypical, overly romanticized to death it might be, but the great expanse of the never-ending African sky is no myth.

It really does feel like the earth's reflection turns the sky into a never-ending search for itself. The horizon always seems deeper, even illusive, as it teases the transparent elastic structure behind the iris into endless adjustment.

For the most part the road from Nairobi to Garissa, capital of Kenya's North Eastern province that lies just a couple of hours from Dadaab, the biggest refugee camp in the world, is nothing more than a litany of monotonous bumps. Despite our scurry across the hard but mostly puddle-ridden path, the world outside the window seemed to veer back in typically dry, contemptuous discern.

Along the route, Kenyan traffic police litter the journey with curious eccentricity. Some cops wave us down with a baton; others instead gesture at their semi-automatic rifles.

It seems Kenyan traffic police need to be rather multi-skilled; as well as being adept at issuing traffic fines they are vigilant for any elements that might point to banditry or human trafficking. This was one of the main transport routes from Somalia to Nairobi after all, and the two-decades-long civil war in Somalia, now compounded by severe drought, obviously facilitated desperate measures, which usually culminated in horrendous crimes including trafficking of human beings.

Although Garissa, our stop for the night, and the closest built-up town to the refugee camp, is still some hours away, the further we venture towards the north-east, the drier the landscape becomes.

Baobab trees, the iconic African tree of life, stick out across the landscape like hunched, disfigured torsos, aged by the scathing dry seasons that have so ravaged the region.

Of course, the baobab spends a large part of the year looking rather ravaged – it is merely nature's Goth look. But amidst the gloom, the baobab's nakedness looks spectacularly eerie.

Even the usually greener acachian trees, identifiable by their smaller leaves, are perched like a brittle stack of wayward firewood. Dry heaps of bird nests still droop from some branches, long abandoned.

Dry riverbeds

Up to four rivers we cross over are dead riverbeds. On one of those riverbeds I see a family erecting a makeshift home. This soon becomes a familiar sight as banks become empty plots.

'Imagine how many thousands of people from here to the coast were relying on these rivers,' Moses Obuye, the cameraman from Nairobi, tells me as we cross yet another dry bank. In areas alongside the long road, thorn scrubs prick out of the bloodshot red sand like dead grey hair on a wounded carcass.

But then we cross the Tana River, Kenya's longest river, and there is life once more – bustling and roaring. The stark contrast reminds us that this, no doubt, is Africa.

We finally arrive in Garissa – a dusty one-horse town, where Kenyan Somalis, relief workers and a handful of camels jostle for space. Men sit outside the brightly painted container shops selling basic groceries and chewing *qat*. Others slide in grease under cars in roadside workshops. And tall Somali women draped in dark abayas negotiate a sale of not-so-fresh veggies in makeshift shelters made of thatched straw.

The town is literally a three-street walk.

'Think of Garissa like you would an outpost . . . caught between the Kenya–Somalia border and civilization back in Nairobi,' Obuye tells me. 'There is nothing around it.'

The world's biggest refugee camp

I am tying my shoelaces when the early morning call to prayer begins to sound over the scratchy loudspeakers at the neighbourhood mosque.

And so just as light begins to streak through the night sky, I gingerly slide myself into the rented Land Cruiser. I am asked if my bed was fitted with a mosquito net to prevent contracting malaria from the team of notorious bloodsuckers buzzing about.

'No . . . and I was eaten alive last night . . . so wait, does that now mean I have malaria?' my voice begins to crackle in mild trepidation.

'Nah – you are on the medication, so you should be fine . . . or . . . well, you will know either way in two weeks,' is the collective reply, along with raucous laughter. Two weeks to malaria, then. I look out of the window and watch the sun rise slowly over the prairie.

The road from Garissa to Dadaab resembles a wide, dry riverbed. It's been so beaten up, it feels as though you're driving in a shallow bowl flanked by river banks and layered in different textures of sand – from the rock-hard to the soft desert grains – giving the easily distracted on wheels more than one reason to drift.

Outside my window, two tall giraffes strike up dust as they glide with elegant nonchalance through the rough, drought-resistant vegetation beside us. Moments later, we slow down and allow a herd of camels ambling through the sandy motorway to pass, but as we motor our way further across the bumpy road, a tiny deer hops across, forcing our Toyota to grind to a momentary halt. I remind myself that we are not in a game park and this is not a safari. Besides, thousands of people have trekked across the wild for days hiding from militia and police by day and hyenas by night, to escape the insecurity of violence and famine in nearby Somalia.

Some three hours later – after suffering repeated whiplash every time our excitable driver plunged carelessly into a ditch at full throttle – we reach the headquarters of the United Nations High Commissioner for Refugees (UNHCR) in Dadaab.

According to the UN's security system, the entire North East province of Kenya is classified at a security level four – indicating a level of 'substantial threat'. Trips to the various camps that make up the Dadaab complex need to be taken under a security escort to mitigate the risks, some of which include raids by bandits and other fun and games by forces loyal to al-Shabab.

In reality, the thousands of refugees undertaking the gruelling journey from Somalia are at a far greater risk of encountering bandits or stealth attacks from al-Shabab. Though it cannot be ruled out, heightened security measures seemed to me to be a purposeful attempt to set a security standard, 'just in case'.

Twenty years later

Throughout the journey, I had wondered what a refugee complex widely billed as the largest in the world would look like. The widely distributed aerial photographs from archived UN material from the early nineties showed the staggering scope of the settlements. Thousands of tents, enveloped in a coil of dust, lined the dusty plateau uniformly like obedient soldiers. The white of the tents a stark contrast to the brazen brown emptiness of the surroundings.

In an area spanning fifty square kilometres, just two hours away from the Kenya–Somalia border, three camps – Dagahaley, Ifo and Hagadera – were originally set up to host a total of 90,000 people. Twenty years later, with more than 380,000 people registered as refugees in the Dadaab complex, I was naturally curious as to how the camp had changed, how it would 'look'. I also wondered that if the camps were indeed overflowing with people as we had been told over and over again, where on earth were the new arrivals shacked up?

We are quickly ushered into the UNHCR reception centre in Dagahaley. We are greeted by the sight of a few hundred people standing behind barbed-wire fences waiting to be registered as refugees by both the Kenyan authorities and the UN, so they might be given a ration of food, a mat, a pot and a white plastic sheet to cover the hut they are to build out of branches, twigs and sticks from the surrounding trees, or the remainders thereof.

At Dadaab, each camp sees thousands of new arrivals, culminating in an estimated 800–1,200 people filtering in each day. The registration process is arduous, and some only complete their registration days after their arrival – sometimes, even a week – this, after walking for anything between five and twenty days to get there in the first place.

Slow burn pain

Inside the Médecins Sans Frontières (Doctors without Borders) (MSF) base in Dagahaley, a hospital made out of a collection of makeshift structures of wood and steel, hundreds of children are being treated for severe malnutrition. On each bed in the paediatric ward an anxious parent, usually a mother, sits, resting tentatively with her infant.

The sight involuntarily invoked memories of images of those Somali and Ethiopian children with deep-set eyes and sunken cheekbones splashed liberally across television news bulletins all those years ago – in the eighties and nineties – with disturbing regularity. After all these years, it seemed surreal to be covering a story dripping with embarrassing visions of déjà vu.

The doctors and nurses here say that the first few days after arrival are the most crucial for these children's survival. Far too many are in critical conditions. Over the past two months (May–June 2011), the number of babies needing immediate care has doubled, precariously stretching the capacity of available medical infrastructure. One nurse tells me that it is simply impossible to keep up with the demand and priority is driven by the most needy. Needless to say, many parents and children are traumatized after making such a long, difficult journey but theirs is of a secondary concern.

In the outskirts of the Dagahaley camp where we go following the trip to the hospital, we find seventy-odd unmarked graves, jutting out of the earth in a plot of land between the tents and huts. These are the graves of infants and young children who had died shortly after arriving – their graves conspicuous by their tiny lengths and by the freshness of the dug-up soil.

Some of these graves are merely a few days old.

Here, the community congregates around us as we try to arrange an interview with a mother whose child is one of the deceased.

She appears to laugh when asked about the circumstances that led to her child's death and her somewhat whimsical response disturbs us.

There we were, trying to converse with a woman who had walked more than a hundred kilometres to save her family from starvation only to see her child buried in an unmarked grave in a dusty track of land, away, and abandoned by the world. This was now an informal refugee camp set up on the outskirts of a refugee camp too full to accommodate new arrivals.

And so she laughed. But why did we expect her to beat her chest and spill tears, offer us a *normal* picture of grief when the entire context defied any semblance of normality?

Tens of thousands of tents and wooden huts, held together with branches, stems, and topped by a plastic sheet distributed as part of the UNHCR rations, dot the plateau.

In fact, between 40,000 and 60,000 are thought to be living outside the boundaries of the complex – existing as refugees beyond the current scope and control of the UN.

These people had yellow tags on their wrists, indicating that they had been registered, but they were in the middle of nowhere with little food, no sanitation, very little livestock (though donkeys perused the drought-resistant weeds with some fervour and dropped faeces around the camp with equal venom), waiting for something to happen.

And they just keep on coming, braving the desert, digging roots off trees to feed their children, begging for water and hiding from bandits as they look for a place to just survive.

This, then, is the humanitarian crisis on our hands.

We call it a day.

POSTSCRIPT

Around 250 children died every day from malnourishment, while the death rate reached between five and seven per 10,000 per day in parts of Somalia, forcing the UN to declare famine in parts of Somalia: the first such declaration in three decades.

As the repercussions of food shortages took hold of the region, and questions began to be asked about culpability over the existence of famine in the twenty-first century, the humanitarian disaster soon became an agonizing reminder that this was merely a symptom of a larger story involving a two-decade-long civil war that has devastated the very social fabric of Somalia.

As it stands, Somalia remains without an effective central government or functioning health sector. It would seem quite reasonable to me that the country has scant opportunity to manage a series of environmental shocks, including drought, desertification or climate change, when it can hardly call itself a country.

By early 2012, the Dadaab refugee camp in Kenya was in disarray. Up to 450,000 people were now living in the refugee complex and though people were only trickling through, at least two zones in Somalia were still categorized as famine zones. However, it is the deterioration of the security in the camp that has been the most startling development. Two MSF doctors were abducted and the camp was sprayed with a series of grenade attacks and shootings that forced many humanitarian workers to leave . . . pushing the camp ever closer to the edge of the earth.

All of Africa: in a day's play

My parents were quite upset when I revealed I would be going to the Democratic Republic of Congo in late 2011 to cover the presidential and legislative elections there. They said it was unnecessary, and that the news channels were reporting incidents of violence across the country and predicting there would be a breakdown of law and order by the time election results were out.

So I told my folks not to allow journalists to sway them.

'I'm telling you again, don't trust the media,' I connived.

Unperturbed and quite used to my balderdash, my mum replied, 'Why can't you just get a wife and settle for a desk job?'

Well played. But no.

It is a beautiful sight: watching a thunderstorm rock the Nairobi night skyline. Driving on the roads of the Kenyan capital the following morning is somewhat less pleasant.

With last-minute arrangements already causing some dithering, the first leg of our journey to cover the elections in the Democratic Republic of Congo (DRC) almost turns disastrous when one smart Aleck instructs the local driver to take a 'slip road' to the airport in order to avoid Nairobi's monstrous early morning traffic. The slip road starts as an impressive sand track but soon enough turns into a mud pit, complete with dancing cars and tilted trucks – left mostly immobile after making some wrong moves on the gooey roadway.

It seems we might miss that flight after all.

To put the drama into perspective: we need to catch a plane from Nairobi to Kigali via the Burundi capital, Bujumbura. Once in Kigali, we need to buy a sandwich and soda, hop into another vehicle and make a three-hour journey from the Rwandan capital to the eastern DRC town of Goma – all by nightfall.

Even stray cats and dogs stay indoors after sundown in Goma.

'You wouldn't have thought the adventure would've started just on the way to the airport, eh?' my colleague Peter Greste teases.

I laugh nervously because he is mostly right.

On our right, the Kenyan national park stretches out as far as the early morning mist allows the eye to see. To our left, scores of slum dwellers go about their business, carefully dodging the sludge as they try to rebuild their settlements demolished by the municipality overnight. On the track, men dig trucks out of the mud.

When I woke up this morning, I hadn't imagined such a start. But I am also unsurprised by the muddle; this, after all, is Nairobi.

Coordinating multiple transfers – by flight, sea or land – across several countries is always difficult. But when it involves generators, editing equipment, body armour, lighting, sound kits, tripods and fifteen bags, expect to be sitting at Kigali airport for some hours explaining why it looks like you are on your way to open a Universal Studios in the Congolese rain forest.

What happened to the days when journalists just carried a notebook and borrowed a pen? Or simply tapped phone calls?

While Nairobi could be described as the quintessential African city – a cesspool of sights and sounds to indulge, frustrate and corrupt – the thoroughness and perceived incorruptibility (not that we tried) of the Rwandan customs officials as they checked every detail of our mammoth package left us bemused.

Customs even made us remove the polyethylene wrapping around our generator case because plastic bags are banned in Rwanda.

In words, Kigali is impressive, if peculiar.

Although the country is still classified as poor and heavily dependent on foreign aid and tourism, there is an order and cleanliness that is almost unnerving. Spotless roads, neat pavements for pedestrians, drivers that follow the rules – you can tell a lot about how a country is managed by the way the people drive on their roads.

There is obedience in the air and a sense of pride in the management of the city. It squashes a myriad of stereotypes and begs new questions.

The route through the land of a thousand hills, as Rwanda sells itself, is quite majestic. Banana trees, jungles of flamboyant wide leaves sprout out like the propellers of green helicopters perched on the hillsides. Maize and tea plantations sit by the side of the winding road; boys stand tilling wet fields and girls carry straws of sugarcane on their shoulders.

Every single plot of this fertile land seems to have been used for some agricultural activity.

And every once in a while, we pass grassy football pitches where barefoot children chase leather on the lush grass between flimsy wooden goal posts: the only reminder that we are on the continent after all.

There is something sinister, almost ominous, in the air when villages have signboards for micro-credit banks and study classes for college students, or when a signboard at the airport advertises that the Rwandan police can be contacted via Facebook.

An African country with a green agenda, an emphasis on technology and infrastructural development – can it really be?

I was warned about the drive through Rwanda. Eventually 'you'd turn down a winding road and cross the border into Goma', I was told.

And then it would be a different world. A world which Rwanda has played a dirty role in creating.

Story goes that Rwanda had been built off the back of sustained instability in mineral-rich DRC.

Unless you are a humanitarian do-gooder, a diamond merchant or an arms dealer, it is unlikely that you have ever heard of Goma, a town in the state of North Kivu in eastern DRC.

If parts of eastern Rwanda resemble what rural Africa would look like in heaven, Goma and the eastern DRC region might just represent everything that ever went wrong on the continent.

Blessed with minerals and cursed by armed groups competing over resources and challenging a frail national authority, this is perhaps where democracy in the DRC will face its sternest challenge.

Goma: the last outpost

I

Flashes of lightning illuminate Lake Kivu as thunder crackles from deep within the sky above. It would seem as if nature's melody has rendered me faithless, but the storm causes the lights to trip and disrupts the Internet connection and forces me to reconsider. I stare at the mesmerizing placidity of the lake, gently shivering after every strike of the spiffy clouds above.

The Ihusi Hotel overlooking the lake is a meeting place – or hunting ground – for UN types, election observers, haughty journalists and other undesirables. Naturally, UN cars line the parking lot. French-speaking receptionists ignore requests made in the Queen's English and poll monitors insist on parading around the bar at night in their election-observer vests, as if sipping cocktails could ever be free or fair.

The road from the Rwandan border into Goma is bustling with activity. Construction sites suggest the city is undergoing a facelift. But when the neatly tarred road ends, another Goma presents itself in the form of the gigantic BDGL roundabout. On the scarred island in the middle, children kick a football around in the dirt, while others loiter about looking utterly bored. To add charm to the peculiar, a donkey wrapped in the flag of a local candidate running in the legislative elections is taunted and petted by passers-by.

A twist in the road leads to another roundabout. This one has a golden *chikudu* at the centre of the island and is flanked by a well-kept garden. People wander over to take a snap of themselves beside the golden replica of the iconic wooden bicycle.

Naturally, these conflicting scenes tell a tangled tale of destruction, development and electoral farce. Around the perfectly trimmed garden, craters for potholes appear in clusters on the roads, but there are also signs that improvement is underway. Men in orange vests work on the tattered roads and, by night, street poles light up the city centre, providing a sense of urban normalcy.

'These improvements are just an electoral farce,' I am told by the sceptics, while Joseph Kabila loyalists shoot back: 'These promises are a work in progress.' Both sides, of course, are somewhat correct, and delusional, though you might hear stories of a third force behind most things in Goma. For example, if you are into conspiracy theories, the road works are a gift from Rwanda to Kabila. Indeed, conspiracy theory is a commodity this town is scarcely short of.

Goma is a hive of ambivalence; there are only signs of a possible regularity. But you do get a sense that the town is just the outer shell of a volcano boiling beneath the surface. And I am not just talking about the region's geological features. The town does not have devastated buildings riddled with bullet holes, unexploded mines spread across the main road or one-legged mutants smoking weed and selling blood diamonds at street corners.

But it is one of the main thoroughfares for blood-stained minerals from Bukavu, Walikale or Masisi, en route to the Western world via Kigali, Kampala and Nairobi.

Although Goma was at the centre of a tug-of-war between more than twenty armed groups and nine national armies, a lot of the trouble occurred on the outskirts, in smaller towns and villages, and in the forests.

Residents say that some of the best development took place after the Virunga National Park's Mount Nyiragongo erupted and drowned the city in two metres of molten lava in 2002.

On the road to Rutshuru, close to the airport, evidence of lava lays strewn beside the road in the form of huge charred boulders. In the distance, the guilty volcano sits idle, blowing circles of smoke into the clouds.

At its best, Goma is a spectacular global village of humanitarian workers seeking to perform a miracle in a town fractured by years of instability.

At its worst, it is the last outpost of civilization for opportunists, diamond merchants and mining magnates before they hop into propeller planes and head into the vast jungle in search of treasure.

I am still trying to decide whether I believe there is a difference.

In the town, dirty UN trucks filled with blue-helmeted peacekeepers sway and bounce as they pass.

The clearly branded 4x4s belonging to the NGOs trundle by and, until late last night, flatbed trucks fully equipped with loudspeakers and slogan-shouting dancing supporters crisscrossed the city.

Across Goma, election posters cling awkwardly to just about anything worth holding on to: they are wrapped around lampposts, broken down vehicles, toothpaste billboards and hung between street poles.

The sense that an event is about to take place is palpable. That it is an important election is also clear.

Residents will tell you that since supporting Kabila vocally in 2006, it has just been one broken promise after another. Some allege that even basic services have deteriorated and it's time for the town to stop looking like a complete mess.

This is a city holding its breath for change.

POSTSCRIPT

No self-righteous journalist with the nerve to prance around in aviators while digging around the dust for stories in Africa's hinterlands leaves without at least one encounter with a prostitute. It's simple really. On spotting their prey sporting long sleeves, cargos and a sweaty brow, ordinary women leave their stalls selling clothing or mobile phones, slip on hair extensions, fake nails and really poor quality musk and chase you awkwardly around the town in oversized, open-toed platform heels. It's what they must do to keep up the stereotype.

And so I return from a hard day's work (only reporting mind you; I wasn't in a mine digging for coltan in Masisi) to the Ihusi Hotel to find a beautiful young woman nagging at my behind. She wears a dark blue dress, complimented by the hair, the nails, the platforms – you name it, she has it – demonstrating she has definitely watched *Blood Diamond*.

After we share pleasantries, she goes for the kill.

'You and me, we go to the restaurant and then we fuck fuck,' she says, with an inviting sparkle in her eyes while her star-studded nose twitches in anticipation.

Obviously not used to being offered sex, for cash or kind, I fumble as I struggle to put on my most disinterested face, feigning nonchalance when all I really want to do is laugh, and so I go on to offer a pathetic 'No thanks'.

'Oh, but why?' she moans back, gesturing at my sides.

'Well, because . . . I am busy,' I offer lamely.

In truth, I want to say I don't want AIDS but I don't want to offend her, you know, by being politically *correct* at a time like this.

'Busy? But it won't take too long,' she continues.

You bet, lady, I want to say, but offer a pithy 'No, no, I have to work tonight', which is of course sad, but true.

And just when I thought it couldn't get any more bizarre, she stops me in my tracks and asks, 'Are you Muslim?'

A stutter, a momentary laugh, but my face then mutates into a curious frown as I begin to ponder why religion is going to take the credit for me denying myself a once-in-a-lifetime opportunity to participate in an orgy of structural violence in the DRC. This had nothing to do with being Muslim, Goddamit!

'Yes, I am Muslim,' I reply with some resentment.

'Ah, me too!' she cries with elation.

'Ah, in that case . . .' I reply.

Nah, I am just kidding. But maybe I will see her in heaven.

Walikale: the curse of El Dorado

Walikale is one of those towns you won't spot from the window of a plane. Squeezed between rolling carpets of treetops, you might just detect a brown blot on a green canvas if you strain your eyes hard enough. But beneath the mist and clouds, and among the rough jungle of towering trees, swamps, rivers and waterfalls, lies El Dorado incarnate: the district of cursed gold.

The territory of Walikale – a series of tropical forests, farmlands, fresh water eco-systems and more than a hundred villages (of which Walikale town is the central attraction) – encapsulates the broader story of the eastern Democratic Republic of Congo's North Kivu province.

The territory is important; it was reported in 2010 that 40 per cent of the entire revenue of North Kivu came from the Bisle tin mine that is located there.

But Walikale is not entirely unique. It is but one chapter in a larger narrative, in which the ordinary residents of a region, considered to contain some of the biggest untapped reserves of mineral resources in the world, remain famished, cursed by the wealth of their surroundings.

The town is so remote, and the roads so bad, that it can take up to a week to get there by car, even though it is only a forty-five-minute flight from Goma, the capital of North Kivu.

Not that the territory has an airport – planes land on a local road, while UN helicopters use a football field to transport medical supplies, people, and curry powder for a garrison of Indian soldiers, known as the 'Fab fourteenth' living on a hill not far from the landing pad.

Incidentally, with developed countries scaling down on peacekeeping operations, Indian troops make up most of the UN peacekeepers deployed in the DRC. It is, however, unclear for how much longer India will maintain its 4,000-strong troops in the country if they continue to be snubbed for a permanent seat in the UN Security Council. Meanwhile, the garrisons are high on shrines, chai and Indian flags.

Walikale town itself is a collection – a hamlet of thatched-roofed mud huts and a red-face-bricked school, flanked by a seemingly misplaced church, with its towering façade and tin top dwarfing the surrounding settlement.

The town centre, marked by an abandoned military truck, a flat-top trailer and an overweight pygmy obelisk that locals refer to as the 'Walikale monument' is literally a half-a-kilometre-long hardened track.

Outside their huts, women sit on blocks of cement and breastfeed their infants while talking to neighbours. Along the road, young girls sell fruit from small bowls, while boys sell fuel in plastic bottles.

The sound of children singing hymns drifts through the broken windows of the school's classrooms.

In the market adjacent to the main street, about two hundred or so vendors sell dried fish, freshly cut beef, nuts and wild animal meat brought in from villages across the region. The charred hands of baby monkeys sit among other produce on the market stalls.

If Goma is the last outpost – where businessmen meet in colonial era-styled hotels to make exchanges worth packets of gold, or in warehouses in the backstreets of the town to sew their wares, or on the banks of Lake Kivu where smugglers prepare to slip across into Rwanda – then you can bet that Walikale would be a central part of the discussion.

For the international media, the Walikale district is famed for three things: the armed groups that operate in its forests; its unsurpassed deposits of minerals, including cassiterite (ore used to make tin), gold, diamonds and colten (metallic ore used in the tiny circuit boards of laptops and mobile phones); and a recent incident of mass rape – involving about 387 victims – that took place in 2010.

Ntabo Ntaberi Sheka, a rebel leader and politician, is accused of being one of the directors of the rape and pillage of a series of villages in the territory – and he has an arrest warrant from the International Criminal Court to show for it.

Mass rape is used as a weapon of war in the DRC – with each generation indoctrinated into believing in its power to cultivate a sense of invincibility.

When villages are raided, and their young boys taken to become fighters, they too are taught to use this weapon.

Sheka shadows over the district's forests in a way only a zealous rebel leader might: with local brew and an iron fist. And according to some insiders, nothing gets out of Walikale without Sheka allowing it.

Of course, today Sheka is in the spotlight, but there are long lines of rebels who have operated and continue to operate in the jungles, despite the presence of UN peacekeeping troops.

Experts working in the region and the tormented locals speak of the place with a mixture of distress and childlike enthusiasm. It isn't hard to understand why – it is a place that fascinates and repels in equal measure.

The minerals in North Kivu, particularly in a remote haven like Walikale, where rebels and government forces are able to act with impunity, are an exacerbating factor in the continued insecurity that remains in the east.

The actors who have profited greatly from the mines refuse to leave, and when they do, have continued, in one form or another, to operate by proxy in the region.

And so while the failure of Joseph Kabila, the incumbent president, to build infrastructure and development has been the Opposition's main rallying cry during election campaigning, many in the east of the country are more concerned by their president's perceived tacit business relations with Rwanda, which they believe allows places like Walikale to continue being plundered.

Crucially, while this goes on, the instability in the region and the presence of foreign militias give Kabila's foreign backers a reason to remain.

Word on the street is that Kinshasa, the capital of the DRC, is nothing without North Kivu, that just about everyone in the higher echelons of the political order are involved in the mining and export of minerals in the region. This means that if a rebel like Sheka thrives, it is because someone important benefits from his existence.

In an apparent attempt to clear up the industry, Kabila banned the export of minerals for six months – from September 2010 to March 2011.

But human rights observers say the ban only served to further militarize the illegal smuggling of minerals and did little to stave off the armed groups, while there has also been a failure to create programmes to regulate the industry.

Neither did it advance solutions to the continued pillage of the region's forests and bio-diversity that has been a trend since King Leopold's Free Congo State ravaged entire areas in the hunt for rubber in the 1890s.

Meanwhile, the Dodd-Frank law imposed by the US – designed to create transparency and end the trade in blood-minerals through the forced certification of minerals – only created new problems.

A weak administration, malnourished police force and readymade black market meant that in a country unable to handle the certification process, official exports dried up, allowing smuggling to thrive.

In 2011, for instance, exports of cassiterite were down by 90 per cent. But with US companies shunning the DRC, the leading buyer of these minerals, illicit or not, is none other than China.

Invariably, the DRC is a complex web of interspersed politics, latent corruption, violence and geographical obscurity that often allows temporary greed to triumph over the aspirations of the ordinary.

The residents of Walikale may be impoverished, but human dignity is in no shortage here.

You see it in their daily struggles to cultivate their own gardens, build a life that is outside the insatiable search for quick riches, and in the dreams they have for their children.

But these efforts do not always translate into reality, particularly when the systematic tendency of those in power to manipulate a fragmented society into self-immolating acts of horror, remains.

It would be a little patronizing to conclude by way of a pithy disclaimer that the African continent is far more than the sum of botched elections, bloodthirsty war lords, dying black babies and parched, dusty earth. Of course there is more to the continent than war; there are even days when women in central African jungles go without being raped, and on special occasions, referred to as 'times of glee', even ordinary first-world issues like generational gaps between child soldiers come up at tribal councils.

But you know this already.

I promise to be better next time.

INDIA, PAKISTAN OR AZADI?

Pretty girls often ask what it is about Kashmir that has so piqued my interest.

Being a hopeful storyteller, my usual response involves telling an epic story, piecing together words like an ancient incantation as I recount a life-changing encounter with a serious seer on a holy hill one winter's morn in Sonamarg.

But this playful routine can however only last so long especially if there was no seer, mountain or life-changing experience except almost losing a toe to frostbite after plopping around in All Stars through snow in Gulmarg.

Sometimes there are no pretty girls either but let's just say they do ask.

The truth is I see the story of Kashmir as one of the most poignant counter narratives to our established understanding of the 'civilized world'. The socially acceptable understanding of such a world of course excludes North Korea and Iran; they are obviously too cool for school.

India, Brazil, South Africa and China represent a new subversive counter-weight in the shift of global power – their developing country badge and their regional might offer a veneer of an alternate model of development – but in truth, they offer little to a counter narrative of how the world should function, of how peace and justice might be secured, and demonstrate little concern for lost and forgotten places. Theirs is just a concern laced with self-interest, power-mongering and control of their domains.

What then of a place like Kashmir? Stuck between Western diplomacy and Indian ascendancy, Kashmiri ambitions for national self-determination suit no one. They have little power, little coordination, a disjointed leadership, a history of an armed insurgency and scant media swagger; their cause is like screaming for a lost donkey in the Himalayas.

It is the demonization of China and Israel that has institutionalized slogans like 'Free Tibet' and 'Free Palestine' into global, mainstream activist causes. In contrast, Kashmir battles to stand up to the established Indian narrative. Of course, Palestine and Tibet, despite their banners, bandannas and flags, are going nowhere rather slowly, but Kashmir does not even have that recognizable paraphernalia one could use to pick up chicks with.

Even more telling is the dearth of intellectual support for justice in Kashmir from India's liberal elite. Only too willing to support the Tibetan cause in lamenting China's occupation of the Himalayan region, that Kashmir remains their blind spot is an extraordinary irony. Likewise, lauding Anna Hazare as he stands up to corruption is easy because he waves flags and talks about reform. He does not question state legitimacy. Indian journalists can also fall into the same trap, either obstructing 'the Kashmir story', relying on army press releases, towing the line; it is still the one topic that can turn argumentative Indians into jingoistic retards.

It is only natural that such an anal retentive sensitivity would draw the interest of any dimwitted writer, wouldn't it?

Besides, Kashmir is at a fascinating juncture in its history. Two decades have passed since the insurgency began, and the Valley has shifted its focus: most of the guns are gone and a new generation of intellectuals are moving voices from the streets to the web, turning slogans into prose and spinning trauma into English-language novels. Their cries are prompting new conversations and begging new questions inside India and across the globe. But it is the nature of all such things that gain prominence and mass appeal to become voyeuristic escapades, romanticized populist movements with long-term career opportunities. Kashmir has the chance to tell its story or turn into a commodity.

Pretty girls will be the end of me.

The disappeared of Kashmir

His unibrow twists and arches furiously. The creases on his face tighten. His eyes shift from the door and with his index finger he points towards the ceiling. Then he stares straight at me and begins to speak – his voice like a calamitous clap of thunder, echoing off the cold walls and ringing in my ears.

I have no idea what he is saying, but his tone makes me flinch.

'Take it easy . . . they are here to listen to your story . . . don't be angry,' says Parveena Ahangar, the chairperson of the Association of Parents of Disappeared Persons (APDP), one of the two organizations going by the same name in Kashmir, as she tugs gently at the old man's knee.

But Ghulam Muhammad Wani refuses and embarks on a second tirade, spitting as he pronounces a series of expletives. A friend, who accompanied me for the purpose of translating, whispers: 'I can't translate all of this. He is cursing the hell out of everyone.' The eighty-year-old is short and stocky but cuts an imposing figure. Dressed in a dirty brown *pheran,* he sits on the floor of his living room in Rajbagh, Srinagar, addressing us. His overstretched woollen socks loop around the contours of his feet, stealing dust from the parched carpet below. He tells his story.

A father's anguish

On the evening of 14 May 1996, members of the counter-insurgent Ikhwan group, a pro-government militia made up of former insurgents, now working for the Indian army, knocked on his door and took off with this son, Imtiyaz Ahmed Wani. Suspected of being a separatist fighting for freedom from the Indian state, Imtiyaz disappeared without a trace.

After searching from pillar to post, visiting police stations and army offices, Wani went to the J&K State Human Rights Commission to file a complaint about his missing son. After failing to make progress there, he sold some property, took out a loan and paid a seemingly sympathetic counter-insurgent who promised information about his son. But the money, too, disappeared.

'My son was a gardener with the forest department, earning Rs 2,000 ($45) a month; he did no wrong,' Wani says finally. 'It has been fifteen years since.' During his desperate search for Imtiyaz, a policeman from the Special Task Force came to his house and offered him Rs 1,200 ($30) as compensation.

Over time, Wani was also approached by politicians offering him 'aid' in exchange for his silence. 'I told them to leave . . . it would be like accepting blood money! They robbed me of my son; who will now bury me when I die?' Wani asks the silent room.

Buried Evidence, a 2009 report published by the International People's Tribunal on Human Rights and Justice (IPTK) in Indian-administered Kashmir, estimates the number of missing persons in the state to be '8,000 plus' since 1989. It is, of course, a figure disputed by the Indian government, and S.M. Sahai, the inspector general of police in Kashmir, declares it is grossly exaggerated. 'This number is not correct, and most of the missing persons are fighters who crossed the border into Pakistan, and are still there,' he asserts.

Human rights activists however contend that the government has repeatedly released contradictory figures, indicating a lack of seriousness on the issue. 'One day, they say 3,931 people are missing, the next day it is 3,749,' says Parvez Imroz, a human rights activist and co-founder of the original APDP.

Zahir-ud-Din, a local journalist whose investigation into disappearances in Kashmir culminated in a book, *Did They Vanish in*

Thin Air, concurs that the state has routinely marginalized the issue. One can even pick up on it from the language employed – 'missing' as opposed to 'disappearance' – ud-Din argues.

A familiar story

Following the partition of India and Pakistan, and the latter's attempt to capture the Valley, Kashmir was split into an Indian-administered Kashmir, a Pakistan-administered Kashmir and, later, a Chinese territory, which is mostly uninhabited.

Ever since, India and Pakistan have used Kashmir to exercise bitter foreign policy towards each other, culminating in two wars and a series of skirmishes along the border. While self-determination has always been a project in Indian-administered Kashmir, it took a rigged election in 1988 to prompt a call to arms against the Indian government's rule of the region; young men ventured into Pakistan-administered Kashmir for training in guerrilla warfare. India responded with a military campaign to suppress the insurgency, resulting in an estimated 60,000 to 70,000 deaths, and Kashmir became one of the most militarized places on earth, with more than half a million Indian troops deployed in the region.

To help put this into perspective, it is worth noting that at the height of the occupation of Iraq in 2008, foreign troops there numbered only 250,000.

Kashmiri novelist Mirza Waheed says that young men did go to Pakistan, and that many did not return, but insists the story has always been bigger than that. 'There have been numerous cases of custodial deaths, torture, illegal detention, extra-judicial killings, also known as "fake-encounters", and they cannot be brushed away.'

Widespread and systematic

The APDP, co-founded by Imroz and Ahangar before they each formed their respective associations, has long argued that disappearances in the Valley have been purposeful, systematic.

Ahangar has not seen her son Javed since he was picked up by security forces seventeen years back. Since the early days of the APDP, she has acted as a pillar of strength for parents seeking comfort and advice in dealing with their lingering loss.

Ud-Din says that numbers have always been difficult to verify, but that disappearances are widespread. 'When people started disappearing in the 1990s we thought that they might have died accidentally due to torture. But thousands cannot disappear accidentally. It happens with a design.' Imroz agrees, saying that while the rate of disappearances may have slowed down over the past decade, it is a phenomenon that is yet to be solved, with perpetrators yet to face justice.

'Both combatants and non-combatants were picked up from home, from the roads, from just about anywhere and taken to detention centres. Their fate are often not known,' he says. 'Enforced disappearances is one of the many repressive measures aimed at breaking the resolve of the people,' says Athar Parvaiz, a journalist based in Srinagar.

Disappearances fit into a larger theme of human rights violations in Kashmir. In late March 2011, Amnesty International (AI) released a report claiming that the 'state of Jammu and Kashmir was holding hundreds of people without charge or trial in order to keep them out of circulation'. AI alleges that a contentious Public Safety Act (PSA) allows security forces to detain individuals when the state has insufficient evidence for a trial. Through this law, between 8,000 and 20,000 people have been detained over the past two decades, with 322 people held between January and September 2010 alone.

Govind Acharya, country specialist at Amnesty International, stresses that while detentions through the PSA can last for up to two years, and therefore pale in comparison with enforced disappearances, the numbers are ominously similar. 'The number of disappearances and the number of PSA detentions cited are coincidental, but they both run in the thousands . . . PSA is a form of legalized enforced disappearance.' Enforced disappearances are forbidden under international law.

But disappearances and detentions are not the only ways in which human rights are being undermined in Kashmir. In late 2010, a US cable released by whistleblower website WikiLeaks reported that the International Committee of the Red Cross (ICRC) had briefed US diplomats on widespread torture in Indian jails in Kashmir and vented their frustration at the Indian government's failure to address their concerns.

In 2009, the Allard Lowenstein International Human Rights Clinic at Yale Law School reported that 'the pattern of legal breakdowns in Kashmir violates basic tenets of international human rights law' and that 'research indicates that India fails to meet its international obligations in Kashmir'. Worse, still, is the report's damning assessment of the 'Indian government's disregard [for] its own standards governing detention'. '[It] refuses to honour court orders quashing detention, and exploits procedural impediments to avoid presenting detainees in court.'

Psychological torture

According to Imroz, the real tragedy of disappearance can be found in the families whose lives it disrupts forever. 'Most of those who disappeared were non-combatants ... and consider how many people are directly affected by the ordeal of a loved one disappearing ... If a family member dies, you mourn and are forced to move on, but when someone "disappears" the entire family, community is disrupted emotionally and psychologically; they all join the search. When does it end?'

He continues: 'It is torturous. Perpetual trauma has gone to their heads. Most of them have become psychiatric patients. The half-widows [as the wives of the disappeared are known] are the worst hit. They cannot go for a second marriage, they cannot inherit from their husband's estate, and nobody accepts them as widows. Most of them have been turned out by their in-laws.'

'It is a huge disruption to the society ... Consider children who have lost their father and breadwinner and are taken out of school, and become child labourers . . . or are refused entry into an orphanage because there is no certification of death, or the complications in sharing property because there is no certainty of anything.'

'Discipline and death'

It is little wonder then that the IPTK report postulates that the governance of Indian-administered Kashmir has taken on the techniques of 'discipline and death' as modes of social control, with the objective of 'assimilating Kashmir into its territory'. This regulatory mechanism has left Kashmiri society traumatized, existing in virtual limbo.

Mirza Waheed has a different take on the matter. He believes that it would be erroneous to label Kashmiris as victims lacking agency, even though they have been victims of a brutal military suppression, or to ignore the fact that any society would devise coping mechanisms in the face of such trauma. 'There is no dichotomy between being traumatized and resilient. A brutalized people have no choice but to be resilient, in all kinds of ways. A mother whose nine-year-old son was bludgeoned to death last summer – what can she do other than grieve or protest? Both require resilience.'

While not disputing this resilience, Imroz emphasizes the lack of institutional and societal support for those suffering from this type of trauma. 'The MSF [Médecins Sans Frontières] have trauma counselling, and they have worked with the APDP, but there is still a lack of institutional recognition of the issue.' Parvaiz agrees, adding that putting aside the romanticism of a resilient society, 'the two-decade long conflict and misgovernance over the years have wrought havoc on Kashmir . . . affecting the social fabric of the society while insecurity about the future reflects in their social behaviour as well.'

Impunity reigns supreme

It would appear that part of the problem is that the Indian government refuses to acknowledge enforced disappearance as the scourge that it is in Indian-administered Kashmir. For the past ten years, both versions of the APDP have assembled every month – on different days – in the Sher-e-Kashmir park – to bemoan the lack of justice and governmental action in addressing the issue. It is not only that the Indian government is refusing to offer an explanation for the disappearances, they are not even willing to address the mass complaints either.

The IPTK report, which Imroz co-authored, documents an investigation of 2,700 graves in fifty-five villages and three districts in Indian-administered Kashmir between 2005 and 2009. The numbers are staggering: 2,373 graves were found unmarked, 151 graves contained more than one body, while twenty-five graves held between three and seventeen bodies!

The study noted that mass graves have always been a tell-tale sign of genocide. But Sahai, the police chief, disagrees, saying that the mass graves belong to fallen foreign fighters and reveal little about the disappearances in the state.

Authorities often claim that unmarked graves are those of fighters from Pakistan, the study notes, adding that such rhetoric conflates 'cross-border militancy with present non-violent struggles by local Kashmiris for political and territorial self-determination'.

According to Acharya, the crux of the issue can be explained in one word – 'impunity'. 'Victims of human rights violations from all sides of the conflict can expect very little from the Indian state of Jammu and Kashmir.'

Through the Armed Forces Special Powers Act (AFSPA), Indian forces engaged in various violations are often protected from prosecution. The government has allowed the UN special rapporteur on minorities and the UN special rapporteur on human rights defenders to visit Indian-administered Kashmir, but has refused access to the UN working group on arbitrary detention or the UN special rapporteur on extrajudicial executions.

Crucially, the UN working group on enforced and involuntary disappearances has also been denied entry, despite repeated requests to conduct investigations in the territory. When quizzed on this,

Sahai is at a loss for words, 'It is difficult for me to comment on this because this issue is of a high diplomatic status.'

Acharya says that 'given the regular visits of others' rapporteurs, it does seem to be a glaring omission', adding that while AI did manage to meet G.K. Pillai, the former Indian home secretary, to discuss their latest report, gaining an audience with the Jammu and Kashmir chief minister, Omar Abdullah, has proved to be quite a task. Although the IPTK report was released in 2009, they are still waiting for the CM's response.

I myself found little success when approaching the chief minister's office for comment. Kashmir has always been a sensitive issue, but if anything, the human rights violations in the Valley are only emblematic of the Indian state's selective observance of international treaties on human rights. Human Rights Watch (HRW) has regularly castigated India for violations in the north-eastern state of Manipur as well, where the AFSPA has cultivated a culture of impunity for the security forces. In the late 1980s and the 1990s, Indian counter-insurgency tactics in Punjab included the use of enforced disappearances, extra-judicial executions and mass cremations. This is perhaps the reason why India has signed – but not ratified – the International Convention for the Protection of All Persons from Enforced Disappearance that came into being at the end of 2010. The convention effectively outlaws enforced disappearance, making states accountable, and effectively turns systematic disappearance into a crime against humanity.

AI is categorical in their acknowledgement that every country has a right to defend itself, but insists that enforced disappearance can never be tenable. Acharya says, 'India does have a robust procedure for dealing with terrorism, as seen from the trial of Ajmal Kasab . . . However, the Jammu and Kashmir government is bypassing the judicial system and imposing arbitrary punishment based on very broad categories by government agents, rather than the judiciary.'

Sahai disputes this, saying: 'This idea that we [Jammu and Kashmir] have a whole new set of rules and that there is no accountability is wrong; we follow the law like other states and places in India. Kashmir is a disturbed area and often human rights groups are used as tools of propaganda by separatists. If our human rights organizations are compiling figures and our judiciary exists to protect the people, what is the need for AI to investigate?'

But Imroz states that state institutions have very little power in the face of the AFSPA. With the judiciary unable to act and the J&K State Human Rights Commission unable to punish, the armed forces have effective legal impunity.

The tragedy becomes further complicated when one notes how Indian civil society, together with the Indian media, 'has done everything short of abandoning Kashmir from the mainstream discourse'. Save for an occasional television programme here and a random discussion there, the harrowing tales of thousands of disappeared people, the broken homes and the daily travails of life in Indian-administered Kashmir are missing from the popular imagination of most Indians. Instead, the narrative begins and ends as Kashmir, the elusive paradise overrun by Pakistani jihadists running around with Kalashnikovs; not ordinary people torn by a decades-long conflict, a disproportionate military campaign and gross human rights abuses.

The Kashmiri people are virtually anonymous in the telling of their own stories. This is partly why ud-Din believes that families nursing broken homes due to the disappearance of fathers or sons need closure. 'While interviewing the former minister of state for home in 1999, I urged him to declare all the disappeared persons dead, as this is the only way out. This alone would end the unending search and the sufferings of the aggrieved relatives. However, the minister refused for obvious reasons.'

New generation: new questions

'The new generation is asking questions . . . the new generation is less afraid to speak up,' Imroz says. 'They realize that they have to get past the rhetoric, rise above it. Kashmiri civil society is slowly rising, and is part of the problem and the solution, and it's up to them to deem what is unacceptable.'

This is a view shared by Acharya, who says the affected families must keep pushing government officials to heed their calls for justice.

'Organizations like Amnesty International can only shed light on a few cases and hope that the other cases will get resolved as well. But it's hard not to be pessimistic about the prospects of justice . . . Of course, as a human rights activist, I'd recommend that the Jammu and Kashmir government takes steps to repeal laws like the PSA and the AFSPA that give immunity from prosecution of human rights violations, initiate steps towards prosecuting human rights violators and ensure that the state does not violate economic, social and cultural rights of those affected by repeated curfews and checkpoints that make seeking an adequate livelihood so difficult.'

But these calls are unlikely to be heard by the Indian authorities – at least not in the near future. And while justice might go some way towards healing wounds and advancing closure, it is unlikely to bring Ghulam Wani's son home or ease this father's anguish. For now, his only recourse is to refuse to pay for electricity, water and other services – withholding a few coins from the state in protest against a silent war.

Wind in the willows: a cricket bat paradise

The old road from Srinagar, to the town of Sangam, en route to the tourist haven of Pahalgam, takes you from the melancholic to the spectacular. The road is flanked by run-down, two-storeyed thatched structures, dusty granite factories and an army garrison surrounded by poorly camouflaged bunkers, stray dogs and dirty footpaths. But the muck is a prelude to a green corridor of hanging trees, soggy poppy fields, freshly tilled saffron gardens and towering snowcapped mountains beyond the horizon of the Pampor highway to Kashmir's south.

'These are Russian poplars; they are thinner than the native ones . . . God knows how they got here,' my companion for the day tells me, pointing at the tall trees as little flashes of sunshine trickle through like disco lights off a crystal ball. Here, in Sangam, some forty kilometres from Srinagar, beneath the shade of a towering Kashmiri willow and lines of kikar trees, is a cricket bat paradise. Beyond the industrial grime of the capital and the pockets of sludge and filth that is the business of any city's periphery, the main thoroughfare leads you to a calmer repository . . . of cricket bat factories, sports shops and billboards bearing the insignia of the biggest names in the cricketing world. It is not exactly Kashmir's rabbit hole – a faraway place of Hobbit miracle workers, unhindered by the scars of a bloody conflict, sculpting cricket bats night and day as a token of love for sports enthusiasts – but it is, nevertheless, quite impressive.

Said to employ an estimated 10,000 Kashmiris, the industry adds an estimated 500,000 bats to the Indian and international markets every year. The variety on offer is stupendous: long handles, short handles, Mongoose bats, autographed bats, half-size short handle bats – and inadvertently millions of thousands of boys, girls, men and women in South Asia will wrap their palms around the handle of a willow carved from the trees of the Valley at some point in their lives.

Kashmiri cricket bats are made from both the willow imported by the British during colonial times to service their energy needs (now known as the Kashmiri willow) and the native, dervish-looking poplar trees.

Behind the façade of shop windows bearing lines of neatly arranged bats, emblazoned with MRF, Reebok, GM, Adidas stickers on the face, splice and spine, is a world of drying planks of stacked Kashmiri willows, unfixed handles imported from Punjab and generator-powered machinery designed to cut planks into a basic cricket blade.

Cricket and conflict

Some say it has been the best summer since 2007.

'This year [2011] has been especially good – first, the calm in the Valley and second, India winning the World Cup have spiralled sales here and across India,' Riyaz Ahmed Ganai tells me in his father's cricket bat factory, Topline Sports, in Mirzapora. The rise of the Indian Premier League (IPL) has done much to boost sales and even forced bat-makers to make new types of cricket bats to suit the new game. When India won the World Cup in March, the demand for bats in India must have risen exponentially, but in the Valley the effect was short-lived. 'Sales did increase and people were excited, but if Pakistan had won the World Cup, the effect would have lasted longer,' Ganai smiles.

'My father told me that when Pakistan won the World Cup in 1992, sales were so good we even sold the bad planks as cricket bats,' he continues, picking up a dark, soggy plank whose dreams of smashing cricket balls were long over. 'Now that has never happened since.' Like everything else in Kashmir, the fortunes of the cricket-bat industry are dependent on a larger political game.

The industry, which produces bats ranging from Rs 50 ($1.10) to Rs 2,000 ($50), is a living, breathing symbol of the more than six-decade-old conflict. It is unsurprising then to hear that the fortunes of both India and Pakistan on the cricket field energize the game, invigorate or diminish sales and influence the scope of shipments to the rest of the subcontinent.

Ganai's father's factory has had to ride out the volatile political conflict which, as well as costing between 50,000 and 70,000 lives, has upset the rhythm of life in the Valley. 'Over the years, there have been so many factors that have cost the business. These include the [political] turmoil but also the earthquake in 2005 and 26/11. Events in Pakistan affect us too,' he says.

A three-month lockdown in 2010 – in response to demonstrations that led to an intermittent curfew, indiscriminate crackdowns and culminated in the deaths of more than 115 teenagers – saw the entire industry shut down for the summer.

Ghulam Mohammed Dar, from Neelam Sports in Sangam, says his shop sells around 5,000 to 7,000 bats every year. It operates on the principal of 'just in time', or *kanban* for the purists, and their policy, like that of most factories dealing with products susceptible to seasonal variations in demand, is not to keep extra stock.

So, in 2010, when the business was closed during the crucial summer months, Dar had no bats to send out when the time came to deliver. 'No workers pitched in to work and with everything on lockdown, we could not manufacture bats as usual,' he says. 'As a result we lost 50 to 70 per cent of our sales.'

His business was hit hard. 'So we had all these bats – thousands of them waiting on order – and we could not send them,' he regrets.

It was only when the chinar trees shed their leaves in October and November that they were able to get back to work. 'Usually in summer . . . about 2,000 bats a month are sent to India. But with the lockdown, we had to send some 10,000 bats in October and November alone,' Ganai explains. 'But so far it has been good this year . . . All we need is for Pakistan to win every series, and we'd do well,' he laughs.

It has been some time since we entered Ganai's factory unannounced, interrupting him as he filed the shoulders of a newly cut bat, gesturing that he needs to go back to work, to toasting that wood . . . for the rest of us cricket lovers.

Kashmiri Pandits: why we never left our home

Sanjay Tickoo remembers it well. It was a warm summer's day in 1990 when he found a poster pasted on the outside wall of his home in Srinagar, the capital of Indian-administered Kashmir. It was written in Urdu, which Sanjay could not read, so he took it to his grandfather and asked him to translate it.

'As he read it out, tears rolled down his cheeks . . . it instructed our family to leave the Valley or die,' Tickoo tells me as we sit in a café on the banks of the Jhelum River in Srinagar.

But, unlike the estimated 100,000 Hindus from the Valley – known as Kashmiri Pandits – who embarked on a mass migration south to Jammu following the start of the insurgency against Indian rule in 1989, Tickoo's family refused to leave.

Instead, Tickoo, who was in his early twenties at the time, decided to take the threat to the local newspaper, where he paid for it to be placed as an advertisement in the classifieds section. 'It was published on the back page. I wish I still had a copy, but they published it as is,' he recalls.

No sooner had it been published than shocked Muslim neighbours and friends congregated at Tickoo's home, apologizing for the misdeed and promising that his family faced no threat.

They urged them not to leave.

A question of numbers

The Hindu minority in Muslim-majority Kashmir shrank from an estimated 140,000 in the late 1980s to 19,865 by 1998. Today, Tickoo says there are fewer than 3,400 Pandits in Kashmir. Others put the number at 2,700.

But Tickoo, who now heads the Kashmir Pandit Sangarsh Samiti (KPSS), an organization that looks after the affairs of the Pandits who remain in Kashmir, says that the plight of the community is complex. 'Over the past twenty years, we estimate that 650 Pandits were killed in the Valley,' adding: 'The figures of 3,000 to 4,000 killings as suggested by some Pandit organizations outside the state is propaganda, which we reject . . . Not that 650 is a low number, because even one killing should not be ignored, but we must get the numbers right.'

While Tickoo's organization says that 399 Pandits were killed between 1999 and 2008, and 650 in total, this pales in comparison with those estimates that put the figure at 3,000, but exceeds the state's suggestion of 219 between 1990 and 2008.

But collating the numbers, or even unravelling the language of migration and exodus, is part of the historical ambiguity that surrounds the Pandits' flight from the Valley. And it has been made all the harder by the fact that Pandits outside Kashmir have dominated the narrative, while those inside have remained largely silent.

On the subject of how many Pandits fled Kashmir, Mridu Rai, a lecturer in Indian Studies at Trinity College, Dublin, writes in *Until My Freedom Has Come* that the figure of 700,000 put forward by Panun Kashmir (Our Own Kashmir), a group advocating a homeland for Kashmiri Pandits, 'refers to a much larger collection of Pandits who had departed [from Kashmir] at different times over the centuries'. She adds that the language used by Pandits who left the Valley – 'exodus' or 'in exile' – serves as 'an indictment of the Indian state for not protecting them within their homeland and then for neglecting them outside it'. These terms also create a single narrative of victimhood, when, in fact, it is difficult to ascertain why individual Pandits left Kashmir.

While Tickoo dismisses claims that Pandits were 'ethnically cleansed', he says that relations between the two communities did sour when the insurgency began. People left because they felt threatened. 'I am not saying that Kashmiri Pandits and Muslims were brothers in arms, living in each other's homes or something before 1989. Yes, there was an unmistakable tolerance and respect for each other . . . violence was unheard of . . . but it would be a lie to say something did not change when the trouble started.'

From hateful slogans that bounced off the mosque loudspeakers to comments whispered in the streets, there was a sudden change in attitude towards Hindus. And these shifting sentiments were used by politicians on both sides, helping to stoke fear among the Hindu minority. 'Until today, we don't know who posted that threat on my wall,' Tickoo muses.

Fifty-one-year-old Motilal Bhat, the president of the Pandit Hindu Welfare Society, formed in the mid-1990s to rebuild relations between Pandits and Muslims, says the early 1990s was a time when myth-making prevailed. 'Those who left thought they would be gone for three or four months, and that they would return when things improved . . . no one expected to stay there for years . . . Kashmir had always been a peaceful state,' explains the soft-spoken headmaster.

He dismisses the figures presented by the KPSS and says most of the killings took place after the mass migration. 'I think the government's figures are correct,' Bhat says. 'I reject this figure of 650 and even the figure 399. This community was made up of small numbers by proportion and, yes, we had around 600,000 to 700,000 people, but maximum people left around 1990/1991 – and the major killings took place after 1991.'

Both communities did display a great deal of chauvinism. 'There was a strange perception at the time which saw the KPs [Kashmiri Pandits] thinking that no matter what they would be protected by the Indian army, while the KMs [Kashmiri Muslims] thought that if anything happened to them, the entire Muslim world would come to their rescue.'

'As we have now seen, both were proved wrong,' he adds matter-of-factly.

People soon realized – whatever their political persuasion or sympathies – that they were at the mercy of both the security forces and the separatists. Bhat contends that Kashmiri Muslims, who 'regretted' the departure of the Pandits, were too slow to react. 'It was too late, and people had already left . . . they should have come forward for the minority. It is the moral duty of the majority to look after the minority and include them . . . if you are in a minority you face a psychological threat, a vulnerability.'

And the Pandits who stayed behind were sometimes treated with distrust. 'The question on everyone's mind at the time was: If all the Pandits have left, then why are you still here? Consequently both sides often saw us Pandits as informers. We suffered intimidation from both sides.'

This is a sentiment Suman Vikash Bhat, a thirty-three-year-old assistant professor of Microbiology at Islamic University of Science and Technology, shares. He says that during the 1990s, when militancy was at its peak and large numbers of soldiers were killed, it was common for the army to take out their frustrations on the civilian population, irrespective of religion. 'They would often respond by beating civilians and there was a lot of these crackdowns where people would be gathered . . . for sure they would give us ordinary people a thrashing . . . They used to sometimes pick people up . . . both sides did so . . . but there were also good and bad people on both sides.'

Suman Bhat remembers the late 1980s and early 1990s vividly – the curfews, the crackdowns and, crucially, his Hindu relatives leaving. 'It was easy to feel insecure,' he reminisces, 'the newspapers at the time were full of stories of violence and as we watched the militancy or terrorism or whatever you want to call it increasing, teamed with the fact that people were being killed, it was only natural that the community became insecure.'

But his family's relations with Kashmiri Muslims made them confident. 'My father is a renowned teacher and his Muslim friends urged him not to leave.'

When he moved to Pune in India to study in the late 1990s, however, he began to worry more about his family's safety. 'We would hear about violence in Kashmir on the television or read about it in the papers and often I could not sleep until I got hold of my parents and found out that they were okay.'

Caught in the flood

So why did some Pandits choose to stay? Suman Bhat offers a couple of reasons. 'We did not migrate because we were not financially well off and we thought that it would be difficult to survive in Jammu. My father had invested almost all his money in land and property here ... The other reason is that my father's Muslim friends refused to let him leave; we were told that "we will die, but we won't allow you to go".'

Even now that he is armed with a PhD from the Bhaba Atomic Research Centre in Bombay, which could land him a top job in any city in the country, Bhat chooses to remain in the Valley. 'I returned in 2010 to Kashmir to find that my father was ill; and I could have taken him to Bombay for treatment, but he is a man of the soil and a man of principle. It would have been a punishment to take him away from Kashmir . . . he loves Kashmir a lot, and so do I, and even I do not want to go away from here.'

But even those who remained behind have a story to tell, Motilal Bhat says, 'Everyone has a story . . . everyone suffered . . . the violence came like a flood . . . and in a flood, everyone suffers.'

His sister was killed in one of the three notable massacres targeting the Pandit community. The first, in Sangrampora in 1997, resulted in the deaths of seven Pandits, then in 1998, eighteen were killed in Wandhama, and in 2001, five in Anantnag.

One evening, unidentified gunmen – local parlance for killings no one takes responsibility for – came into his sister's home in the southern district of Anantnag, ransacked the house and shot indiscriminately. A bullet hit his sister's heart and 'she died on the spot . . . three other Sikh girls were killed as well'.

After this loss he cursed himself for staying on in Kashmir. 'But finally I thought it was destiny and that we have to continue working for a better future.'

Return to Kashmir

Unlike Tickoo, Motilal Bhat and Suman Bhat, Poshkaranth Ganju, sixty-five, from the Baramullah district in northern Kashmir, moved to Jammu in late 1990. He decided to leave after his brother was shot. 'The bullet brushed his neck and he survived but we left for Jammu, because of the chaos here . . . We Pandits are a peace-loving people and we thought it was best to preserve our lives,' he says.

But Ganju's family, who had run a textile business in Baramullah for three generations, found it difficult to adjust to Jammu's climate or maintain the same standard of living they had grown accustomed to in the Valley. So, along with twenty other families, they returned in 1996 – six years after leaving. On their return, the family found their house burnt down, but their shop and its contents remained untouched.

They also discovered that their neighbours were willing to pay 1996 prices for moth-eaten textiles that had been lying in their shop since they fled in 1990. 'We came back to conduct business, and the Muslim welcome convinced us that we were safe here . . . though there was a grenade attack outside the shop shortly after our return. We found out later that this was from a rival business competitor and had nothing to do with us being Pandits.'

Ganju says that back then there was little government support for those who wanted to return and that even the community in Jammu voiced opposition. 'Families in Jammu told us not to come, but we told them that our Muslim brothers had welcomed us to come and so we felt confident to return, and so we thought that if the business would run smoothly, we'd stay, else we would return to Jammu.'

He adds: 'Most of the families in Jammu still imagined Kashmir to be the lawless state of 1990.'

But Tickoo emphasizes that Ganju's story is a unique one because living in a temple complex in Baramullah offered the family state protection. 'Pandits in the villages did not receive special security from the state, remember that,' he reiterates.

Motilal Bhat says that in the early 1990s, those who remained were vilified by those who had left – they 'felt betrayed by the families who stayed behind' as if their continued presence in the Valley undermined the experiences of those who had fled to difficult conditions in Jammu.

'Why people remained when there was so much pain and in spite of the fact that many left is a difficult question to answer,' Tickoo remarks with a faint smile.

'Some will tell you that they could not afford moving to start a new life, others will tell you they are of the soil, that this is their motherland and they refuse to leave, and perhaps others will say something else . . . but does this then mean that Kashmir meant anything less for those who left?' Tickoo asks rhetorically. 'Does it mean they feel no connection or their roots are not here? We are perhaps unable to answer why we are here . . . we are just here,' he concludes.

Motilal Bhat explains: 'For those of us who remained . . . we thought we'd watch events play out and then take it on a week to week basis. But these became months and then years.'

But it was not easy, says Maharaj Krishan Pandita, who is in his sixties. Two of the government telecommunications officers' cousins were killed in the violence and his brother was shot (but survived) during the 1997 massacre in Sangrampora.

He witnessed the direct intervention of the state through forced removals under the guise of a 'security threat'. 'People were forced to move from their village and farmers who had to move suffered greatly after the massacre, but since I had a job in Srinagar and my family could move with me there, it was manageable for us, but not for others . . . The one good thing I can commend the armed forces for was that in this case, they didn't move people to Jammu, they just moved people to another locality in the same district . . . but we did lose everything.'

Monica Pandita, twenty-two, one of Maharaj Pandita's daughters, says she vaguely recalls the events of 1997, when her mother and sisters had to move from the village to Srinagar after the massacre in their district, but admits that she rarely thinks about it. 'All I remember is moving to my new school and nobody believing that I was a Pandit because my name is Monica,' she laughs.

'We Pandits are like a wonder here,' she continues, conceding that she has no Pandit friends and adding 'but it is not a problem for me'.

But her playfulness barely disguises a deep-seated concern that as the community shrinks, Kashmiri Pandits may soon have to face the fact that they are becoming increasingly alienated from those that left the Valley. Tickoo says that despite the cultural symmetry with Muslims in Kashmir, very little epitomizes their position better than the difficulty of finding suitable marriage partners within the community.

Marriage is, of course, the Achilles' heel of religious tolerance in South Asia. And Tickoo contends that with only 625 young men among the remaining Pandits, the issue is growing increasingly severe. There is still a stigma attached to the children of the Pandit community who have been raised under the turmoil of the past two decades. And it is the women who bear the brunt of the burden.

'On one hand, they [Pandits from outside Kashmir] are afraid to send their daughters here, while on the other, they say things like our daughters' chastity have been torn by Muslim men,' Tickoo says candidly. 'It is the kind of ostracization that serves no purpose . . . so you find more and more are marrying outside the Pandit community as a result.'

India, Pakistan or azadi?

But stuck between majority Muslim sentiment and an indifferent Pandit community in exile, what would be the best scenario for the

Pandit community in resolving the Kashmir conflict, I ask Motilal Bhat.

'I think the leaning is definitely towards India,' he tells me. 'People want a better life, and joining India makes sense. A lot of this has always been about power and money, and people realize they cannot be isolated [forever].' Kashmir is changing. 'The youngsters who are outside, they are mixing with the world and undergoing a different process. But if the authorities had to go for a census, people have since lost their inclination for Pakistan . . . and people will show the tendency towards India.'

Suman Bhat agrees. He says that despite Islam being inclusive and despite their sense of comfort with their Muslim brethren, Pandits would feel insecure if they were separated from the Indian state. 'Most of the Pandits would love that Kashmir would stay with India, as a state of India, because there is still some insecurity . . . you know living here, one realizes that what Islam preaches and how people sometimes live can be quite different.'

However, he adds that religious insecurity is but one aspect and insists that there 'are serious practical issues like economy, resources and political clout to consider'. 'If we are an independent Kashmir, will we be able to sustain ourselves? Do we have the infrastructure considering that industries haven't developed here?'

Tickoo emphasizes that self-determination is at the top of his list of priorities. 'I am a staunch Indian and we have a significant relation with India but my identity is because of Kashmir, my identity is because of Jhelum,' he says, gesturing at the murky green river behind us. 'My identity is not because of Jammu, USA, Rajasthan or Delhi . . . I'm proudly saying that I am a Kashmiri, and a Kashmiri Pandit.' If his political and social identity and rights could be guaranteed under majority rule, Tickoo would favour an independent Kashmir, but if he had the option only to choose between India and Pakistan, he would most definitely choose India.

A separate Pandit state?

Motilal Bhat suggests that the decision to join India would be a practical one which has little to do with denying the distinctness of Kashmir. And, crucially, part of that shared heritage turns the idea of a separate state into a non-event.

'You cannot differentiate a Pandit from a Muslim, culturally. Even in the names of people, we often have the same names, the same sense of identity, style of living, and other things.

'And this is apart from India and the rest of the world. You can imagine that in a period of twenty-two years after migration, a Kashmiri Pandit living in Jammu is still totally different from a Jammu resident.

'You might have even heard it from a Kashmiri Muslim that their ancestors were Kashmiri Pandits. Any scholar would confirm that to you. They might have embraced Islam in whatever way they chose. How this happened is not the point – the point is that we belong to a single community . . . and we cannot live without each other.

'I've made it clear that it is not possible to live without Muslims. We depend on them and they depend on us.'

Typically, Kashmiri Pandits claim to be linguistically and culturally distinct from Hindus from the rest of India, and though there has been a renewed move to return among those who left, there are questions about whether the young generation would be able to adapt to the unique environment of Kashmir. Poor infrastructure, periodic power cuts and curfews, in addition to high rates of unemployment, low salaries and lack of private-sector investment keep the Valley decades behind the rest of India's faster growing states.

Suman Bhat says, 'People are coming back. Every year thousands of Hindus from Jammu come over. Tourism is flourishing during summer. We depend on this tourism industry. Kashmiri Pandits come over and even visit their old neighbours . . . they love being here. But for the young generation, who were born in Jammu, it's hard to imagine them adjusting to this place. For the elderly people, who lived here and then migrated, I can tell you without any hesitation that they will love to come back.'

He then goes on: 'We have suffered a lot, Kashmir has suffered a lot, but even when I went to study in Pune all those years back, I had it in my mind that I would have to come back and settle down here.'

Motilal sums it up eloquently, urging the leadership to restart talks. 'No one here enjoys the violence . . . the authorities, the government and leadership from all sides must realize that,' he says. 'They have to go for a political solution, they have to break the ice, they have to come forward – in the interests of the common people.'

POSTSCRIPT

I remember crossing the Indo-Pak border with a group of friends in 2004 after watching India's memorable cricket victory in Lahore, and on our arrival at immigration at Attari, a customs official demanded that we relinquish a book my classmate had purchased in Pakistan, entitled *Cries of Kashmir*, a collection of poetry about how the conflict had turned the Valley into a shadow of itself.

Going through our luggage, a tall, muscular Sikh immigration officer in military fatigues picked up the title and flipping through the pages said, 'You cannot take this book into India . . . It is banned here.' We looked around. There was no sign hanging from the roof, or a piece of fax paper in a plastic sleeve with a list of banned books, beads and sex toys. He had just looked at the title, flipped through a couple of pages, sucked his thumb and concluded it was sacrilegious to the Indian state.

It wasn't my book and I didn't care much for it, but I couldn't understand as a tender political scientist wet behind the ears how a country that revelled in its status as a democracy could ban an obscure poetry book for turning a phrase that no one was likely to read. Yes, my mate had bought it – but it wasn't an ancient manuscript bearing secrets of the universe that was about to hypnotize India towards mass euthanasia. This was a silly text standing up to the great Indian democracy Goddammit! I refused to give in.

'This is the kind of book that could cause an uprising in Kashmir,' the Sardar said, riffling through the pages. 'Do you think Kashmiris need this flimsy book to rise up?' I reply instead, with some amusement, as my struggle to take the issue seriously gathers momentum.

'I am a proud Indian,' he replies, 'And it would go against my conscience to allow a book like this into my country,' he says, shaking his head.

'But, sir, this is India . . . not Pakistan . . . this is a *real* democracy, isn't it? I thought that this place was all about free speech and human rights and different opinions . . .' I finger back. 'And look, I am South African, and we are students at JNU . . . we are learning about this land . . . and you are not going to take away a book from us, are you?' I conclude.

'Yes – but I can't do it, I just can't . . .' he trails off.

Just then, another officer walks by and recognizes me as the kid who had earlier filled up a 'comment/complaint form' bidding Indian immigration to create a help desk dedicated to assisting illiterate farmers fill up the necessary immigration forms before crossing the border into Pakistan. The Samjhauta Express was a cheap form of travel and there were scores of old illiterate rustics left to their own devices to fill in forms and find the right queues, and since we had hours to literally kill flies, I took a walk to a makeshift office and made an official complaint cum recommendation that citizens ought to be treated a little more humanely. This gentleman, obviously both warmed and amused by my self-righteousness, instantly urged the presiding officer to allow us to pass, with the text. I am guessing he didn't figure me for a troublemaker, or maybe he did.

Either way he had got the point. And I hope you will, too. I have no allegiance with a teenager made permanently blind from birdshot in Baramullah any more than I have with the ordinary office worker who gets blown up by a bunch of rabid jihadists while commuting in a packed train in Bombay (again, who the hell calls it Mumbai?). Likewise, I don't care for an illiterate father left humiliated in front of his son as he awaits help to fill up an immigration form on a border crossing with any less intensity than for a half-widow in Anantnag, who must go on living in limbo, unsure if her husband would come back dead or alive, if ever.

They are all a blot on our collective humanity.

I often think about that tall Sardarji in his military uniform at the Attari border who seemed to express sincere distress at the thought of a counter narrative filtering around India. I respected his loyalty, even his earnest opinion that by concealing dissonant ideas one could make a country safer, less fractured, even more unified.

As if.

At some point, surely, we all have to stop pretending and take a look into the mirror.

CURRY-STAINED STUD-MUFFINS

Extra! Extra! Screwing Indians wholesale!

I've had it with Indian businesses. Really, I've had it.

Sure, half of them are my cousins and all that, but even shared bloodlines and Sunday *akhni* doesn't make shitty service and bigoted operations acceptable. We all talk about how big ol' Telkom, Eskom, SAA or the SABC rip us off, but no one writes about 'Indian business' and their built-in penchant to make you chew your lip, grind your teeth and wish you had bought that Kalashnikov.

You would think that after a century or so of profiteering, conning and banging the maid, South African Indians would have stopped acting like malnourished cane workers and learnt to be professional businesspeople. But they haven't. Not most of them, at least.

Indian businesses succeed through this strategy: get a bunch of underpaid lackeys to work like zombie machines, then get a bunch of muppet managers who can do nothing but follow orders to supervise them, and ensure they don't walk off with pizza crusts in their underpants. In fact, it would seem that Indian business owners specifically employ moronic sub-creatures as part of a grand conspiracy to institutionalize customer apathy.

'I have incredibly slow and incompetent workers. What should I do?' moans the classic Indian employer.

'Erm, well, you could pay them more? Create incentives? Provide training courses?' replies the voice in his head.

'Don't be ridiculous! Those things are for white *owes*.'

Fact is, it really is difficult to debunk all those stereotypes about Indian businesses and their inglorious treatment of employees (as hard as you may try). If it isn't the perpetually delayed payment of paltry salaries to staff, it's the lunch time, overtime and any-other-time without extra pay that holds true. If it isn't poorly trained workers, it's the verbal abuse those poorly trained workers regularly suffer, in conditions that seldom live up to vaguely respectable health-and-safety standards.

Little wonder then that Indian businesses tend to attract the array of technically challenged mutants that the skilled-labour evolution overlooked and now no self-respecting businessman would hire. You know those desperate-looking cashiers and packers with sad eyes, faded uniforms and overgrown ears that you might have found in the dingiest of supermarket chains in the poorest suburb in the country? Indian businesses thrive on these deformed creatures, their employment virtually an act of charity. Makes it easier to pay them next to nothing, you see – or less than that.

And if feeling sorry for blue-collar workers isn't really your thing, don't worry: even highly skilled professionals are treated with a disdain not seen since the last time Stalin met the Gypsies. Accountants would rather join the circus, optometrists would rather become sailors and administrators would rather milk their mother-in-law's pet monkey than work for a fellow Indian. (True story that last bit. Saw it in the *Post*.)

Naturally, then, quality service just doesn't exist. It's common talk in the circles of the general brown populace that when Indians run a place, skimping becomes part of the standard business practice, regardless of the obvious benefits of providing certain services or even possible franchise requirements. And in the event of whatever services you do receive deviating somewhat from an agreed-upon deal or advertised promise, or even if it's downright appalling, you can be sure the useless manager you encounter will be 'unauthorized' to deal with your subsequent complaint. I have too much personal experience to write this one off as a mere urban myth . . . Unsurprisingly though, being Indian, there is always a spice to vindicate that quease-inducing pizza.

'It was just the new lemon tikka flavouring on the chicken, sir.'

'What? You expect me to believe that? *Jou ma se-*' And suddenly Indians speak really good Afrikans . . .

On the other hand, I've heard people say that if you play dead when you receive poor service from an Indian business you might just score a longer, more rewarding life. Apparently, your willingness to be rolled over and have your pubic hairs stretched until your balls turn a royal monkey blue, will bring you virgins, wine and the good life in the hereafter.

But not everyone buys the virgins-in-heaven story – not even the Muslims.

The root of the problem is that so many South African Indian businesses continue to provide pathetic services simply because they can get away with it. It is often poor Indian and black consumers, the quintessential voiceless, who patronize Indian businesses and whose concerns aren't likely to be taken seriously. As for the new-age urban middle-class Indian clientele, they are invariably related to virtually every business by some remote family connection, and by nature they are unlikely to stand up to anything, save perhaps for a fleeting moment in the bedroom with the missus. Perhaps.

Of course, some of my older cousins had the mighty balls to face apartheid and risk being sent on a long vacation (which some historians refer to as being 'in exile') or, worse yet, be killed. However, now that apartheid is over and there is money to be made, even Indian community newspapers that stood tall on their former anti-apartheid glory unashamedly ignore the crass exploitation, racism and new bigotry as they turn the other cheque.

I sometimes forget that Indian community papers are also Indian businesses; I suppose it is incumbent on them to become bastards themselves, and their community-newspaper business model wouldn't allow any news that could sabotage that potentially profitable advert from the nearby butchery. This is why it is particularly amusing to hear South African Indians complain about being the soya in the grand South African club sandwich. 'We were second-class citizens under apartheid, and now with this damn affirmative action we are still second-class citizens.'

You have to wonder what they were told when they left India. 'By order of her Majesty the Queen, you may play maharajah with the natives . . .'

No?

Affirmative action might be flawed – then again so is powdered milk. Indians might have good reason to feel bummed from both ends – but too little is made of their role in the unhappy orgy. It is often the case that Muslims and Hindus will complain about a lack of cultural sensitivity in their majority black–white workplaces, with regards to cultural festivals, religious goings-on and other minority shenanigans. Yet quite frequently, it is the unregulated, non-unionized Muslim- or Hindu-owned workplaces that are even more unholy and uncompromising than the multicultural settings.

It is a strange cacophony: business acumen might run through their genetic make-up, but Indians are reluctant to believe that a successful business is anything more than the act of making as much money as possible. Keeping your employees smiling with a decent pay cheque, a lunch break and a clean toilet is really not on the memo. If you want work satisfaction, upward mobility and a decent salary, go work for a white company – this, unfortunately, is brazen common knowledge among the brown.

But it's not all that bad. If you know someone who has a cousin who once worked with his brother's neighbour's mother's stepdaughter, you could even score a discount on that unmarked item . . . In all seriousness, though, Indians are incredibly charitable. Some percentage of their profits will almost always end up sourcing a blanket for the homeless or a brick for an orphanage. Come earthquakes in Haiti, Chile or Istanbul or a tsunami in Sumatra, Indians will pull out the cash from under the mattress and donate as if their own *nanima* were there. Like that, Indians can be very generous; ultimately they are just a bunch of selectively emotional sods, willing to make a plan, bend the rules or burn you that DVD.

Unfortunately, this attitude still doesn't cut it; perhaps guilt for being imperious dickheads at work is the reason they are so charitable. Then again, Indians are strange. While most white kids dream of becoming the next A.B. de Villiers or Dale Steyn, Indian kids look up from their PlayStations and talk about opening a supermarket, just like the *ballie*. That's fine; I can totally understand why opening a supermarket would be so attractive for a nine-year-old. The problem is they really go on to open it (or audit it, at least), without ever learning to piss straight.

Not too long ago I spent time on the dark side: I worked the aisles of an Indian wholesale and I experienced the Machiavellian egos of the contemptuous *larnie* who ran the place as I packed the trolleys of other big retailer dicks. You *really* don't want to go there. Fact is, it doesn't matter how incredibly big, respectable and important some Indian businesses have become, their indentured past is really just a curry stain away.

And again, it doesn't matter if the owners are wealthy enough to be sitting on the Isle of Capri drinking tea in a silk zardosi sari, or important enough to be playing golf with Robert Mugabe, customers are treated like imbeciles with masochistic tendencies if they bother driving all the way back to the shop to return a faulty product. No matter how sophisticated they may be in their private lives, for an Indian businessman, a return is about as welcome as a black daughter-in-law.

It wasn't always like this – well, that's what the older folk say, at least. The Indians who graduated from cutting cane to becoming farmers, and the traders and their assistants who arrived here later as businesspeople, are said to have operated in a more dignified manner. Incredibly, some Indians made it really big by being honest businesspeople, as they chipped away at the sensible and not-so-sensible needs of rural and urban consumers. Business was apparently about craftsmen selling a trade, an art or an expertise, using soft, cordial dialogue that created the strong foundation the community now proudly sits on. Moreover, the strong religious and work ethic rooted in family values, entrepreneurship and determination allowed these early Indian businessmen to prioritize education, cement community values and secure seventeen-inch rims in severely hostile terrain.

This, they say, *is* the house that Jack (Devnarain) built. Touching story that. But you would think there would at least be clean toilets for the staff by now.

POSTSCRIPT

I was surprised by the heated response to the original version of this article. Having built up something of a reputation for treating all sorts with an often-snide disregard, I figured the piece would have been received in the few-sacred-cows spirit of the blog. Instead, the Accidental Academic quickly erupted into a war zone, with readers questioning my integrity, accusing me of bigotry and comparing my writing to playwright Mbongeni Ngema's infamous song '*AmaNdiya*' about how black South Africans have been discriminated against by Indian South Africans.

My approach to this issue was simple. Cut through the fat, spill some gut and make people queasy where necessary so they take genuine notice of the problem at hand. This is a topic that everyone knows about, but one that is seldom discussed or even mentioned in the mainstream. Moralizing reflectively over the issue would have served no purpose. If the Bhagavad Gita, the Bible and the Qur'an make it eminently clear that any sort of injustice and exploitation is intolerable, what chance would I have by politely reminding my cousins of their obligations (which they've been ignoring for as long as I can remember)? This topic needed to be gripped and shaken wildly – like an empty pump during an asthma attack.

Alas, many of my educated Indian readers turned defensive, and if Azad Essa had an embassy in their area, they would have burnt it to the ground. I might as well have drawn the Prophet. Even my white liberal friends accused me of inciting hatred, while a couple of black readers added some affirmative-action rhetoric about it being unfair discrimination.

So here, for the record, is my position on writing a piece such as this. Our knee-jerk overreaction to politically incorrect humour or analysis – except, perhaps, when it has to do with easy-to-target black politicians – is not only unhealthy, it is self-defeating. I think we have reached a stage in our history – now, some twenty years after Mandela was freed – when our default settings ought to change from taking immediate offence at politically incorrect conclusions or discussions, especially from a participant observer, to considering at face value the ugly truth he is seeking to expose.

Important things need to be said, even when – *especially* when – they're hard truths. In this case, of course, not *all* Indian businesses are hideously evil operators out to dupe employees and customers alike. But you already knew that.

I never knew Fatima Meer

The iconic anti-apartheid activist, writer, teacher and mother, Fatima Meer, left this world on 12 March 2010, having suffered a stroke two weeks earlier. With the passing of Dennis Brutus, the resilient anti-apartheid and anti-war activist, poet and troublemaker, in December 2009, South Africa lost two remarkable human beings in quick succession. Both refused to get aboard the gravy train that emerged from a shifty new South Africa, remaining true to their principles: unyielding, stubborn and brilliant.

I started writing the original version of this piece three days after Meer's death.

A number of activists, writers, politicians, morons and other opportunists will be writing long-drawn tributes to Fatima Meer in the coming weeks. Some of the personalized tributes will be less bearable than others: 'I met Fatima at the mall', 'She bought *dhania-jeera* from my aunt once', 'I tried to assassinate her but I was just doing my job' – and the like. Unfortunately, in many cases, describing her remarkable journey as one of the most incredible stories of the anti-apartheid and anti-poor-people struggle will merely be a side effect of the writer's unashamed desire to take the opportunity to raise his or her own market value as a well-connected, blessed storyteller, a nauseating and wilfuly pathetic attempt at pontification to immortality by association.

And now that I discuss Fatima Meer here, I become one of the losers I have just described. Except, I am not going to tell you how she taught me hopscotch, how she inspired me to care about others or how her memory gives me goosebumps.

Because I never knew Fatima Meer.

I have not read any of Fatima's twenty-five books. I was not even born when she lectured. And I was probably playing cricket when she was patrolling Chatsworth and attempting to help the poor and suffering natives.

Fatima Meer was, to me, like that elusive relative or acquaintance you may know of: the one your father, cousin or drunk neighbour told you about one night when you sat smoking pot on the roof; the one who lived such an incredibly rich life (apparently) but who you never got to know – and, worse, never even visited once.

We all have one of those.

'You know, this man went against his family's wishes,' says your narrator, as he exhales the good stuff. 'He moved to the Transkei in the 1960s, where he built the first school for kids with special needs. He was a medical doctor but education was his thing. You know, he loved people so much that when he was detained for a week in a special holding cell for being a "*kaffir*-lover", he met Madiba in passing and was so inspired he joined the arms struggle working as a doctor for . . .'

And on it goes. 'You should go talk to him one day, he lives just down the road . . . such a fascinating man . . . what he will tell you, you won't find in any history book . . .'

But, of course, you never did grab the opportunity. Just like I never did.

How many times did I drive past Burnwood Road in Durban, the very road that swung alongside the Kennedy Road dump, where Fatima Meer lived in a modest house? And every time as I drove by in a characteristic scurry, I would look at the bend that led to her home – and further on to the local Makro – and I would remind myself: 'I have to go see her soon!'

But I never did. And sometimes I actually made it to the Makro.

And now the great woman is gone, her house marked as a possible national heritage site. All the while I sit here, sheepishly writing my half-baked story of gutted regret, when I could have been 'out there' lapping up the lessons she so willingly passed on to those who cared. But I'm quite sure I'm not the only one headed for a reality check.

Today, if you walk into the sociology department at the University of KwaZulu-Natal, you will struggle for clues that would point to a time when an emphatic, important and moving character called Fatima Meer shook the corridors and pummelled her way to becoming the first black female professor at the white university. To those who knew her, Meer was as tough as she was compassionate, and as insistent as she was giving. Crucially, she was able to circumvent rhetoric uniquely by pushing her discipline beyond the lecture halls.

But there is no Honours Board, no library, no Chair of Sociology – no photo frame even – that links the university to this great servant.

Because she was a compassionate and determined pioneering public sociologist who literally connected the theoretical mumbo jumbo of the academic world with the travails of the real world outside, it is incomprehensible (and morally repugnant, actually) that returning sociology students will never know their seat was once warmed by this insistent foot soldier of anti-apartheid activism whose life they probably aren't being taught about. A bizarre mix of internal politics, incompetence and laziness can do that.

It doesn't take long for the maggots to set in, but it took five days before the university's press-relations department mustered up a release telling of her demise. And you can bet there will be a move to name a 'Fatima Meer' something or other, now that she is gone. Perhaps a library, or a book counter or even a departmental toaster.

The question now is this: is it too late to commemorate Fatima Meer's legacy substantially, or will she simply be deified for lesser ends?

POSTSCRIPT

Fatima Meer received a state funeral, which I attended along with hundreds of other mourners. Even Winnie Madikizela-Mandela came to pay homage. (Gosh, that woman has some presence.) It was my first time at a state funeral.

Naturally, I found the soldiers – or the coast guard or whoever – carrying her coffin to be quite patronizing. I was glad that her closest friends later echoed the sentiment that the funeral was hijacked by the African National Congress in a feeble attempt to 'claim' Meer as their own: the type of memorabilia they can store in a museum as a relic from the good old days. 'Look, there's the Freedom Charter, and there's a Madiba shirt and that's Fatima Meer's body . . .'

The irony, of course, is that Meer was anything but an emblem of a successful struggle veteran who paraded in and out of flashy events with her activist credentials tied in a bun. She was just Fatima Meer, fighting against values and not labels. The apartheid struggle wasn't personal; it was simply the right thing to do. Likewise, when the ANC seemed to have lost the plot, she was right in the front, coaxing the new powers to do the right thing. Again, it wasn't personal.

In the end, almost a thousand people came to the Durban Exhibition Centre to pay their last respects before her body was taken to the Grey Street Mosque for her Islamic funeral rites, and then to the Brook Street Cemetery to be one with nature.

I stood and watched until the final grain of sand filled her grave. I said goodbye for those who were absent and whispered one last prayer that God might leave behind some of her bravery, for the rest of us.

The brown woman's burden

Indians around the country are up in arms after a new study revealed that one in three Indian women in South Africa would marry a black man by the year 2018. The study, funded by the Race Still Matters Institute in Orania, argues that the increase in 'Maluti Masalas' will significantly shift the racial plateau of post-apartheid South Africa.

The research project, which sampled a large number of Indian women from Durban, Cape Town and Johannesburg, is the biggest study of professional Indian women ever to take place on the continent. It found that a resounding 42 per cent of the women interviewed said they'd prefer a black man to their current Indian husband, and 23 per cent said they'd had a relationship of sorts with a man of a different race at some point. Crucially, nearly two-thirds of those interviewed conceded that they no longer found Indian men appealing as life partners, while more than a quarter said they could see themselves 'with no one else but a black man in the future'.

Researchers say that the shifting trend has less to do with black men and more to do with the diminishing pool of suitable Indian partners. According to the report, 'Indian men are clingy, insecure and refuse to return the favour'.

The findings seem to have knocked the air out of the Indian community, who claim, as usual, that they are being specifically targeted by a third force. Community leaders are said to be outraged;

the South African Hindu Maha Sabha, the Jamiatul Ulama and the 1860 Foundation released a joint statement in which they accuse the Race Still Matters Institute of being 'purposefully tasked with a mission to sabotage the celebrations of a 150 years of Indians in South Africa'. The statement also accused Dr Fadila Arnold, director of the study, of being a 'bloody agent' and of having 'white tendencies'.

'First they stole our jobs, then they took our suburbs and now they're trying to hijack our women,' read the statement. 'Dr Arnold is just a Cape Malay who is bitter that the Zuma government has arranged such a lavish celebration of our indentured forefathers and not *her* forefathers – whoever they are.'

When asked to respond to these claims, Dr Arnold denied that the study was part of a campaign to detract from the celebrations. 'I am not from the Cape, or even Malay,' she said. Instead, she explained that the results should be seen as a 'positive development' and 'proof of the increasing integration of Indians into South African life'.

Dr Arnold claims that the Institute was first commissioned by a leading women's magazine (owned by a prominent black woman of almost cult-like status) to track the love interests of professional Indian women and their white bosses; but they soon realized that all Indian women really wanted to do was shag their garden boys.

'It is all about the construction of desire, and Didier Drogba is the key culprit here – he has changed the way women see black men,' she said. According to the study, around half the women interviewed said they would score with the Côte d'Ivoire and Chelsea soccer star if put on the spot. 'Drogba represents everything Indian men wish they could be: he is tall and dark and can last the full ninety minutes.'

The study explains the phenomenon by noting that as Indian women have moved their rotis and sweetmeats out of the kitchen and into the South African boardroom, they have invariably found themselves working alongside powerful males from other race groups, black males in particular. This has led to an inevitable shift in their taste in partners. Factor in their own increased influence in terms of decision-making, spending power and seven-inch-high-heeled sex appeal, and it seems they believe that Indian men are just incapable of handling a woman with power.

'Contrary to popular opinion, black men are refined. They don't stare you down like those morons at the Suncoast Casino,' said twenty-seven-year-old Sapna Kalyan, who has dated a black man for the past three years. 'You just have to make sure they've been educated in a private school, and then it's just like going out with white guys. It's not like I'm dating a darkie from the township, you know.'

Tasneem Baker, twenty-four, concurred that black men understand what women want. 'Most of them have had so many partners, they just know how to please you,' she said.

Baker felt that overcoming her racial prejudices was the most difficult part of her change in attitude. 'But the more time you spend with them [black men], the easier it becomes,' she concluded.

Likewise, Kajal Modi, twenty-six, a beautician, said that it didn't take brain surgery to understand why modern Indian women would prefer a *real* man. She believes that Indian men are mommy's boys and, despite their promises, their wives invariably end up trimming their mother-in-laws' toenails.

'It's like the umbilical cord is superglued and stapled to their navel,' Modi teased superciliously.

Some sociologists have argued that this movement bears the markings of a gender revolution that started in the 1960s. They claim that it is a purposeful and possibly even vengeful shift in thinking.

'For generations Indian women have been putting up with their spouses and boyfriends fantasizing about white women,' explains Professor Thomas Pattman from the School of Sociology at the Old White University in Randburg. 'They know their husbands exchange pornography on their computers and ogle every white chick at the office, so they figure their time has come. They no longer want to end up with an impotent Indian boyfriend who's forced to take a suitable Indian girl to mommy after messing around with all the hot and easy coloured chicks in Wentworth or Eldos. The modern Indian woman has dreams and ambitions. And she watches porn!'

The study also captured the imagination of the Native and Racial Studies Institute in Pofadder, where anthropologist Dr Dingane Zwele commented that 'it does feel as if the Indian woman is attempting to erase her indentured past', and that to seek such 'self-cleansing' with a black man is not unheard of because 'black men are really the new whites'.

Dr Zwele believes an Indian girlfriend is every black man's goal. 'Black men know that it's generally harder to get an Indian woman than it is to get a white woman because with Indian girls you get that straight hair *and* the spicy chicken curry,' he explained knowingly. 'It is the perfect marriage of two opportunistic Melville yuppies.'

Dr Zwele believes the fact that Indian fathers are now far happier to give away their daughters to black men may prove to be the singlemost powerful step towards tangible race reconciliation in the country. But Sarona Haripersad-Zondo, a thirty-one-year-old HR manager at a large accounting firm in Johannesburg, disagreed on this point when interviewed at her Rosebank home with husband and actor Siyanda Zondo. Instead, she argued that reducing Indian–black interracial orgies down to a poorly conceived political statement is regrettable.

'It's more complicated than that,' explained Haripersad-Zondo. 'For one, I just can't identify with Indian men. All they are concerned with is status and cars, and they have this impossibly narrow idea of the world. Black men go so much deeper.'

Her husband grinned widely at this point in the interview, and then added his perspective. 'It's thrilling to walk into a spice shop with a hot Indian ass on my arm,' he laughed. 'It really fucks them up! You know how these Indian ballies can be.'

Zondo noted, however, that despite the many benefits of being married to this season's black must-have – an Indian girl – adjusting to the intercultural nuances can be quite taxing. For example, he says that his wife expects to be 'taken care of financially' when the natural thing to do would be to split the bills. 'But once you get over that squeaky voice, you can overcome anything,' Zondo smiled, squeezing his wife's small frame.

Another couple, Tandai and Nasreen Mulasikwanda, of Umbilo, Durban, both in their late twenties, explained that in their case religion and not race was the biggest obstacle to overcome. Mulasikwanda says that he was pleasantly surprised to find Indian Muslims so open-minded about skin colour. 'But they often ask if I am the *muezzin* from Zanzibar,' complained Tandai (also known as Bilal).

Psychologist Dr Frantz Burger believes that experts are, in fact, missing the most fascinating aspect of this study: that the research has shed new light on the behavioural patterns of Indian women after decades of focus on the brown man's burden.

'We all know the allure of white women and the inability of brown or Indian men to resist their charms. Indian men feel their status is elevated if they're with a white girl. But this new study turns the issue on its head, so to speak,' he explains with academic enthusiasm.

He says that one needn't look further than the Tiger Woods two-dozen-white-women scandal to get into the psyche of Indian men. 'He is a semi-black man dropping white girls to their knees. Indian men wish they were him, simple as that.'

Dr Burger says that the findings of this study not only put Indian manhood at the edge of a new precipice, they also shifted the value system of the colour-coded pecking order.

'If white males no longer represent the pinnacle of human ambition, could this truly be the end of white cultural supremacy?' speculates Dr Burger.

But Dr Arnold rubbishes such conjecture as merely a pipe dream. 'One needs to consider that until e.tv starts showing tasteful soft porn with a representative black cast, Indian men will continue to lust after white women,' she concludes in her study. 'There will always be enough conservative Indian families in small towns with an assembly of submissive virgins to take home to mommy.'

POSTSCRIPT

The best part of being able to write satire – particularly bludgeoning satire like this – is having the opportunity to raise potentially unthinkable thoughts without quite saying enough to name the shame. Of course, this piece is laced with stereotypes: generalizations that we South Africans survive on every day in our private lives. Some are playful, some are racist; some dictate our behaviour and actions, as well as the friendships we make or lose.

'Race', 'ethnicity' and 'culture' are as fluid as they might be farcical, and they mean more to some than to others. Either way, if the glove fits . . .

This testy work of defiance is a previously unpublished piece, but I suspect that if it had appeared on my blog it would have incurred the wrath of the various self-satiating human-rights well-wishers out there who would have spammed me with a mindless barrage of misinformed hate. Suffice it to say, there would have been name-calling along with the defensive trite that night-time keyboards seem to muster up with disturbing regularity these days. There would also probably be the lone ranger skirting the outposts of wonderland, wanting to know more information about this fascinating study. (I always laugh when someone writes in to complain that one of my studies doesn't exist.) And there would be others besides. Satire can do all the things you can't do with a regular article – quite like a mistress.

So let's get by the muck, shall we?

The truth is, this piece is about Indian men as much as it might be about Indian women. And Indian men are – *generally* – a funny bunch. They'll date girls but frown when their sisters get a boyfriend. They'll fantasize about white girls (and even pay for sex with them) but be sure to marry pristine virgin Indian barbie dolls (and then ensure they get rid of any guy friends they may have had). They'll playfully tease the secretary at work for her sexy leggings and then suggest to their spouses they should work from home.

In short, most Indian men are a bunch of stunted hypocrites who think women need to be shaded from harsh truths, politics and swearwords (unless they're giving the lessons). They don't want to be intimidated by their women, let alone challenged by an alpha female of a wife; rather, they want the docile option who understands her place and can be moulded into shape when necessary. So when your average Indian man – whether Christian, Hindu or Muslim – meets an independent spirit looking for a partner and not a quasi-father, they dub her 'too modern' or 'not homely enough'. In other words, 'she'll be difficult to use as a doormat'.

Hence we have the situation where thousands of modern professional Indian women long for their Indian Prince Charming to ride in on a progressive steed and not on a mule called 'cultural baggage'. But such princes are not to be found (except in minor metro-*kraals* perhaps, but then they're usually gay) – so 'our' Indian ladies are increasingly turning to white men for friendship, and even love.

From what I hear, white men are supposedly less superficial, more likely to take you to the theatre or engage you in stimulating conversation, and have less expectations of you in the kitchen. Sure, they might not come with the 'chivalrous' (or is that 'debilitating'?) notion that you are their economic responsibility like Indian men do, but you're getting a man and not a sponge who still lives off his parents at the age of thirty. It is also a fact that, despite knowing that most white men don't wash their hands after visiting the loo, professional Indian women find them more open-minded and amenable to the ambitions of a modern woman with career goals. And another fact: Muslim women find befriending white men easier than Indian Muslim men because 'white guys understand you can be just friends with girls', whereas Muslim men never seem to be able to get over their madrasah brainwashing, which insists boys and girls cannot mix without some kind of underlying sexual intent. (It's possible this holds true for all species of humans, but *no one* in the Indian kingdom believes men and women can just hang out without sucking face.)

These issues aside, the iron truth is that, while professional Indian women profess to be open-minded and voice their disdain for Indian men as they battle to find a like-minded partner without any hang-ups, they will rarely date or marry black men. Of course, this will probably change over time, but for now their open minds and free spirits start and end with white men. Even a dark Indian boy is usually a problem.

In return, the Indian male fascination with white women can be considered largely puerile. As an Indian boy, you're 'permitted' to sleep with a white girl (obviously) and date her (if you're lucky), but marrying her is usually out of the question. She is just your subconscious attempt to claim back your dignity, live out the porn flick you downloaded last week and preen your social CV. Because only the choicest Indian girl selected by mommy dearest will do.

And black women? Ag, dare not tell anyone they feature in your wet dreams.

Indian Muslims and their black Bilals

I

As a child, I used to attend compulsory Islamic-instruction classes in the basement of the neighbourhood mosque every afternoon after school. I always wished I didn't have to go. Madrasah, as it's known, was boring and pointless, and it took me away from playing street cricket – the sort of thing school-going kids ought to be doing. My teacher, the *ustadh*, was a scrawny small-town man with an inferiority complex and an unhealthy affinity for doling out a hiding. Madrasah, to me, was a form of conscription: compulsory service for all kids needing discipline. Often, I returned home only to watch the sun descend over the Palmiet Nature Reserve, leaving me with just supper and homework (that destroyer of kids' dreams) to finish the day.

Learning to read the Qur'an effectively meant learning to read the Arabic alphabet and then transferring that knowledge to the classical Arabic of the Qur'an without the aid of translation. We then progressed to memorizing these verses, again without even an explanation of what we were memorizing. As a result, the best students at madrasah were the most accomplished parrots, and it seemed to my ten-year-old brain that God loved hearing us say things we didn't understand. But the parrots revelled in the opportunity, reciting verses in a cacophony of tongue-twisting vowels, complex emphases, deliberate breaths and impeccable pronunciation – each textured to send you into spiritual orbit. They would deliberately hypnotize our senses, each layer of verse engaging us with a melody that bid you to the Divine. It helped that some of these students also went for the morning Hifz–Qur'an memorization classes, where they conspired with the ustadh to perfect their recitation. The age-old tradition of memorizing the Qur'an is an astonishing one, continuing an incredible discipline that started centuries back: a demonstration of human potential that ensured that through human memory alone God's word could never be forgotten. Yes, these guys were *that* good. Unfortunately, this was all they were good for.

For me, being Muslim had little to do with being a pet parrot in a cage. I was a kid and I wanted to play, take rides on magic carpets, listen to stories and fables. While so many of my classmates memorized everything and knew nothing, I just knew nothing. They were at least eloquent idiots.

My father, in a bid to gain my sister and me a reprieve from our weekday ordeals, would contrive to have an occasional fender-bender. He didn't particularly like the brainless curriculum at madrasah either, and he was still scarred by the sessions of his own childhood. My mother, conversely, was determined that someone should instill in me some Islamic decorum, including how to pray, what to think and how to wash my arse. I love my mother, so I went. Besides, knowing how to wash your arse in the desert is a nifty skill to have.

I thank God I was eventually allowed to leave madrasah when I was twelve. My father decided the corporal punishment meted out to me every damn day by the ustadh was no longer acceptable. 'He's been there for years now and he still can't piss straight. What more could they possibly teach him?' he rightly philosophized.

I've never admitted as much to Dad, but I was a real little bastard at madrasah. I likely deserved every lashing dished out to me. While I was a sweet and obedient white-arse licker at my ex-Model C primary school, calling out to Mrs Southgate in my whiny–needy voice, I became the broody demon from beyond at religious classes, refusing to answer anything properly. I was the kid coming from the fancy education, wearing a khaki uniform and long Boer socks, who thought he was better than the rest. Well, perhaps it wasn't that exactly, but so it seemed. Madrasah, you see, allowed me to drop the façade. This was the early 1990s; I had to impress my white teachers at school to make sure they didn't think this whole multi-racial experiment was a mistake. Back then, the onus was on every single Indian and black kid to convince white people that we were in fact a civilized lot – sort of how the onus now is on every Muslim prat to prove to the world that we're not all bearded zombies with a penchant for flying planes into skyscrapers. There was no need for such pretence at madrasah. I was there to let my socks down and be a brat. The ustadh could judge my upbringing, but not my civilization.

Looking back now, my behaviour was unacceptable. I really should have been a better parrot. In my defence, though, my teachers were obsessed with promoting rituals ahead of spirit and traditions over values. Our madrasah classes were so archaic in their zeal, the ustadh so fixated with pronunciation, that we never even got to learn about hating the Jews or blowing up America or the heresies of communist Russia or whatever else our indoctrination was meant to include . . . My ustadh, despite his good intentions, represented all that troubled me about my brethren. Terrified as hell to ask questions, so willing to be manipulated in the name of heaven and far too quick to judge, he took 'literal' to a whole new level. Everything was seemingly reduced to walking into the toilet with your left foot and entering the mosque with your right. Seriously, if there was a revolution going on outside, we wouldn't have had a clue.

There *was* actually a revolution going on outside. The white government had nobly admitted that non-white people were human after all. Black people sat next to me on the same bench. We spoke. We copied each other's homework. And they didn't even steal anything.

For those of us who attended multi-racial schools, classroom education was fused with a changing culture. You could feel the nuances, the pretensions, the paranoia of racism or its opposite number, overcompensation. I remember coming home one day and revealing with glee the news that a black kid had been appointed class monitor. My young scepticism for the rainbow-nation drivel being meted out at school – all the pretty colours sitting in a row – was especially hard to shed because of the sanitized Indian world I returned to each day – a world that spoke of 'maids', 'dirty shack-dwellers', 'thieving garden boys' and 'Malawian beggars'.

II

Every Friday the local Sparks Road Mosque courtyard, like so many mosques across urban South Africa, is swathed in black women dressed in black abayas, hands outstretched and faces suitably sombre as they implore the Friday faithful for a bob or two. They form two perfectly straight rows, effectively ensnaring anybody who dares venture between them. For a couple of minutes every Friday, ordinary men are rid of their suburban existence as they become glorified jihadists, fighting off the furious advances of a throng of needy women. A chorus of '*Salam alaikum,* Allah will reward you, bhai' resonates through the noon air, annoyingly interrupting the anticipation of a handsome lunch. As our jihadist fights his way into the mosque, trying his best not to be guilted into reaching for his wallet, a woman with a sickly baby catches his eye. 'Zakah, Sadaqah, Lillah – anything, bhai?' she implores, invoking the charitable tenets of Islam. He flings a couple of rands in her general direction and is safe.

I've found the bent-boned look these women sport strangely incongruous. They look far too young to be suffering osteoporosis, so I offer them a sheepish smile in return for their earnest advances. Besides, I'm told a smile from one Muslim to another is a kind of charity anyway.

This tradition of hanging around the mosque on Fridays, dressed like a Muslim, is beguiling. Of course, some of these dear souls are 'real Muslims', convinced that while Zuma may be the new Messiah, Islam really is the path to salvation, with or without a charitable donation.

It's on Eid al-Adha, the more depressing of the two Eids, that the queue of black 'Muslims' outside most mosques reaches a crescendo. This particular holiday is cœlebrated with the mass slaughter of goats, sheep and bulls, as Prophet Abraham's obedience to God for offering his son as sacrifice is commemorated. It's a legendary story about submitting to the Divine, with God famously showing his mercy by offering Abraham a heavenly lamb to slaughter instead of his son. Little did Abraham know his selflessness would draw thousands of new, pretend and part-time converts to mosques everywhere to collect whatever free meats its patrons deigned to distribute to them. It's quite a sight, made even more curious by the large platoon of Indian men, armed with batons, battling to contain the crowd baying for their meat. It is irreconcilable in its absurdities, suggesting both beauty and farce in what is essentially organized religion.

Anyone can join the queue, of course. No one asks you to read the Kalimah before you're proffered a bloodied liver or heart, but most guess it would be safer to at least dress the part. You wouldn't want to go there and rough it out in a queue for two hours only to be told to wear a scarf and try again next year. In that respect, it's a lot like an *American Idol*-type show, except Simon Cowell doesn't wield a baton.

Black people aren't the only ones converting to Islam for the sake of a free meal or a couple of silver coins. Just the other day I saw a white woman kitted out in an abaya and scarf begging outside the Sparks Road Mosque. There are generally a fair sprinkling of Indian people in these queues as well; after all, not every Indian is a rich Gujarati-descended businessman living in Morningside. But it's the deep-seated culture of dependence that the richer Indians have fostered with black converts that is one of the curiosities of Muslim life in South Africa.

Indian Muslims in South Africa often believe they are doing the religion a favour by approaching poor black folk in rural areas and 'educating' them about *Deen* (roughly: the righteous path that Muslims must tread), reminding them about the last day and then closing the deal with some charity.

Only an imbecile could think that a religion that seeks to promote itself based on its ability to provide a welfare net could ever make any sense. Likewise, so many in the community seem to believe that the compulsory 2.5 per cent reduction of their assets (*Zakah*), coupled with a vociferous call to Islam, is the be-all and end-all of what God has asked. The only thing dirtier than the idea that Zakah compensates for otherwise dodgy behaviour is the widespread tendency to make the newly brainwashed black kids sing Islamic songs for middle-class Indian Muslims. 'Look, we saved these poor bastards, and now we will go to heaven' seems to be the motivation.

There is nothing wrong with advancing ideals that encourage cleanliness, honesty, family values, accountability and love for one's neighbour. But too often this Muslim-flavoured redemption comes at the cost of personal heritage. It doesn't seem to matter that the latest singer was a Zulu boy from a rural village with his own ancestors to consider, traditions to follow and multiple funerals to attend. If he wants to make it in this world and be rewarded with virgins in the next, he clearly needs to be coached in an Indian–Islamic ethos . . . For their part, the 'converts' realize they need to disguise their other life, act the part, wear a mosque hat, mutter some Urdu and perhaps change their names to Bilal. Maybe then the Indians will come teach them maths.

Here's the irony, though: even after they've turned their black countrymen into their own image, the local Indian Muslim community still battles to approach black Muslims as equals. This is, of course, not something the community is willing to admit, and understandably so, but it does reek of a rather disturbing hypocrisy that decries Western cultural hegemony in the mosques but assumes itself superior to the black masses.

This is Africa reeling under the missionary position all over again.

III

The Grey Street Mosque in Dr Yusuf Dadoo Street in Durban is a magnificent sight. Originally built in 1904, and then rebuilt and redesigned by a pair of heathens in the '20s and '40s, the mosque is a powerful emblem of a bygone time. The sandstone façade of a fearless Islamic design is tightly wrapped in the one-time British imperialism that characterizes the Victorian-era feel of Durban's CBD, and the mosque stands like a citadel overshadowing the banalities of daily life, crime and informal trader squabbles in the street below.

People still talk about the mosque as the largest in the southern hemisphere. They obviously don't get out much. But the mosque remains deceptively spacious, with chandeliers dangling luxuriously from the ceiling, plush red carpets stretching invitingly underfoot and fish circling the ablution area for the faithful. If God loved money, he would live here.

As one of the country's most celebrated mosques, it ably encapsulates the eccentricity of the city's vast array of cultural deposits and its many faces and smells, while beautifully reflecting the vibrancy that makes Durban a remarkable African city. But beneath its vaunted surface the mosque sticks out as yet another racist dinosaur.

As a mark of petty discrimination, self-importance and overwhelming stupidity, the trust deed of the Grey Street Mosque was an exemplary creation. When it was developed nearly a hundred years ago, the deed stipulated exactly who wielded the mosque chequebook. Five Memons, two Surtis, one Konkani and one Urdu-speaker, or 'colonial Muslim' as he is referred to, were the only ones accorded the lofty status of mosque trustees – and in that order.

The story goes that the Memons and Surtis were traditionally Gujarati merchants or traders. While speaking different languages, they both came to South Africa as passenger Indians, and they both came with the idiotic idea that their lighter skin and so-called passenger seat on a rat-ravaged ship gave them the right to treat the often darker, recently converted, former indentured labourers as second-class humans. They both dominated the original mosque committee because they were on the top of the food chain. Thus the sub-humans became known as the 'colonial Muslims' or Urdu-speakers, while the Konkani, in spite of being some derivative of an Indo-Arab lineage and perhaps even lighter-skinned than both their Memon and Surti counterparts, was too small a community in Durban to contest their sole seat in the committee.

At some stage in the city's history, Indians were running the CBD, with Grey Street forming the business and cultural hub of the *casbah*. The specific ethnic make-up of the mosque committee was deemed to reflect those closest to God; this was *their* mosque complex because they had paid for it.

The demographics of the city centre have changed dramatically since the early twentieth century. But, as far as my research can ascertain, the deed hasn't. There's been a huge influx of East and West Africans to the CBD, and a good measure of drug trafficking with a side order of Pakistani chicken – but the mosque remains an Indian–Muslim community project, a living anachronism of a historical inequality.

This is 2012, damn it!

Black Muslims may be welcome in the mosques, welcome to pray shoulder to shoulder with their Indian brothers as they collectively kneel before God in a show of equality, but they are still considered *lesser* equals. They still cannot be trusted with the responsibility of running the financial and cultural affairs of the mosque.

To me, this particular aspect of the Grey Street Mosque represents everything that is wrong with Indian Muslims and their 'black Bilals'. Yes, the committee sends cash to the disadvantaged mosques in Chatsworth or at the Bluff or in random rural areas, and this charity is obviously laudable, but they don't encourage autonomy, just institutionalized subservience. There is no purposeful attempt to empower; it is simply a mechanism designed to maintain control.

Even back at madrasah as a kid, I often wondered if it was apt or ironic that the muezzin, the man who gives the call to prayer, was almost always a black guy, just like I had read in my Islamic history books. Our ustadh would give us our new lesson about a verse we didn't understand, lash us a couple times for mucking about and then advise us to pray with him leading the procession as a quasi-Arab. Dressed in the traditionally flowing white Arab thobe like most other Indian indentured *maulanas*, he was happy to give 'black Bilal' the privilege of performing the call, while he got to act out the Indian fetish of being an Arab and leading the prayer.

For those not well versed in Islamic history, one of Prophet Mohammed's closest companions, Abu Bakr, paid for the freedom of a black slave named Bilal who had pledged his life to Islam. As the story goes, Bilal had a strong voice so he was subsequently given the honour of making the *adhaan*, or call to prayer, ('that song', as my white friend used to call it, before I shot him), which sounds five times a day at the mosque. Bilal went on to become a very important figure in Islam, standing tall as an iconic companion of the Prophet. Islam uses this example often to pronounce the faith's disdain for racial profiling: even a former slave could stand on mosque walls and make that call, as well as lead the faithful in prayer. At the time it was revolutionary, but my Indian uncles, with their subjectively biased understanding and overly literal interpretation of the faith, think it's sweet to perpetuate history with a black muezzin.

As kids we were often tasked by the ustadh to call the *bhangi-saab*, Durban-Indian parlance for the muezzin, from the back alleys of the mosque to perform the ritualistic call to prayer. We would race down the cemented stairs, skip a few and land on a platform that housed a washing line, our faces skimming the dripping clothes as we zigzagged our way through to the muezzin's front door.

After years of shouting 'Bhangi-saab! Bhangi-saab!' as I searched for him as a kid at madrasah, I discovered that the phrase literally translates to toilet cleaner in Urdu. You see, when no one was watching he could double up and clean the loos too.

IV

There may be more black men leading the prayers today than there were twenty years ago, but the discrimination remains tangible.

Very rarely are black Muslims taken as seriously as Indian Muslims, either as human beings or as Muslims. As a former heathen and now a trustworthy Muslim guy, the black Muslim may have better access to a loan or a stable job because he is unlikely 'to gamble it all away' or 'turn up drunk', but alas, he will remain Junaid the garden boy or Bilal the muezzin for the rest of his life. Indians know that based on *their* version of the *dawah* system (the invitation to join Islam) many converted black people are dependent and reliant on Indian Muslims as benefactors – we *know* we've bribed them. And this is his job now. He may be a black Muslim, higher than that ordinary hobo on Broad Street, but he is still just another darkie with a Muslim name.

An entire system has been created that effectively excludes the little black Muslim from the important decision-making, from the right to consider himself a religious and human equal. And so he has become the Indian try-hard, the pseudo-Indian.

The sad fact is that black Muslims are well versed in the part they must play. They appeal to the charity element of Muslim life, and the game goes on and on. Indian Muslims treat black Bilals and Alis and Fatimas as a people who always *need* something. The fact that Indians still have their maids and garden boys, and see black people on television as still starving 'in Africa', and working as waiters, factory workers and cleaners but very rarely in their father's stores as managers, accountants and decision-makers, suggests that it is almost impossible to break this cycle of expected subservience.

Black Muslims are meant to beg – even if they are working for you. 'We are doing them a favour' and 'At least they are Muslim' seems to be the prevailing mentality.

Apartheid might have signed off in 1994 to be replaced by a new democratic country, with new ideals, rules and expectations; schools may be increasingly multicultural and dynamic; ideas of colour may be slowly disappearing as the rainbow merges into a vibrant ribbon without differentiation . . . But too much of the past remains the same.

Shilpa Shetty, Zuma's bastard and the end of my India

I

There was very little South African about me as a kid. There is something to be regretted in that realization, I suppose, but then again I'm glad I wasn't running around with the old South African flag, waving it merrily each time we *didn't* participate in an international sporting event. I was raised instead on a diet of the Bollywood myth and it wasn't too long before I believed that visiting my ancestral village, marrying some uneducated *chhori*, chewing tobacco and dancing on a donkey cart would be my destiny.

My childhood home was always perfumed with the heady wafts of cardamom and cinnamon, but ours was not a home in some backwater Gujarati village. This was Durban, the great South African seaport city in the twilight years of white supremacy. By day the potent rush of chilli powder and onion wafting from our kitchen was sensory caffeine, shocking my senses out of their morning slumber. By night, the golden images of popular fifties' and sixties' Indian cinema – Bollywood – would bounce off the cream walls of our cosy TV room. The high-pitched songs of Asha Bhosle would test the neighbours' tolerance as our home was turned into a bastion of nostalgia, indulging my father's love affair with the place he called home: India.

By the age of eleven, it was the stories of Mughal India and the fables of Akbar, Salim and the beautiful Anarkali (who was allegedly buried alive for being a whore) that enthused my imagination. I might have watched Franco Zeffirelli's iconic *Romeo and Juliet*, but I knew just as much about Laila and Majnu, the legendary Arabian love story that ended, painfully, in his madness.

I sometimes thought that I was an Indian kid living in South Africa by mistake. I guess you can blame my father.

My father brainwashed me with stories about Indian independence, about the creation of what he called a rogue state, Pakistan, about the iconic Jawaharlal Nehru, the esteemed Mahatma Gandhi and the understated Maulana Abul Kalam Azad (to whom I owe my name), who collectively fascinated him no end. I had to watch that overeager idiot Ben Kingsley play Gandhi a hundred times on the VCR . . . It was no wonder, then, that my naïve sense of justice came with a Bollywood song and dance and eventually sprouted a colourful secularism and tolerance for diversity.

While I am not entirely sure of the source of my father's continued obsession with India, I am pretty certain that it was borne of his first extended stay in the country, as a student in Bombay in the 1960s. Or perhaps it had to do with his return to South Africa instead.

Having lived a simple but culturally rewarding life in India, perhaps he could never quite accept being treated like a second-class citizen on his return to apartheid South Africa. Factor in the inevitable sentiment that when 'the blacks' did eventually defeat apartheid and 'take over', South Africa would surely turn into a banana republic and the Indians would eventually be told 'to go back home'.

So I'm guessing it helped if he could imagine alternatives.

It was hardly surprising, then, that I knew more about India than I did about my own country. Sure I used to watch *Pumpkin Patch*, speak Fanagalo and visit cousins on their sugarcane farm in Tugela, but I visited India three times before I had even seen Table Mountain. My first trip was in 1992 when I was ten. Whereas on his first visit, my father had taken a ship to India via Lourenzo Marques (now Maputo), a journey that took three weeks, we could now reach

Bombay by a burly Boeing in no more than a day. But even as more Indian South Africans began visiting India in the 1990s with the advent of cheaper air travel, it wasn't as popular a tourist or business destination as it is today. India was regarded as the dirty shit-hole our ancestors had escaped from. It was full of flies, cow dung and dusty streets. It was thoroughly backward and we should consider ourselves lucky we were *here*.

My paternal grandfather had come to South Africa as a trader's assistant in the 1920s, and was mostly successful in securing a better future for the family, so we could all become overworked businessmen, doctors or teachers. I knew in detail the story of his desperately poor childhood and the million-and-one sacrifices he had made. (Apparently he once tried smuggling gold out of the country by melting it onto the chassis of a car. He was arrested. But what a legend.)

So while the majority of my South African Indian friends thought of India as just a filthy place where people took dumps out of moving trains, where beetle-nut spit turned roads into bloodstained death-traps and where men yanked out their johnsons at the mere sight of foreign flesh, I had a slightly different perspective. For one, my cousins in Gujarat were wealthier than any of my South African friends' families and they showed me an India that I never thought existed. You'd never guess it, of course, because they were humble as pie, and yes, India was still undeniably the dump described. Coming from a country with steering locks and burglar guards and muggings and hijackings, I was even jealous of the freedom my cousins enjoyed, roaming on their motorcycles, carefree, uninterrupted, without curfew or danger. Still, my father always wanted us to see the 'authentic' India, and second-class train travel ensured that we would return with no illusions. Even then, my fascination for the place only escalated, making my cousins and the friends I made along the way laugh at the thought that someone from the outside, who lived in a land of pristine clean air, with gorgeous beaches and surrounded by white women, would ever want to actually 'move back'. They couldn't wait to get the hell out and go to America. Or Amrika. Shake head. Shake head.

I just liked it in India. There was an incommunicable energy that matched my temperamental frequency – a dirty façade that begged the persevering among us to dig a little deeper. The *real* India was an old woman, dressed in a simple khadi sari, lines drawn on her face, fingers and feet, and scarred by centuries of defending, protecting her offspring from marauding invaders. India was really a loving granny.

Whenever I returned home to Durban, I'd tell my friends about how awesome India was, would scrawl the names of my favourite Indian cricketers on my SpaceCase and paste photos of Aishwarya Rai inside my cupboard doors, claiming her to be the most beautiful woman the world over. I was proud that she was Indian, with her fair skin, long legs, green eyes and lavishly high cheekbones, yet at the same time managing to maintain the soft Indian feminine features and coy demeanour that made her seem deliciously traditional. She was my Sita, the standard-setter for all Indian womanly virtues, competing with white women from Europe and trumping them. This was something new . . .

II

In 2004, as part of the requirements of my masters' programme, I got the opportunity my father had been dreaming of all my life: to study for a semester in India. It had been five years since my previous visit.

The Jawaharlal Nehru University (JNU) in southern Delhi exists in a time warp. It's really a game park featuring all sorts of bizarre creatures not seen since the Marx brothers' movies. The campus is overrun by cows, peacocks, dogs and kurta-communists still waiting for the Soviets to fund their Hare Krishna Bolshevik revolution. A cow smooching a dead tree outside the sociology department or a lonely dog howling at the moon near the international relations school were all in a day's studies.

Since the campus catered mostly to graduate studies, it was an unusually mature environment, filled with thousands of really serious folk looking to join the civil services. Every night the peasant intellectuals, alumni of the university, journalists and philosophers would descend upon the Ganga Dhaba, JNU's open cafeteria which serves as Delhi's Faraway Tree, a haven of secret prose, hosting a trunk of clandestine intelligentsia hoping to become future politicians, writers and fascinating alcoholics. Students converged on the tree stumps and cement blocks, sitting around a makeshift fire in winter, sipping chai or Nescafé and laying into bread omelettes and aloo paranthas as they articulated their customary disdain for the ongoing perestroika of Indian economic policies or American foreign policy or, most likely, the local slapper sitting a couple of stumps across.

The dynamics on campus were dizzyingly weird. India's affirmative-action or reservation policy, which attempts to redress the effects of the caste system and gender disparity at universities and workplaces, generally favours students from previously disadvantaged backgrounds. This meant I was surrounded by rural, conservative men and, of course, plenty of women. The resulting campus demographics were a general mismatch of farmers' sons in lungis and middle-class women rolling about in fashionable jeans and daddy's cars. It was old patriarchal India colliding head on with a new, independent, tighter-assed India. And it showed. As educated as some of these men might have been, they were really a bunch of clean-shaven rustics trying to rear feminist cattle.

Just outside the campus, the emphatic new India roared, with shining shopping malls, modern cineplexes and Nike showrooms standing tall among the muck, grime and malnourished stray dogs in an eclectic assortment of a new global ambition. In the open Priya mall down the road from the university, random sacred cows (the real kind) doddled past McDonald's (beef burgers banned), stood idly outside the fabulous United Colours of Benetton showroom and dropped dumps outside the Barista café, where yuppies drank imported Lavazza coffee. A few blocks away, penniless street children ate scraps under Sony flat screen billboards. It was as if distinct shades of wealthy and poor sat on top of each other in an upside-down latte, with little bits of cow dung sprinkled on top. The normality of this visually abhorrent inequality was institutionalized: the rich had no qualms or fear in broadcasting their wealth, while the poor were Gandhian stoics in a culture of shared acceptance. The societal structure was firmly entrenched; India is a billion people, after all, and a holy mythology of subservience keeps the poor at bay. (No such luck in South Africa, of course, where inequalities are raged against by means fair and foul.) The difference now, compared to my previous visits, was the rising amount of in-your-face wealth on display; India's economic success was begging to show itself, and it wasn't pretty.

Friends from class – mostly charming pot-smoking white Europeans of the female variety – would peruse Delhi's enigmatic nightlife, unintentionally luring the prowling eyes of rich Indian men, the new invincible elite. These were the confident offspring of a generation of successful industrialists or important government officials, and they were responsible for shedding India's coy culture for shameless affluence. In other words, they were nouveau riche douche bags, with massive egos, dripping dollars, fancy fast cars and eternal blonde-fucking ambitions. I visited a high-end bar once and had to play boyfriend to a couple of classmates to keep the unrelenting Indian erections at bay. I didn't go back.

At university, discussions often revolved around tradition versus modernization, the iconic Indian debate that still professed an earnest fascination with India's battle to manage its soul during its tryst with modernity. To me, though, the clear penchant to slide ugly truths beneath shiny new skyscrapers and shopping malls with pristine tiles was a rejection of the idea of India I had gained as a youngster – its sense of development, society and space. This was no struggle between modernity and tradition; it was rather a case of tradition being tradition because of a lack of opportunity (like your average forty-year-old virgin). Those with the means were cashing in on the economic boom and embracing the brave new world without a second thought. But India was not designing or carefully regulating her entry into the unfettered global economy; she had dived right in, holy cow and all.

I couldn't help but feel that the country, paraded for centuries as the all-encompassing epithet of a grand old woman, as 'Mother India', the source of all life, merciful sustainer, dogged martyr of peace and justice, had in reality turned into a cougar in high heels, ready for a night out on the global town. This old woman in all her wisdom, with a bosom of cultural capital accumulated over thousands of years, was perhaps just another pompous whore after all.

III

In 2007, South Africa hosted the first T-20 cricket World Cup. The Proteas were set to play India in what turned out to be a quasi-quarterfinal fixture in Durban. It took some effort, but I managed to drag my dad along, with my two cousins, for the historic game.

On the night of the match, Kingsmead was a sea of blue. Indians came in thousands: old indentured patriots, new illegal immigrants and everyone in-between, flocking to support the motherland. Indian flags outnumbered South African, and the stadium became a coconut-grove bhangra bash.

Nothing demonstrates the veracity of my split personality more overtly than an India–South Africa cricket match. For me, this was a once-in-a-lifetime opportunity to watch a powerful Indian outfit take on the perennial-choker Proteas in a World Cup match under a sublime night sky in my home town. I wore my Indian cricket shirt and a jester hat stitched in the colours of the South African flag.

Most of the South African Indian supporters, despite their roots, wouldn't have known the first thing about the country a couple of years back, but India was beginning to make a name for herself on the backs of Shahrukh Khan's lip-synching, dramatic Zee TV soap operas, Shilpa Shetty's curves and the economic rise of India the Superpower. It was suddenly cool to be Indian or be associated with this new incarnation of the motherland, which somehow resembled the 'modern Indians' we were meant to be in South Africa.

I watched in disbelief as this young Indian team, without its old

Tendulkar–Dravid–Ganguly guard, went on to thump South Africa out of the competition and Indian fans danced to the tune of victory. I looked around the stadium and saw a new pompous culture permeating my city as the bass of the frenzied tabla and urging chorus of *Chak de India* reverberated off the plastic seats and the aluminium advertising boards. I watched Indian flags rise as the celebration surpassed the match itself. This was Durban, not downtown Delhi, yet a song from a Bollywood movie resounded victorious across the stadium without anyone batting an eyelid in dissension. This had turned into a 'home victory'.

I was dumbfounded at the cultural displacement before me. Thousands of South African Indians brought up on American cultural symbols of Levi's jeans, Nike sneakers and Coca-Cola rose to celebrate a new cultural power.

India went on to claim the cup, a fine victory for an ancient civilization that had just turned sixty years young. And the success of the competition heralded a new era for cricket: the Indian Premier League (IPL), run by a wannabe Fifa cartel of flash money and slippery personalities. In many ways, the IPL, with its draconian methods, bullying tactics and uncultured mining of its most-prized resource, the game of cricket, is the epithet of the new India.

How odd that it was born right before me, in Durban.

IV

In 2008, I returned to JNU as a visiting researcher for a couple of months. Going back to JNU was inspiring. Everyone was just as warm as I remembered and everything just as dysfunctional. This time I was prepared to handle the 'new' India – and I finally got the opportunity to take a trip to Kashmir, an elusive prospect that I had been looking forward to for years.

When I first embarked on the Global Studies masters programme, which included semesters in Germany, South Africa and India, I became close friends with a student named Wajahat Ahmad, from Indian-administered Kashmir. I didn't understand him at first because his default position was a static wide-mouthed stare that made him seem slightly retarded, but Wajahat cooked a mean potato curry and we quickly became friends. We sat many a night in the dining area on the fifth floor of the Hindenburg international student house in Freiburg in Germany talking about religion, politics and Kashmir into the wee hours of the morning.

Wajahat is a child of the insurgency. He grew up in a conflict zone, where families were terrified for their lives, where soldiers and insurgents knocked on doors on cold nights, and where kids were better off in boarding school. He, too, was eventually sent to Delhi.

Being the eternal cynic, I always listened to Wajahat's tales of Kashmir's wounds with a pinch of salt. I would tease him that Kashmir had no industrial base to survive independently and that aspirations for independence based solely on the nostalgia of majestic chinar trees and the revolutionary poetry of Faiz Ahmed Faiz or Iqbal were juvenile.

In turn, he would mock my apparent affection for India, ruthlessly judge my proclivity for enjoying Indian cinema and call me a 'fucked-up South African' for having a split personality.

I tried to remind Wajahat that the only reason why people knew about Kashmir was because of the spate of Indian movies made in the 1950s and '60s that showcased the 'Switzerland of the East'. We couldn't watch a damn Hindi movie in our house without my father pausing the VCR to point out the Kashmiri version of a Venetian gondola called a *shikara* and tell us about an experience he'd had on one, or that the snow-capped mountains behind Shammi Kapoor's head were the illustrious Himalayan mountains, or, much to my mum's disdain, that he was meant to marry a Kashmiri, live on a hill and survive on fresh air.

This was the Kashmir of my dreams, a land belonging to fairy tales and folklore, an untouched reservoir of natural splendour, a gross poetic anomaly to the rest of India's grunge. With Wajahat's tales of childhood and family now added to the mix, I felt delirious when I finally managed to arrange a flight from Delhi to Srinagar in late January 2008.

But nothing could have prepared my eyes for Kashmir.

Under the glaze of a shy winter sun, flanked by snow-covered mountains and immortalized by the iconic Dal Lake, Kashmir looked to me like an aged empress. Her majesty and her tumultuous tears shimmered in the early morning air; her former glory apparent, yet seemingly a melancholic lifetime away.

In 'the city of bunkers', as Wajahat once wrote of Srinagar, army bunkers sat uncomfortably on street corners, outside mosques and temples, crammed against walls between businesses. People walked with their gaze lowered, not as per Islamic injunction but to avoid eye contact with nervous soldiers. Grown Kashmiri men addressed young soldiers as 'Sir', and after sunset the city became a ghost town, the result of a self-induced curfew for survival. The air was dense with a palatable uneasiness that I found at once both captivating and terrifying.

I felt sorry for the soldiers. Most of the estimated half-a-million troops in the area were unhappy to be posted there. They were far from home, in unfamiliar territory. The Kashmiri people naturally despised them, the guerrillas terrified them since they apparently feared God and God alone, and the winters were caustically bitter. Their nervousness was plain to see.

Indian soldiers repeatedly mistook my good looks for that of a local Kashmiri, and my penchant for travelling with locals by public busses and unmarked vehicles didn't help my case; without provocation I would be frisked aggressively. But I deliberately and stubbornly chose to wait for my harassers to complete their rough duties until they finally asked for an identity card. At this point I'd promptly whip out my South African passport and tourist credentials, and they would just as promptly become over-friendly weirdos. In so doing, they unwittingly gave away the Indian army's PR game.

This is why South African or Indian tourists wonder what the fuss is all about in Kashmir. They visit the famous Valley on tourist packages, travel in marked busses and rest in houseboats and secure hotels, and pose with touristy soldiers beside 'beautified' bunkers.

The frenzied Kashmiri violence of the 1990s might have simmered down over the past few years, but it is not easy to forget that around 70,000 people have died in the unrest over the last two decades. And even though India wasted little time in marketing the region as an incredible tourist destination with a spate of new flights and transport infrastructure planned to further the 'normalization' of Kashmir, the tension I felt in the Valley was authentic. In reality, it was always only a matter of time before a stone was thrown or a soldier let loose a stray shot and the entire region would erupt. The spate of violence in 2010 and the relative calm of 2011 attest to the unique cycle of 'terror' and 'enforced peace' in the Valley.

On my return I concluded that whether or not you felt Kashmir ought to be independent was irrelevant – this was a people under occupation.

V

The India I dreamt about as a child held me in her bosom and gave me something to be proud of. What else was I proud of back then?

At the end of apartheid, it was too early to make a call on the new South Africa. Sure, we sang happy peace songs in 1994. I was a kid, I didn't live in a township, I went to an ex-Model C school (schools reserved for white kids under apartheid) and I had no idea what the country was really about. At the same time, I refused to be the Indian kid who obsessed over the English Premier League, watched Hollywood films and listened to gangsta rap (or, secretly, Mariah Carey). So I took India with me to school because it filled the temporary vacuum in the cultural white hole.

Of course, the India that my father had lived in five decades earlier was a very different place, and his rendition of the land reflected this. Back then India was an infantile democracy with kwashiorkor trying to survive in the big, bad world – a huge new nation with hunger pangs, and Pakistan on its tail. The greyish melancholy of pre- and post-Independence life was often captured in the music and cinema of the time. It was no surprise then that the

Soviet Union consumed Raj Kapoor films like cheap vodka as they celebrated the Charlie Chaplin-like struggles of the Indian urban working class. Once you dusted off the muck, back then it was a country far easier to understand than the political animal it is today.

The widespread image of India today is that of an age-old civilization reconciling itself with modernity. There is also the image of an all-encompassing subcontinent rapidly earning worldwide respect and prestige as an economic powerhouse through its expert skills base and work ethic. And Bollywood does the rest with its idealized scripts and fantastical utopias of unity, democracy and historical intrigue. But Bollywood is a prime example of celebrated Indian-ness that tells you very little about actual Indian society, which, in itself, is quite revealing.

In essence, India has been able to represent itself as a new brand for those looking to reject the ongoing Americanization of the world. It is less aligned with contemporary Western values (but it is aligned enough to generate interest from those parts), and it is, crucially, less pervasive than other non-Western cultures. Self-righteous Indian popular cinema is unashamedly promoted as family viewing, and is consumed in the Middle East and in many parts of Africa as worthy substitutes for 'corrupt' Hollywood narratives. At the same time, Indian culture is considered less of a threat in comparison with China's rigidity and the fundamentalist hostility of global Islam – thus it is truly the Western world's best chance of a weedy ally in the farcical clash of civilizations.

India today is the last bastion of exoticism. Whereas it was considered 'hippie' to don Indian fashion, speak of 'shanti' and watch Amitabh Bachchan movies in the 1970s, it is now seriously hip to visit a Sufi dervish, read *Shantaram* and watch Amitabh Bachchan movies (yes, he's still around). Not only does it make economic sense to tie up with India, being among the largest consumer bases on the planet, it helps that the Indian work ethic and cultural values are seen as amenable to the global marketplace. In many ways, modern yuppie India, despite its claims to be anything but, is actually about mimicking white, American lifestyles. Yes, it wants to and needs to maintain its own identity, but you always get the feeling that it is only a matter of time before it takes a liking to rump steak. It is that all-encompassing, all-confusing tradition-versus-modernity conundrum that sweeps people off their feet and helps legitimize the contradictions.

Throw in a couple of the obnoxiously powerful business heroes of the Indian diaspora residing in the US and UK – men who are only too keen on tightening the imagined umbilical cord to the motherland as they wax on about their beloved India, further fuelling the nostalgic hullabaloo of the all-encompassing, inviting Mother India – and it really is quite impossible to imagine anything but a gross post-modern cultural orgy of goodness.

What we are given is a romanticized version; even its poverty is splashed on one huge airbrushed canvas that serves to beautify India's tragic poor as 'resilient, colourful characters' making their way in a country that is simply too big, multilayered and complex to expect rapid improvements: think *Slumdog Millionaire* here.

One consequence of this celebration of modern India is the glossing over of so many difficult questions. What of the unceasing Indian diaspora? And the massive military repression in Kashmir? And the unrelenting and inhuman caste system? And the blatant disregard for human rights in the north-eastern states of Nagaland and Manipur, and the Indian government's horrific treatment of illegal migrants, or the pathetic state of its minorities?

And while the poor conditions of India's large Muslim minority have been relatively well covered, especially with the emergence of the Sachar Committee Report some years back, not much is spoken about the chronic discrimination and archetypal caricatures of Christians in mainstream media. Even less is spoken about the anti-conversion laws in some states, which boils down to trampling on freedom of religion, a pioneering pillar of India's secular democracy.

Internally, India is fraught with debate about its leaders, its draconian policies toward the poor, its shifty capitalism, its unhealthy call-centre consultants and its supersonic modernization rate. But beyond its borders, Indian issues are slipped under an ethereal

Persian carpet. The world prefers to talk ill of Iran, North Korea and the Taliban, or about the growing political threat of China and its litany of human-rights abuses, as if there was a Tiananmen Square massacre every weekend.

Today, it is not a case of denying India's charm, history or its unparalleled diversity. But I am no stranger to her methods and no longer shocked by her holy bigotry.

I am not sure if it is an irony that, whereas my father returned to South Africa after studying in India with an unequivocal love for the country, my return from student life there raised serious questions that tainted my aforementioned affair with the land. Maybe it was apt. I wasn't returning to apartheid South Africa after all. I was returning *home*.

I am not saying that India is not more than the sum of its flaws. That would be shortsighted. I am not suggesting that India is not a part of who I am. That would be a mistake. Evidently, there really is no point in my attempting to shed the memory of the subcontinent to arrive at some equally delusional but fashionable Afro-friendly 'I'm from Aaafrika, maan' strap-on philosophy, because that would just be a lie. Next I'll be saying that my pseudo-black skin is the new black or that I'm actually Zuma's bastard.

But wait, I am all that.

I am a perplexed fist of identity, the knot at the centre of a tug-of-culture, holding on to dear life between bloodlines, Indian ancestral roots and African dreams.

Indeed, we all are this perplexed diversity. It's perhaps the only thing that makes us the same.

I used to cringe every time Wajahat flippantly addressed me as that 'fucked-up South African'. I didn't like it because he was specifically referring to my split persona. I didn't think it was fair because it made me feel as if I was always searching for *my* history amid my convoluted sense of space and belonging.

I didn't like it, mostly because he was right.

Acknowledgements

The response and support from friends to the news that I was turning the Accidental Academic into a book continue to surprise me.

I must first thank readers, cover designers and voters on the blog for creating the buzz that eventually gave birth to the first edition of this book, *Zuma's Bastard*. An entire machine in many parts of the world got this baby breathing, and while I surely cannot name everyone, I am particularly grateful to:

In Hong Kong: Maseena Ziegler, for forcing me 'to start a blog' in 2008: 'be bold, be brave, be brilliant' is what she advised.

In South Africa: Ari Sitas, Aisha Lorgat, Bianca Tame, Nomkhosi Xulu, Amanda Kinners, Shaun Ruggunan, Adarsh Maharaj and Steven Gordon, for providing unparalleled feedback at UKZN. This project started under your collective tutelage and I am forever indebted.

Yusuf Osman and Fathima Hassim, and all the lads in Johannesburg for opening their doors to me during those dark days when I came as a cash-strapped journo to cover a story or complete a course in Jozi.

Noorjehaan Joosub, for starting the Facebook group that led new readers to the blog.

Aliki Karasaridis, for the tremendous feedback and support as Thought Leader editor.

Shafinaaz Hassim, for not only suggesting the ridiculous crossover, but also convincing me to believe in it.

Aasia Fredericks and Mariam Mahamed, for giving me the initial lowdown on the publishing world and how to con publishers into giving me a book deal.

Zahira Kharsany, for all the social-media insight that put us one step above the rest.

Shubnum Khan, Zuhayra te water Naude and Nanda Soobben, for kindly drawing remarkable cartoons in the lead-up to this experiment.

Saleeha Idrees Bamjee, for designing the wicked cover and for lending her talented pen over and over again to the design of the campaign.

Fatima Cassim, for the endless online company into the depths of the night, for the punning titles, and for designing my original book proposal.

Tim Richman, from Two Dogs Books, for his part in taking a risk and giving me a voice and, in so doing, breaking all the rules.

Khadija Patel, for bringing insurmountable wisdom to the mother ship, patiently offering guidance in editing and marketing at any given time, on any given day.

Gulshan Khan, for co-editing the initial manuscript and being my trusted partner-in-crime throughout the creative process of so many of these articles.

Fathima Paruk, for being my friend, confidante and marketing heroine, without whom there would have been no adventure.

To Khadija, Gulshan and Fathima: thank you for believing. Even more than I did.

Ferial Haffajee, for engaging me back in the time when no editor would even reply, for lending an ethereal magic to the idea, and for agreeing to write the foreword even before I had found a publisher.

In Qatar: Mohammed Ziyaad Hassen, for the sporadic brainwaves, support and for coining the famous 'liberal agenda'.

Ayesha Jacub, for the challenging questions and unyielding support in marketing the project.

Tarik Mousa, for taking the piss every day by asking me, 'Are you done with your award-winning-international-best-seller?' and, of course, for clapping in the hallway.

Mohammed Alsaafin, for the stimulating discussions, honest feedback and tireless friendship.

Carla Bower, for her friendship, support and industrious efforts in helping make my writing make a little more sense.

In India: Meena Kandasamy, for her steadfast belief in the book and for throwing unconditional blessings to help it on its way.

Karthika V.K. and her wonderful team at HarperCollins India, for listening, reading and giving this baby much life and love in the subcontinent. A special thanks to Neelini Sarkar and Debasri Rakshit for dancing through the edits graciously despite my stop and start, million-and-one edits, re-edits and re-re-edits along the way. Thank you for your patience and enthusiasm.

This book is theirs as much as mine. But please forward all hate mail to me.

Copyright Acknowledgements

A number of articles in this collection have been adapted from writing that previously appeared on Thought Leader. Several of them later appeared in magazines and newspapers in differing versions. The publishers are grateful to the following for permission to reproduce articles from their publications in this book:

Al Jazeera for
In search of an African revolution
The road to Dadaab
The world's biggest refugee camp
All of Africa: in a day's play
Goma: the last outpost
Walikale: the curse of El Dorado
The disappeared of Kashmir
Wind in the willows: a cricket bat paradise
Kashmiri Pandits: why we never left our home

Al Huda for
Across the divide with my Jewish cousin

Mail & Guardian for
Slip on those heels and grow a penis

Daily Maverick for
Fore! I smell the blood of a Schabir Shaikman

Leadership Magazine for
I never knew Fatima Meer